Olden Days is Twin Peaks for sadists, a grueling southern goth-ic of fetish, business, and violence. Connor de Bruler grounds his work in an effortless present inhabited by characters all bro-ken by their pasts. It's a mystery of murky waters that never shies from the gruesome depths it plunders and will leave a residue you'll never quite wash away.

— Kyle Yadlosky, *Creep with a Camera*

If Dashiell Hammett and Bentley Little decided to team up and write an homage to Flannery O'Connor, they might have created something like Olden Days. In a story driven by pov-erty, perversion, and pure lyrical lightning, de Bruler's writing scorches on the page.

Brandon Nolta, *Iron and Smoke.*

olden
---
days

First Montag Press E-Book and Paperback Original Edition July 2018

Montag Press
ISBN: 978-1-940233-55-0
Design © 2018 Rick Febré
Photograph © Courtney Niskala

Montag Press Team:
Project Editor – Charlie Franco
Managing Director – Charlie Franco

A Montag Press Book
www.montagpress.com
Montag Press
1066 47th Ave. Unit #9
Oakland CA 94601 USA

Printed & Digitally Originated in the United States of America
10 9 8 7 6 5 4 3 2 1

For Joe Felicia whose experience as a PI was invaluable to the writing of this novel. I don't think I could have written the character without you. And for Zachary Amendt. You published the story that finally made those closest to me see what I've been trying to say.

connor de bruler

olden
---
days

"We have reason to be afraid. This is a terrible place."
—John Berryman

"There's a dog on the road,
and a wolf in the cellar."
—Chuck Falkland

BOOK A.

0.

Victoria Vandergreven went missing in the fall of 2007, leaving behind her diary, her purse complete with her cell phone and wallet containing fourteen dollars, a walk-in closet's worth of clothing, a pack of menthol cigarettes hidden inside her soccer cleats, a book of matches, and eight droplets of blood leading to the front door of the upper-class Charlotte, North Carolina home.

At nine o'clock that night, when her mother kissed her on the right cheek before bed, Victoria was already asleep with her headphones on. Later, her father claimed to have heard Victoria walk down the hallway to use the bathroom at eleven-thirty. By morning, she was gone.

The initial facts suggested that the seventeen-year-old had been abducted. The responding officers were familiar with Victoria—Vicky G to her only two friends at school. She had strange, luminescent gray eyes, glowing as if her pupils were made of zinc, a complexion the color of tannin powder, soft cheeks, and straight amber hair. More importantly, at the time of her disappearance, she had a fresh and easily distinguishable slash on the left side of her face. According to her parents, Marc and Bishop Vandergreven, she had been out of school since late September, continuing her junior-year studies from home while seeing a psychologist once a week to recover from the trauma of her assault. Police were aware of her previous case: Three girls at school had cornered her in the bathroom and attempted to deglove her face. They got as far as slicing her face from her left temple to her chin with a razor box-cutter before the school courtesy officer discovered them, responding to Vicky's screams for help. As of that last night, all three of the girls were in custody and continued to exhibit little remorse. The one girl who had done the cutting had told Vicky earlier in the week that if she kept on with her former boyfriend, an exchange student from Holland, she would cut off her face. She had confessed without pause or crying only three minutes into her questioning. The other two girls had only agreed to help her because they were jealous of Vicky's looks, and the attention she received from boys. They denied any knowledge of their friend's intentions to use a razor and thought they were just going to restrain her to keep her from running away. These two were under house arrest while the third, the razor-girl, was in general population in the Mecklenburg county jail the night Vicky was allegedly abducted. The boyfriend from Holland was away as well, visiting Nashville for three days with his host family.

Without any prior suspects, by the time the parents were under scrutiny, it was discovered that the blood leading to the front door wasn't Vicky's. In fact it wasn't even human. By the end of the day, the crime lab had reported the blood samples to be DEA 1.1 positive, a blood type common to domesticated dogs. But the Vandergreven's did not own any pets. The crime scene investigators, who could find no evidence of a break-in, had discovered shoe prints on the window sill of Vicky's room which led with scuffs up the exterior wall, directly onto the roof of the home. There, they found a stashed half-empty bottle of Popov vodka and a dozen spent menthol cigarettes, like a river of dead caterpillars flowing into the rain gutter. A young technician, following a hunch, had crawled along the edge of the roof to the tall wisteria growing on the side of the house and discovered loosened shingles and debris on the thick vines consistent with the tread patterns of Vicky's missing shoes as described by her parents.

Months went by. Winter came. The police had questioned everyone Vicky had known in her neighborhood and in school.

With no leads, the head of the abduction task force stepped aside when veteran homicide detective, Beaumont Cutler volunteered for the case.

Cutler kept his focus on the parents, rotating them every two hours for day's worth of questioning, matching their narratives, while trying to capitalize on any contradiction. He brought in more acquaintances, people she hadn't known but who knew of her. 'Shoe leather,' he called it, as in: 'Gotta use shoe leather.' Her father's family in Scotland hadn't heard or seen from her, so she hadn't snuck across the Atlantic. From what little the police could gather, she had nowhere else to go, no one else she would likely turn to for shelter. Cutler had grilled the Dutch boyfriend for eleven hours and had come up with nothing. Cutler obtained a warrant to excavate both the front and backyard planting beds that might have been disturbed. They searched for human remains, or the remains of a dog. They unearthed the septic tank and still found nothing. Under Cutler, the lead detectives returned to their original theory of a teenage runaway. For one thing, her interests had been strange. She was a fan of crime investigation programs. The Vandergreven's DVR was filled with recorded episodes of Dateline and 48 Hours. Her DVD collection was almost exclusively horror films, especially old Italian productions from the 70s, and Japanese slashers. Her book selections were just as macabre. She had two separate notated editions of The Dying Mule by Kareem A. Hrabal.

Her diary entries were depressive and vague:

God smokes the lamb's breath,
From the ram's horn
Atop the mountain of loneliness,
He seeks reprieve from the pain of thorns,
That forged his sense of holiness,

The detectives came to believe the evidence suggested that she had staged her own disappearance. It was no longer a question of 'how', or even 'why', but 'where'. The detectives only then turned their focus to the book of hotel matches from the soccer cleat for the first time. It came from Moore Campgrounds Ltd.: a log cabin rental agency in Cosby, Tennessee 180 miles west above the Pisgah National Forest. Her parents were vehement they had never heard of it and that Vicky had never once in her life set foot in Tennessee.

On his way there, Detective Beau Cutler called the Cocke County Sheriff who agreed to escort him to the cabins. The drive took more than three hours in heavy rain. He hated the Appalachian Highway almost as much as he hated the autostrade south of Rome where his mother's family still lived in the vicinity of Salerno. By the time he reached the outskirts of Newport, a hail storm was ravaging the streets of the tiny hamlet. Detective Cutler managed to park in the police station lot after averting a head-on collision with a piss-yellow Plymouth Voyager skidding along the freeway exit on a river of sleet pellets. The driver had been startled by a sudden burst of lightning; a tell-tale sign of hail. Cutler was greeted in the lobby of the modest police station by Sheriff Forrester. They laughed at and hugged one another, instantly realizing how similar they appeared. Several officers also noticed they're apparent doppelganger status. They had the same short haircut. Their body weight had   a similar, slightly overweight, stocky build that suggested they had once been muscular. They were both six-foot-one exactly, staring directly into each other's pupils as they spoke. Detective Beau Cutler was half Italian on his mother's side and had grown up in Newark, New Jersey before relocating to his adopted hometown of Charlotte at twenty years old. Sheriff Nathan Forrester was an un-enrolled Cherokee Indian with distant Irish and German roots from Louisville, Kentucky. He moved to Newport, Tennessee after the police academy. It was his third year as the elected Sheriff of Cocke County. He made Cutler a cup of coffee and offered him a slice of cake. One of their officers was celebrating his birthday Forrester explained. Cutler, feeling his weight, refused.

Moving quickly to the case, Cutler had brought Sheriff Forrester sections of the case file and the book of matches as a courtesy. The Cherokee lawman wasn't especially interested. He skimmed the report, but spent more time holding the evidence bag with the book of matches. He was familiar with the Moore Campgrounds. He told Cutler about a 911 call from the cabins that previous winter. A pimp had been using the cheap cabin homes to house his working girls for the local timber men. The girls were mostly Mexican and Honduran, trafficked up through Alabama, Memphis, and eventually Knoxville where they were sold off in groups to small-time pimps. The ones who performed the worst, the girls who couldn't make as much money because they bled too much or cried too often ended up in little places like Cosby and Johnson City. Those were the girls he encountered, he said, the ones who wouldn't make it to places like Richmond, Louisville, Indianapolis, and Detroit. The girls who had already proved themselves were headed for the motels on the Las Vegas Strip, San Francisco's Tenderloin, Miami, and all the five-star hotels across the Mid-West and

Southeast.

"Appalachia is a dumping ground for the worst of the worst on both sides of the transaction," Forrester told Cutler.

Cutler nodded and wondered whether it was possible that a young girl of means could end up in the trade.

Forrester nodded and explained to Cutler that while he hadn't seen it happen firsthand, he had heard about it from the local the news and in late night cable documentaries.

"Hell," he said, staring out at the hail as he spoke.

"That shit they're making out in Siberia as an alternative to Heroin— they call it Krokodil on the internet— it's here. I've seen kids out there with rotten limbs like monsters after learning how to make it on message boards, good kids, kids from old money, maybe that was the girl's problem."

Forrester paused and continued to tell Cutler about the 911 call from the cabins. A young woman had claimed to be alone in a cabin, she had been drifting in and out of consciousness, scared, unable to speak in clear sentences with the dispatcher. She did manage to give her address and explain that a man with a bag on his head and a shotgun was stalking her from the woods outside. The dispatcher said that a male cadence could be heard in the background of the telephone call, laughing hysterically at the girl on the phone with the dispatcher. The dispatcher asked her if the man with the bag on his head was with her inside the cabin. She told the dispatcher that no it had been her guardian angel who was in the room with her, but she explained that she doubted the angel could protect her from the man outside. Cutler listened carefully to the story as Forrester recalled it. Forrester told him that once the officers arrived on the scene, the girl, who had only been thirteen-years-old, was dead in the cabin, a syringe hanging from her foot. The back door to the cabin was intact. The, and all the windows were shut and locked, unbroken. One of Forrester's deputies had to break down the front door to get in. The cabin had been rented to a Greg Larson of Knoxville, Tennessee. The camp steward had said that he had fled the scene before the cops had arrived. The girl was turned out to be a some runaway from Charleston, West Virginia. Cutler asked about who this Larson was. Forrester told him that Larson had left the country from the ATL airport three days later. That much they knew. His involvement and current location was an ongoing investigation.

Cutler asked about the man with the bag on his head and the shotgun outside, and if any evidence had been found in that regards.

Forrester shrugged.

"There probably never was one," he said. "It's a common image to hear about around here. Anyone could have imagined it. You think about things like the Zodiac killer and The Town that Dreaded Sundown and realize that she was probably just relaying her own drugged-out hallucination. Forrester was convinced that the real killer was Larson. His theory was that he had shot the little girl up with a enough smack to kill a horse and laughed at her while she did the best she could to save herself on the phone with dispatch, imagining the man with the bag over his head, until she died because her body stopped breathing."

The two men paused and looked out the window, the hail outside piling up in waist-high mountains.

With no one to safely drive the streets, the two old cops were trapped in the police station for the night. The staff had pulled out several cots and wool blankets, laying them side by side on the conference room floor. A few of the deputies slept in the hallway, others on the couches in the lobby. While Cutler slept he dreamt about snow falling on an empty field. There, he was walking through a frozen tundra landscape somewhere out in the West, somewhere he had never been. He could hear snow crunching beneath his boots, and the impotent howl of gusting winds. Brickle strands of dried weeds whipped at his clothing, snapping in the frigid currents. He In the distance, he could see the silhouette of a Bison, and an outline of a home beyond it. He knew inherently, as he always did with the rampant familiarity that his dreams offered, that the house in the distance was not a safe place. Next to him, Sheriff Forrester stood there sipping a hot cup of coffee and pointed to the Bison. 'Not too many of them around anymore,' he had said as he gestured with the steaming coffee toward the homestead in the distance.

"That's the Murder Palace," he said.

Cutler woke up at mid-morning and thought little about the dream. He ate eggs with the other police officers and helped Forrester scrape ice from the many squad cars. By afternoon, when the roads were cleared and freshly salted, they drove out to Cosby where Cutler got to see the rental cabins. Contrary to what the matchbook would leave someone to believe, the cabins were ugly, squat and covered in peeling vinyl siding. Even from afar it was clear that the roofs needed repairs. Every lot was numbered with a wooden stake. The rental office was located half- a- mile away from the cabins across the lake where an elderly woman with bad hearing ran the desk with her daughter-in-law, a thin blonde woman with a solitary gold front tooth. There Cutler showed the two of them several pictures of Victoria Vandergreven. They remembered her immediately. She had been there four months earlier. They recognized the fresh scar when he mentioned it. To prove their word, they took out the guest list and showed Cutler and Forrester her signature. She had signed in for a night as Lupita Lopez. The women initially denied her a cabin since she looked young, but she had shown them a Nebraska driver's license with the same name that confirmed that she was a young looking twenty-five. She had come alone, paid in cash, and left early the next morning without a word. Neither of them knew what she was had been doing in the area. Both women remembered her speaking with a thick accent that they couldn't place. The old woman said she hadn't spoken English worth a flip. According to the dates, Cutler calculated that this quick stay was a month before she actually went missing. He asked the women if she had met with anyone while she had been there. They couldn't recall there being anyone. When asked, the ladies confirmed that she had left nothing behind.

At this point, Detective Cutler thought of the trip as a false lead. But, he wondered, how could her parents have missed her for an entire day and night? It's clear from the women at the camp that she had been to Tennessee at least once. After Forrester and Cutler inspected the cabin, and drove back to Newport in silent thought. There Cutler spent the night in a motel, watching television, faxing the office, and making telephone calls. He felt an emptiness that he couldn't articulate – something about the dream. He used to tell his wife about his dreams, especially the dreams that he thought as prophetic. Every day he saw patterns and connections all around him, which was precisely why when he was younger he had decided never to try LSD in junior college. At the time he was smoking enough weed on a daily basis to fumigate a small apartment, but when given the chance to try LSD he turned it down, not because he was worried that he couldn't handle the ferocity of a true hallucinogenic experience, but because he worried, subconsciously at least, that the chemical so beloved by rational cultural crusaders like Tim Leary and Terence McKenna and even Aldous Huxley would grind away the fantastical components of his otherwise regimented, analytical brain. He was afraid that people like Leary, Mckenna, and Huxley, who were still seen by the reigning oligarchy of the time as unmoored, loose and eccentric in there thinking, were, in his opinion, far too analytical in their thinking to a point of handicap. Cutler, a lifelong aspiring cop, knew innately, since his grade school days, that what gave him and in turn any successful detective an advantage was their vibrant imagination. And so it was never unfortunate to him that hallucinogens were disqualifying for any police force, since he was never tempted to try it and possibly mess up his uncanny pattern awareness. Pot, on the other hand, he was fine to lie about, which he did to become a cop. There were other detectives who did not think like he did, who instead put themselves in the broken mind of a criminal, or the mind of a scared, little boy, the mind of sex-crazed young woman in her first-year teaching position, or of a spree killer. But they could not think the way the discombobulated, irrational masses thought, and that was there undoing as detectives – by focusing on wild personality theories as opposed to the obvious. There were times, when Cutler doubted his abilities, when he felt that his creative hunches hindered his regimented, rational side, leading him astray. When he was a rookie, he would sit up in the morning with his wife and relay his dreams to her as if he were searching for an interpretation from her. As he lay on the motel bed in Tennessee, a divorced, lonely, older man now, he thought about the vivid images related to the Vandergreven case from his last dream: the bison, the homestead crime scene, and Forrester's comments.

When he got back to Charlotte, the police had already gotten a schoolmate of Victoria's into custody. They were holding him on a simple marijuana charge just so Cutler could ask him about the fake Nebraska driver's license. The kid, a brown-haired Ashton Kutcher look-alike, had been caught only once manufacturing and selling fake licenses for other kids at Victoria's school looking to buy alcohol. Cutler walked into the interrogation room, draping the chair with his still wet coat, setting down the Starbucks long black coffee between them. He took a slow sip before saying for starters, "Victoria Vandergreven, from your school? You remember her?"

The kid had his head lowered, his shaggy bangs covering his eyes like a sheepdog. He shook his head no.

Cutler tapped his finger on the plastic cover of the paper cup.

"Of course not. Is that why you put the name Lopez on the I.D.?"

The kid peered through his bangs.

Cutler had his attention.

"You know, Lupita Lopez from Lincoln, Nebraska?"

The kid said nothing.

"Look, I already know everything about you and you're side business. We have examples of your handiwork. It's fuckin' good. Maybe a little too good, too good that my conscience doesn't want you on the street or at school. Maybe so good that I want to see you stay in here for a while?.."

The kid scratched his temple.

"Don't believe me. Where do think we got your name from? You're customers sold you out for a slap on the wrist – misdemeanor under-aged drinking, no mention of the fake ID. We got one from Jose, from Michael, Alonzo, and even little Alex, who honestly looks fourteen. And for a kid entrepreneur like you, you sure are having some bad fuckin' luck with all this coming around right now. You just celebrated your birthday last week. Eighteen. Shit, that makes you an adult, though still not old enough to drink. You've got nothing of that youthful stupidity left to lean on. Nothing's coming to save you. Do I have to convince you of anything else?"

The kid's face went pale.

"It would be in your best interest to assist me in my investigation of Victoria's disappearance. Now, you do remember your good old friend Vicky G don't you? Trust me, you have nothing to gain, and everything to lose by being silent about somebody else's girl."

Here the kid spoke for the first time.

"We weren't friends, never," he said in a low voice. "Unlike everyone else, I was afraid of her."

"Why?"

"It's hard to explain," he said.

"Try me."

"I don't know. She was just so weird. Everybody thought she was so great, but I saw how she just controlled them. I used to see her up in the teacher's lounge, welcomed there like she was one of them."

"Bullshit! You can't lie your way out of this. No one thought she was great. I've talked to every one of her teachers. I've talked to the janitors, and all the coaches. Nobody remembers her. She was invisible. It's almost as if she didn't even attend the school. We do know that she had two friends. Now tell me about the I.D that you made for her. Why did she want it? She wanted to buy alcohol and cigarettes, right? She had vodka stashed on her roof. She had cigarettes. Both of which she left behind."

"She just wanted one. She didn't tell me why. She just wanted me to make sure that she would be at least 25 years old."

"Why 25 and not 21?"

"She wanted to rent a car."

Cutler took out his pad and paper.

"There you go. These are the things I'm looking for," he said, scribbling notes. "Now, what else did she ask for?"

"She didn't want her name on it. Which was cool because that made it easier for me."

"Did she say why?"

"No, I don't know why."

"You don't really care, you just want to take the money, right?"

"Usually, but I didn't that time."

"Give me a break, kid. Don't tell me that she didn't pay you."

"She didn't pay me anything. I didn't ask her to," the kid said.

"You made her a fake license for free?"

"I just changed around an expired license that I had. But no, I didn't ask her for money."

"Why?"

The kid hesitated.

"Did she offer you drugs? Sex? What?"

"I saw her in my dreams, watching me. She's still see her in my dreams. She's always there. She watches me. I wanted her to go away."

"You're not making any sense," Cutler said.

"Ever since, I can't stop worrying about everything. I can't sleep. I'm afraid to close my eyes at night. I can't eat."

Cutler set his pen down and looked at the kid.

"You've got something else to tell me? Better let it out now."

1.

The Citigo hadn't been burning long. He could still make out its color in the dark of the alley; a little green Škoda pushed onto its side, blocking his exit, near perfect circles punched through the glass by the thrown paving stones where the Molotov cocktail had been tossed inside; the winged arrow logo pointing to the sewer like an omen. The tall dark man stood in the center of the crowd and stared up toward the sky wondering if the cold drizzle would take care of the flames. Firefighters pushed everyone back as the green Škoda's windshield glass popped in the heat. A policeman in the green-paneled Mercedes wagon spoke with some old Turk.

The tall man turned around and stood beneath the short eave of a closed shop trying to get out of the rain. He took out a pack of French cigarettes from the breast pocket of his checkered flannel shirt, set the filter in his pursed lips, and cupped the weak flame of the hotel match. A cop he hadn't kept his eye on flashed a light in his face as he exhaled. He didn't flinch.

"Ausweis bitte."

He took the red passport from the left pocket of his wrangler jeans and gave it to the officer who shined a light on the photo then, in one vindictive jerk, back into his pupils.

"Hast du nicht etwas gesehen?"

The tall man removed the cigarette from his lip.

"Ek ferstay nikt. Kein Deutsch. Ek ist Ungarisch. Magyar vagyok," he said in a thick Hungarian accent.

Another officer called his interrogator back over to the old Turk. He handed him back the passport and told him to stay put.

"Bleib hier. Geh nicht weg"

The tall man set his hands in his jacket and, with the cigarette perched in the corner of his mouth, strode through a break in the crowd down the long street where the flickering light of the burning car ended and the neon cross above the closed pharmacy door turned the dung-coated pigeon spikes a glowing radioactive green. He kept on down the street, reading the signs at each corner, retracing his steps through X-burg. He took shelter at a bus stop once the rain had picked up and smoked another cigarette while he read the map. He was close to Tempelhoffer-Damm.

The street light above the bus stop shattered, pelting the rounded glass overhead. He ducked behind a trash can. Another light, one of the fluorescent tubes lining the top of the open structure, burst from its plastic case. The next gunshot sounded, echoing as it ricocheted off the curb.

He caught a glimpse of something across the street.

Another shot. Another light above him gone, a section of the world erased.

He could see the muzzle flash in the empty concrete window beyond the scaffolding.

The last light near the bus stop died with the next shot.

He took his chance and ran across the block, swerving and taking cover behind the massive claw of a JCB, his own breaths reverberating off the wet, dirt-caked metal. Taking a fresh pair of plastic gloves from his jacket pocket, he checked his pulse. Pausing for moment, he listened to rain, staring at the black window below. There was an entrance in the courtyard of the unfinished building. He scooped up a ball of mud and tossed it at the silhouette of a cherry dogwood, knocking the tree and just barely shaking the branches. He then grabbed a loose chunk of asphalt and lobbed it at an extended ladder. The chunk knocked the ladder sideways. Three more shots pulled up long streaks of splattered mud between the rungs. Hoping the shooter was looking the other way toward the ladder, he crawled out from under the JCB claw and ran through the courtyard and inside the husk of the building. Inside the air was dry and empty. Bits of glass scattered through layers of sawdust and grit crunched under his weight as he went up the makeshift stairwell, then pulled the 9mm from his belt loop, crouching at the foot of the stairs. A pale face on a thin neck turned toward the sound from his direction. There were three in total, all now turning away from the hollow window. He fired four times, seeing each of their panicked, adolescent faces in the flash from the Beretta. The spent shell casings struck and rolled across the floor.

He stepped over them and toward the window where he grabbed the miniature .22. He folded it expertly and placed it quietly on the widened sill. The figure closest to him had baggy jeans held up by a woven belt with a gold buckle plate in the shape of an American dollar bill dotted with cubic zirconium diamonds. He looked through his pockets and found ten euros and a handful of firecrackers. The other two bodies held iPhones, which he smashed, a few more bucks in change, which he stole, and a few clove cigarettes, which he tossed back onto the blood-soaked floor next to their bodies.

Outside, the sky cleared. Leaving, he walked past a football court, its goal posts made of tough, welded steel pipes, closed off from the street by three walls of concrete brick and a row of galvanized fence. He smelled Tempelhoffer-Damm before he could see it, the musty odor of tobacco trapped in propane-fired heat mingling with the metallic scent of pooled rainwater, dried up disinfectant, urine, and wafts of jellied grease from the dõner stands and chicken rotisseries. Where the sidewalk ended, he crossed the street-car rails to the station's entrance. He stood alone on the platform alone for some time. A subway sped by without stopping before the next arrived. When it stopped, the doors opened slowly. He sat upright in the orange-cushioned booth and stared out at the platform.

When the subway reached his stop, he exited as the doors opened even slower this time. He left the platform until he was sure the CCTV cameras were out of range, and set the black plastic bag he had been carrying inside the janitor's bin in the corner of the tunnel that ran under the street.

He walked along the curved street to the AstroTurf lawn of the Hotel Columbia, its cafe and the bar closed. No one was behind the small front desk. He rode the iron-gate elevator to the third floor and took out his key. The world appeared abandoned.

His room was cheap and plain: one bed, one desk, a wardrobe, and a small television, the bathroom was the size of the elevator car, half of it eaten up by a narrow, walk-in shower. He took his clothes off, and showered, then put on a pair of boxers and a white shirt. He grabbed his satchel from the wardrobe and set it on the twin bed. From the hidden pocket under the lining, he took out a stack of slim, small booklets and set them beside one another on the table. He had seven different passports: two from Peru, two American, one Mexican, one Canadian, and the Hungarian passport from his jeans. He glanced at his portraits in each of them, then decided on the first American passport. He was bald in that picture. The name was Alan Webster.

He sat up in his bed and read a German porn magazine titled, Busen. In one section, the women were naked in a some kind of park in Slovakia, having sex with each other on picnic tables. He knew the park, he had been there once. It must have been early in the morning when they took the photos as there was dew on the grass beneath them. The park was empty as the morning light broke through the evergreens that ran through it. It looked cold. Studying the pictures closely he could see that their skin was goose-bumped.

2.

The airport had still been crowded in the early hours of the morning. He had eaten breakfast on his layover at Charles de Gaulle. Over the Atlantic, he struggled with his seat adjustment and drank whiskey before falling asleep. The cabin lights woke him as they prepared to land.

At ATL, he walked through the corridor that connected the gates with his only bag slung over his shoulder, seven hits of acid, a bag full of scopolomine, and 3fl oz of colloidal silver woven into the base with a scent barrier. He found the Sweetwater Bar and sat down in a booth.

The server approached him while he was changing the SD card on his cellphone. He ordered a beer and a plate of French fries.

The beer had gone flat by the time the woman sat down across from him. She was dressed in a black sweater and a gray peasant skirt. He could still see some of the violet lacquer she had scraped off around her cuticles. Her eyebrows looked thinner. She stole one of his fries.

"You didn't order me anything," she said.

"You're gonna throw it up anyway. What's the point?"

"The point is to keep the waitress at bay. We're in the U.S. now. There's no such thing as privacy."

"The waiter will come four or five times anyway. That's his job. They always say, 'I'm going to be taking care of you today.' That's a thing now. They tune out our chit-chat before they say that."

"Must be nice to speak something other than English ."

He didn't respond.

The server approached them.

"Y'all doing alright? Ma'am do you need anything to drink, something else to eat?"

"Water with lemon," she said.

"She'll also have a Tanqueray martini."

"Scratch that. Make it a Manhattan," she said.

The server kept his eyes on the woman.

"So that's a water with lemon and a Manhattan from the bar?"

She nodded.

"I like y'all's style," he said. "I'll be right back."

The tall man dipped a French fry into the stainless steel cup of ketchup.

"You know, I used to be a waiter."

"Why did you order me a drink?"

"Because I don't want you to go into a shaking fit."

"What the fuck went wrong?"

"Nothing went wrong? You seem on edge. Jumpier than usual. Lift up your shirt."

"We're in the middle of the airport."

He ate another French fry.

She scanned the room and lifted up her sweater.

"Take off the bra. Pass it to me underneath the table."

She pretended to scratch her back as she undid the straps.

"Nobody's looking. Do it," he said.

She gave him the bra under the table and he tore it to shreds.

"Give me your purse."

She slid the leather bag across the table.

He checked for a moment, rifling through the pockets, thumbing through her wallet, before tearing out the inner lining. He set the red silk on the table like a handkerchief.

"Has anyone actually wired you?"

"No," he said, feeling the leather on the edges of the bag. "What's a Gucci bag to you anyway?"

"A couple thousand."

He set the inner lining back inside and gave her back the purse.

"Then learn to sew."

"Even if I did get touched and had to take a deal. Do you really think you could take me out in public like this?"

"Everybody I do gets done in public. I'd scrimshaw an epic into your ribcage right on that goddamn bar top. But that's why you pay me and not some ex-Navy seal, isn't it?"

"You should have been a wise guy the way you talk a big game, or maybe a Southie hooligan. Did you learn to talk like that in prison?"

"No," he said, smiling. "It's the schoolyard where you learn to talk like that. Prison's where you learn to back it up."

"You're too much."

The server came with her drinks.

"You sure you don't need anything to eat, Ma'am?"

"I'm fine."

He turned to the dark man.

"You still doing good? That beer must be getting warm?"

"I drink slow. It's fine."

"Alright, then. Just holler if you need anything."

They thanked him.

She looked across the table, cupping her hands around the martini glass.

"Why did you order me this drink?"

He didn't hesitate.

"I shot three kids," he said.

"They saw your face?"

"They shot at me. A little survival .22. A pipe job. The most a German street punk can get his hands on. But he was a pretty fucking good shot."

"When?"

"Just after."

"You're sure they weren't Russian."

"Could have been payed off. They were taking out the street lights around me. They had a chance while I was out in the open and didn't take it, so maybe they were just dickin' around."

"If one of them was that good of a shot, he could have been setting the stage for someone else."

"Maybe," he said. "But nobody else showed up."

"You used the same gun?"

"Yeah, the 9mm. It's clean."

"You think they're gonna link the casings."

"Probably, but they're more likely to wonder why an entire block got shot out by some kids with a .22."

"You pitched the 9mm?"

"Janitor's bag. The train station. No cameras."

"They'll find it. They're Germans."

"So what? The gun's got no prints and its registered to some dead guy in Lindau."

"They'll connect the dots."

"At least, it won't come back to me."

"You sound confident for a guy that just tore up my bra looking for a wire."

"I trust myself, not you."

"You're gonna throw me under the bus one day aren't you."

"Things like this don't last. Sooner or later, somebody's

gonna screw something up."

She took a gulp of the Manhattan.

He passed her a silver USB stick with the Siemens logo on the side.

"Is it on here?"

He nodded.

"That and about a gigabyte of creepy porn."

"Why's there always kiddie shots on these things. I mean, what the fuck? Seriously?"

He downed the rest of the beer in one swallow.

"No kinder porno this time. But the shit on there's weird enough," he said.

She ate the cherry from the glass.

"I don't need to know. As long as the data's on there."

"So," he said, pausing for a moment. "What do you have for me?"

"White Toyota pickup. Garage B. Level 4."

"Yeah?"

She ran her fingers through her hair.

"Yeah, it's got an Indiana license plate. The money's in an envelope strapped to the bottom of the front seat."

"How about a gun?"

"We're in the U.S. Go find one," she said, passing him the keys and the ticket.

The money was under the front seat like she said. The fake registration and insurance card had been placed neatly atop the owner's manual in the glove compartment. He had a license with the same name as the registration. The gas tank was full. He kept the car running and checked the tail lights before driving through the garage to the tollbooth. The pickup had been there for weeks and had racked up a significant charge.

"God fuckin' damn it," he mumbled as he fished out his wallet and paid the attendant.

He made his way north, out of Atlanta. The fresh asphalt was quiet on the worn tires. He kept the windows open in spite of the autumn chill. There were brakes in the gray clouds exposing the dying red sun. The sky had a granular appearance like sand mounds still visible at high tide.

It grew colder as the light faded. He rolled up the windows after crossing the state line, the Toyota crawling up the narrow stretch of country interstate, passing the park welcome centers, gas stations, and chemical silos. He listened to a racist talk show on a distant, static-filled AM frequency.

Just before full dark had consumed the road, the silhouette of an owl passed over the truck. He tilted his head head below the rear view mirror and caught a glimpse of its wingspan glowing in the truck's headlights, against the beryl-colored horizon.

The highway north of Georgia, entering the Carolinas, didn't bend correctly, and lanes broke off without warning like shards of melting ice. He turned the dial and found another radio station he liked. The DJ had a soft voice. She sounded kind. She was Southern. It was a religious station, some kind of ministry extension.

The white pickup eased up an incline. At the top, he could see the red lights wading in the river of darkness before descending into the valley to join them. He took an exit for a town he didn't know, and pushed on through the woods. He caught glimpses of derelict homes eaten away by time and gravel driveways that looked like snow-covered ground in the passing glare of his headlights.

Exhausted from the jet lag, he needed rest, a quiet place, a surface that wasn't moving beneath him. He pulled into the parking lot of a Motel 6. He circled the empty lot twice, then drove down the road to the EconoLodge instead. There were a couple of girls in the back lot opposite the sticky bushes. He got out of the car and made eye contact with one of them, nodding toward his car. She was a short Latina woman with dyed blonde hair. Her jet-black roots shone through the peroxide strands, her stomach sloping over her tight jeans, her eyes thick with mascara, and her lips bulging with a deep red lipstick. She took the long way around the bushes and slid past the dumpster. He got back inside the truck. She opened the door to the passenger's seat and slammed it behind her.

He offered her a Gauloises.

"I've never seen those before," she said.

"It's a French cigarette. But they make them in Poland now."

"You from there?"

"No," he said. "Just got back from Europe. Business."

She took one from the red pack.

He lit a match for her.

"A gentleman," she said, sucking on the filter.

"There a liquor store 'round here?"

"Yeah, but the place closes at sundown. This is South Carolina."

"Beers?"

"There's a brand new Publix down the road. I can't go in with you though, they know my face."

"Okay."

He started up the engine.

"You might want to save your money though. I'm kind of expensive."

"Yeah?"

"Twenty for a mamada and fifty for missionary. I'll sit on it too for fifty, but I don't do nothing in the ass."

"How much to party for awhile?"

"Two-hundred for an hour," she said, blowing smoke at the windshield.

"So ten hours would be two-thousand then."

"Don't waste my time, dude."

He took out a roll of bills and handed it to her.

"You should count that. I'm not sure if it's everything."

She set the money in the cup holder

"No," she said, firmly, stubbing the cigarette out on the dash. "I'm out of here. Open the door."

"Just chill out. It's not too good to be true. I'm not gonna chain you up. I'm not gonna kill you."

"Fuck this," she said, pulling up the automatic lock.

He pressed down on the gas pedal.

She began to scream for help.

"I'm a criminal," he shouted. "I'm a drug-trafficker. I'm not a plumber tryin' to get blown after work. I've got money to blow. I just got back from Europe for fuck's sake. When I'm in Vegas, or Miami, I'll pay twelve-thousand a night for a girl. But I can't really do that around here can I?"

"You're the one who set the price. I'm just payin' it. Now count your fucking money and do your job."

She took the money from the cup holder, spun with her right arm and punched him hard in the face with a fistful of rings.

He swerved.

She opened the door and rolled out of the truck, smashing up on the curb as he bounced off the street.

He pulled the Toyota into park on the sidewalk and

watched her in the rear view mirror. Her face was bruised, she had hit the ground hard. Her arms were skinned and bleeding. She ran off into the kudzu, the blackness swallowing her.

He ate dinner at the Hooter's and tipped his server twenty dollars. She asked him if he was serious and took the money.

He walked across the road to a rough-looking bar and ordered a Bourbon. He drank in silence, tuning out the college football game on the mounted televisions overhead, ignoring the monotonous chords of the country song playing on the touch-screen jukebox. On his third glass, he stepped outside onto the patio and lit a cigarette. A gathering of white men in gray work uniforms, their names stitched onto their breast pockets, tossed darts onto a plywood bulls eye.

He turned to a fat man clutching a Miller.

"Where can you get girls around here?"

The fat man paid him no mind and walked away.

He listened to the cats fighting near the trashcans, then went back inside.

"Another one?" the bartender asked.

"Just pour me a Guinness," he said.

"You look down, Chief," the old man said, as he poured the beer from the tap.

"Chief?"

The old man paused and let the head settle at the top of the glass.

"I didn't mean nothing by it. I call everybody chief. I thought you was a Mexican. I didn't mean no offense."

"Don't worry about it," he said, taking the beer. "Let me ask you this though."

"Which is?"

"I'm not looking for a hookup and I'm not looking for

trouble. Just a point in the right direction."

"You lookin' for dope?"

"Where can I get a girl?"

"Pendleton Avenue."

"Pendleton, huh?"

"You make the square right out of here, and find the North Polo RV park on Pendleton. It's right behind the Greenpoint Market."

He slipped the bartender a hundred when he shook his hand.

"Be careful. There's always a cop around there."

"I am a cop," he said. "And you never saw me here, got it?"

The old man nodded.

He drank the beer and exited the bar.

3.

Starla used to get up early and pull the dead magnolia leaves from the warped gutter around the trailer, scratching ice loose with a garden trowel in the wintertime, picking out acorns with her bare hands, brushing away the cobwebs and dead cicadas once late August came around. She'd balance herself on the sawhorse since Lonnie refused to buy them a ladder. Next, she would lie on her side, even in the rain, and check for squirrels and raccoons beneath the cinder blocks with an old hockey stick. Most times she knew there weren't any, but it kept Lonnie at ease.

For two years, that had been her morning routine before making coffee and rolling a couple of joints. Lonnie would wake up later, cook his own eggs since she couldn't do them any justice, and smoke the first joint. He sipped his coffee like he was sucking venom from an open wound. She wasn't supposed to talk in the morning. Neither was he. IHe thought it was bad luck to talk before ten.

She put up with the rituals for a long time, but only let the beatings go on for a month. He had hit her a few times in the past, slaps mostly, open-handed swats on the cheek or the back of her head, but it wasn't until she fought back that he really started to beat the shit out of her. He did things like lock her in the bathroom, or lock her outside without any clothes on. She'd called her brother with a fat lip and a steak over her eye when she'd had enough. Her brother took four days off work just to drive down from London, Kentucky and put the fear of God into him. Knowing that the ties of family make people do crazy things, Lonnie left town real quick and moved back in with his sister a few counties over. Her brother insisted on giving Starla a handgun. She opted instead for a can of mace and a dirk.

Still, she checked the windows with the mace in her hand.

LaShay started hanging out more just to keep her company, sleeping there most nights of the week. She sold down at the end of the bamboo grove and, when business was good, gave Starla a cut.

She quit her job down at the Exxon, afraid that Lonnie would find her alone at three in the morning with nowhere to run, and took a full-time position as a closing stocker at the nearby Greenpoint Market where she could walk to work now that the Sable had finally given out. It did mean that she had to walk home alone in the dark five, sometimes six, nights a week.

Behind the mini-mall where the lights never shut off, where the buzzards congregated in the afternoon and raccoons pilfered the trash bags once the sun had gone down, there was a short path that had been blazed in the evergreens between the main road and the trailer court., It was along this path that Starla headed home in the pitch black with her apron slung over her shoulder, her bandana still tight around her unkempt hair, with only the ember of a menthol cigarette and the moon to light her way. She had done it so many times, she knew the path by feel. The woods ended abruptly at the construction site. She crossed the plateau of soft clay dumped behind by the tires of the concrete trucks, leaving behind a course of inch-deep bootprints. Three porta-johns stood on the hill like tombstones. She saw fire in the distance and heard the bass boost of a sub-woofer. She moved up through the thistles, taking immense strides down the bottom half of the incline over the brambles and wild blackberries which tore into the seams of her already worn Levi's. At the bottom she parted the brush, feeling the heat of the bonfire on her cheeks. LaShay stoked the embers with a bamboo staff. Jim Jones blared through the speakers of Andante's souped up rice rocket.

"Somebody got a re-up," Starla said, tossing her cigarette butt into the fire.

"I ain't trying to talk business after work."

" 'Cause you ain't all that obvious," she said. "You running the quality control division now? I can smell you across the fire."

Andante smiled and cranked the music a notch lower. He stuck his head out from the open door of the Honda.

"We got Papa Johns on the counter you want any. I done filled your fridge up with beers too."

"That Busch Ice shit you get from the Vietcong palace?"

He clicked his teeth.

"Coors," he said.

"Fancy."

"Fuck you, Fixico."

"Fixico the Fixican," LaShay said, stoking the fire.

"You're already gone, aren't you?"

"I'll bounce back," she said. "Hey, if you're coming back outside, would you grab me a beer?"

"Sure."

She walked up the wooden steps and let the screen door slam behind her. There were two pizzas on the counter beside the ashtray. She tossed her apron onto the couch and set her bag in the hallway before stepping into the bathroom. She took off her bandana and ran her fingers through her hair while she studied her face. The mirror was flecked with toothpaste. She took off her pants and pulled on the pajama bottoms she had left near the sink that morning and walked back into the kitchen. With a slice of warm pizza in her teeth, she grabbed two beers from the fridge. She shook up the Coors and tossed it to LaShay who held it out and let the foam spurt out of the can in a white streak, sizzling over the red coals. .

"Bitch."

"Y'all got a bowl started up?" she asked, chewing on the pizza.

Andante handed her a blunt from the ashtray in his center console.

She took a drag, then looked at the tip.

"That burning as uneven as fuck," she said, holding the smoke in her lungs.

"This is number two. We're pretty dumb."

"Zig-zag wrap?"

"White grape White Owl. Tossed the guts in the fire."

"Two Gs?"

"Just one this time."

Starla exhaled and coughed.

"You ghosted that shit," LaShay said.

Andante offered her another hit.

She shook her head.

"Nah, let it hit first."

She swallowed more beer.

"They don't piss test at Greenpoint?"

"Not unless you cut yourself."

"That's lucky. They were militant about that shit when I was on the line at HP."

"No shit, it's a line. You gotta clock in and clock out like a fuckin' robot."

"True."

"I like nights like these," LaShay said. "I don't have to work tomorrow. I'm high. I can taste the shit out of this beer. I got paid. I got good shit. It's all good."

"Nighttime is whenever you need it to be. The produce manager at Greenpoint starts drinkin' at one-thirty. He goes to bed at six."

"What time does he have to get his ass up?"

"Around three, three-thirty. He clocks in at four."

"I used to do that shit," Andante said.

"Yeah?"

"When I was planting roses and petunias upstate. It got so bad that summer even the Mexican's didn't want to work in the heat. I'd get up at three, be on the farm at four-thirty. We were done by noon, right when the sweat was about to cover your back. I used to hit the Pub House till they closed up the second time. I was asleep by seven."

"Andante workin' legit?" Starla said, sipping the Coors. "How long ago was that?"

"Like three or four years back."

"Lancaster?"

"Lynwood. Way up there."

Starla tossed the pizza crust into the fire.

He passed her the blunt and she took another hit.

"So tell me," she said, holding the smoke in her lungs. "Does your lower back ever smart when you sit down?"

"Are you kidding me? It hurts to lean over."

She exhaled.

"That's probably 'cause you're full of shit."

LaShay laughed.

He took back the blunt and gave Starla the finger.

She returned the gesture and finished off the beer.

Three logs collapsed into a pile of coal. A swarm of orange fireflies escaped into the trees.

"You feeling good yet?" LaShay asked.

"I'm feeling something," she said.

"I got a bowl packed inside. You want another hit?"

"Sure."

LaShay walked up the wooden stairs and struggled with the screen door.

"You alright there?"

"I got it."

She returned with a skull-shaped pipe and lit the weed with a green Bic, covering the top with the shroud and striker wheel.

Starla inhaled the residual smoke.

"So, I heard you got problems with some nigger at work," Andante said.

"Watch that tongue," LaShay said, staring into the fire.

"What? I ain't white."

"You ain't black neither."

"Yeah, but come on. I'm a person of color," he said.

"Not enough," she said.

"Still though," he said, turning to Starla. "I heard you got problems."

"Who'd you hear that shit from?"

"Steve in meat."

"Little Steve? What's he know."

"Says you been asked out by the same dude a couple times and that he's straight crazy."

"I seem to attract the crazy for some reason. What else?"

"Nothin' else."

"Then he doesn't know much."

"What else is there?"

"He's just some punk with a crush. He's a college student. Young and naïve as hell. Wants to get with a grown-ass woman."

"Fuckin' men," LaShay said.

Starla could feel herself ticking, blood rushing to places she had not known it to circulate before. Strange lines of technicolor plasma quartering her field of vision. Torrents of fire surrounded her. The music blaring from Andante's speakers had become a sinkhole; some kind of auditory vortex pulling her toward the car. Or was it holding her up? Or pushing her forward into the fire?

"I think I'm a little too high."

"You're tripping balls," he said in a lucid, matter of fact tone.

She crushed the beer and tossed the aluminum into the fire.

"I better call it a night then," she said. .

Starla woke up to her cellphone alarm: an unholy, electronic screeching capable of reviving her from the most comforting sleep, or the worst hangover. She reached out to the nightstand, knocking over an empty glass and her paperback copy of The Dying Mule. She stepped into the bathroom and started flossing.

"Ooh, girl! That bitch across the way got herself another man."

"Some deadbeat redneck?" she asked still looking at herself in the mirror.

"Uh uh, this one's fine by my standards. He's dark and pretty young too."

Starla walked into the kitchen, brushing her teeth. LaShay was eating a slice of last night's pizza over the sink, one hand parting the blinds.

"He looks damn fine."

Starla spit toothpaste froth into the sink before leaning

forward to peer out the window.

"Strange."

"Look at that shit. That bitch ain't got no business wearing a damn red nightgown like that," LaShay said.

"She's probably a hooker."

"You think?"

"I bet."

They watched the stranger get inside a white pickup and drive off. The older woman across the gravel road waved to him in the open doorway of the trailer.

"Well, I don't know. Maybe she's got some skills."

"I doubt it. She's a hooker."

Starla returned to the bathroom and finished brushing her teeth.

LaShay poured them both a cup of coffee and set the Newport Reds on the table.

"You want some of this pizza?"

"No, I'm gonna stop and get an egg and cheese."

"Okay. Sugar or cream?"

"Just cream, no sugar."

Starla didn't bother taking a shower. She sprayed herself with the last spurts from the perfume bottle on her dresser and took out clothes that didn't smell of smoke. She held her boots in her hand as she returned to the kitchen.

LaShay was turning the dial on the radio.

"Put it on the Lancaster station. That one comes in clear," she said, sitting down at the folding table.

"I don't wanna listen to that crap."

"It's good morning music," she said. "It speaks the truth."

"Shit. Truth about what? A bunch of depressed-ass white men losing they're dogs. Fuck Country. "

"It's about struggle," Starla said, tying her boots with an

unlit Newport in her lips.

"I'll tell you something about motherfuckin' struggle. I'll tell you about some real strife. None of this feeling sorry for yourself 'cause you a drunk piece of shit."

Starla reached for the coffee and took a sip.

"So what did y'all end up doing last night?"

"Nothing, really. I hung for a little while longer before Andante dipped out, doused the fire, went to sleep."

"Andante drove home?"

"You know he did. Nobody's gonna stop him. I ain't lettin' him spend the night here."

"True," Starla said, lighting the cigarette.

The radio static increased. LaShay kept turning the dial.

Starla sipped her coffee and let the cigarette smolder over the ashtray. She punctuated her sips with brief drags before returning the crooked filter to the wedge of the glass ashtray.

"Your brother still in Kentucky?" LaShay asked.

"Of course," she said. "He's not coming back. Not for a while."

"How come?"

Starla paused.

"Um, well, I heard this on Facebook from Karen so, you know, it might not be all that, but apparently, he got into some trouble after he whipped this rowdy guy's ass outside the strip club where she works. He plead guilty and asked for a diversionary program."

"So he's on probation."

"No, he's gotta take some anger management courses and it's gonna fuck up his hours at 84 Lumber. He got put on a late shift and he's pissed. It'll be awhile before I see him. I'm just glad he hasn't lost his job. He already pissed dirty once and they looked the other way. I'm not sure how deep in the shit he is."

"You gonna call him?"

She looked around the kitchen and stretched her shoulder.

"I'm gonna wait. See what happens."

"That's what I'm talking about, right there."

"What?"

"That's that white-people shit y'all always pull."

"The fuck you talking about?"

"The minute one of your own gets in a rut, you just walk away and don't pay them no mind. It's like you don't wanna look at somebody once they fuck up or start crying or lose a job. Y'all make each other feel so alone, and when white people feel like they gettin' to be alone in the world they don't suck it up like the rest of us. Y'all start blaming us for your shit. 'Oh, them niggers got all the privilege now.' 'If my kid was black, we'd be gettin' a scholarship.' 'How come all them Mexican's live in the same house?' 'How come them Jews only work with other Jews?'"

"Are you telling me I should call my brother?"

"Let him know you love him. He came down here when you was getting beat. Don't be a coward."

"You don't know my brother. He'll think I'm judging him."

"It don't matter what they say or how they sound. They can say 'Fuck you' and you still know it meant something that you called. People don't say what they mean. Ain't nobody genuine like that, 'less they drunk as shit."

"Everyone except you, right?"

"Bitch, please."

She turned off the radio and stubbed out the cigarette.

Starla leaned back in her chair.

"What time do you go in today?"

"I've got an hour."

"When you get off?"

"Seven-thirty."

"So eight?"

"Yeah, maybe later. What about you? Whatchu got going on today?"

"North Polo, then down by Crescent Lake."

"You need to be careful. There's cops out on Crescent Lake."

"You know where I stashed the bail money," LaShay said, smiling

"I'm serious."

 LaShay took out another Newport Red.

"So am I."

"Why do you have to get me all down and shit before work?"

"Say's the bitch that wants to listen to a motherfuckin' Country station in the morning! 'I done lost my dog and my wife and my stepsister too' are you fuckin' for real?"

Starla smiled and sipped her coffee.

"I'm not sure what I'd do without you."

"You'd be alright."

Starla took out two more cigarettes and stuck them in the front pocket of the backpack with her loose pens and lighter.

"I used to roll joints every morning while he made that cheap-ass-shit coffee. He said I rolled them too tight. They burned crooked and he couldn't get the roach out clean."

"It's been almost two years, girl."

"I'm not lamenting."

"Then why are you talking about that shit?"

"I'm just remembering. I wonder how mad he'd be if he saw me now, with you."

LaShay got up and stood over Starla who pushed back from the table. She sat down in her lap and kissed her.

The predawn mists settled into a layer of dew across the knolls and onto bald patches of red dirt. The leaves were dying now. Yellows and faded greens filled the gaps in the canopy. She couldn't find any reds or browns; no true autumn colors yet, just brittle vines and lichen-covered bark where the pines stood and the dying foliage dropped. She walked along a sidewalk the same color as the sky, passing the unkempt hedges where the town ended. Leaning over the dead blackberry bushes, she could see a deep valley of endless kudzu below. The sidewalk continued along the ridge of the valley, bridging the gap of the fractured downtown. There was a universe in the damp kudzu below her: squirrels, robins, broken mason jars, dull lengths of copper wire, trash bags, paper cups, the fat tips of yellow mushrooms sprouting up from the detritus.

She stepped over chipped concrete toward the red-brick tower of the Methodist Church and finally across the street to the old McDonald's with the roof of splintered wooden shingles. The scent of fry oil wafted down the road long before she pulled open the glass door. Men in reflective yellow vests queued up behind all of the three registers, while Spanish-speaking women in black collared shirts with accents from Sinaloa to the farthest islands of the Caribbean pushed along an assembly line of cheap food from the kitchen behind them. She ordered an egg and cheese on bagel and began to eat it outside on the curb, checking her phone for the time. She had ten minutes. The neon barber shop sign on the corner lit up and, through the murk of the tinted business-park glass, a disembodied hand flipped the hanging 'closed' sign around to 'open.' She wiped a piece of fried egg from her lips, and tilted

her side to adjust her belt. There were a few bites of the breakfast sandwich left, a thick chunk of the bagel crust smothered
in the once emulsified corner of processed American cheese.
She wrapped the remainder in the hollandaise-streaked paper
and tucked it into the corner pocket of her bag, away from
the loose cigarettes. She returned to the cracked sidewalk as
pickup trucks and a septic tanker sped past her. Birds chirped
overhead. She didn't look to see them.

Starla walked back to the strip mall.

She had eaten her breakfast too late and as a result, the
coffee from earlier felt like it was burning a hole in the lining
of her stomach. Walking through the faded white lines of the
empty parking lot toward the automatic doors, she pinched at
her back pocket to smooth the annoying ripple in her panties.
The bakery girl, Rishad, was smoking a cigarette in her Honda
Civic, its door ajar. Rishad was dangling her short legs over
the side of the driver's seat inches from the asphalt. She had
the radio on full blast; a sedate public station broadcast. Voices
bellowed from the car door speakers.

"Danish humor," the commentator said, "is like most
Scandinavian humor: an excessive almost Japanese spectacle
of slapstick and objective absurdity. There's no nuance, no
subtlety."

Rishad acknowledged Starla with a brief nod.

She returned the nod.

The Greenpoint Market was one of the last thriving
buildings in the strip mall known only to outsiders as the
Lancaster Commons. Beside the health-conscious supermar-
ket, wedged in the stucco cove along the grime-filled walkway,
there stood the remnants of an empty Radio Shack. Beyond
that stood a Dollar General that would never go out of business, a Mexican restaurant which had changed owners three

times since she could remember, and the Cedar Frog: a failing sandal boutique.

Starla reached into her pack and took out her wrinkled apron, the pocket of which bulged with out-of-stock tags, box-cutters, and accumulated wrappers. The automatic doors parted letting her in and she set her pack on the customer service desk to finish tying her apron. Bugs gave her a smile and a wink with his one cross-eye.

"How you doin', Miss Starla ?"

"Just fine," she said.

She passed through the immaculate chip aisle that ran to the meat counter and into the backroom. She just managed to clock in a minute early and stood in front of the cramped manager's office to toss her things into a small locker.

The red-headed scarecrow of a floor manager that they called Devin had his legs crossed; his skeletal hands gesturing with each syllable as he spoke with his distinct Iowan accent. Maurice, sitting across from him, was scratching at his receding hairline, a look of frustration and a bad hangover evident in his wrinkled, beet-red face.

"Hi, Starla," Devin said, peering out from the door frame of the office.

"Hi, Devin."

Maurice squinted as he massaged his temples, then allowed his body to slump back in the chair.

"The truck's here early," he said. "Also, there's no floats."

"I'll find floats," she said.

"There are no floats. There are never floats. They're all taken up by back stock, why didn't you run back stock last night?"

"I did for the first two hours. Then I had to close the store."

"Why do you always have excuses and no solutions for

me?" he yelled down the hall as she walked away. "Why do you hate us, Starla?"

She smiled and shook her head.

Jones had already salvaged five gray floats for the day's shipment. She could see stacks of auto-shipments piled against the walls, some balanced on worn, uneven pallets. Melting ice dripped from the two floats he had pulled earlier from the freezer.

"I fuckin' quit," Jones yelled over the hip-hop on the radio.

Starla pointed to the back stock along the cracked stucco walls.

"That's against the regulations isn't it?"

"I don't give a fuck. It's not going anywhere till I can get these auto-shipments squared."

"What about ad change?"

"There's no way we'll have time till tomorrow. Your bulk looks like shit. You gotta package up the pineapple rings and papaya jerky."

"Front end swamped?"

"They will be."

She helped herself to the miniature jar of Tiger Balm on the absent receiver's desk.

"Alright, let's get this over with."

She was drenched in sweat well before her first hour was up. By three o'clock, her knees felt as though they might buckle. She never felt she could justify asking for her thirty-minute break before four.

She carted the collapsed boxes to the bailing machine then walked over to the mini-fridge beside the time clock and grabbed a the plastic bottle of Table Rock spring water that she had purchased a day earlier, glad it was still there. She looked around the dust-covered backroom, the step ladders piled in the corner, the orange shop vacs lying halfway in the filthy mop-bucket reservoir.

Marc from food-service kicked open the double doors at the end of the hall and wheeled the cart with a steaming pot of spent grease. He looked like a sailor in his red cap, which he kept folded just above his ears.

"Coming through," he said in a tired voice as he maneuvered the wheels of the cart around the overflowing racks of back stock.

"Smells like french fries," she said.

"Left over from the beer-battered cod today."

"Mmm. Nothing like fried fish to go with your macrobiotic energy shake."

"Of course, what else would you have?" he said, carting the spent oil to the dumpster behind the store. There, the oil would solidify over the garbage heaps along with their recycling and paper trays. At the front of the store, the waste bins were separated neatly by category: garbage, plastic, compost, aluminum, and trash. In the back, Starla and the rest of the staff tossed every bag into the single compactor chute in the receiving bay.

Devin passed her as she screwed the top back on the water bottle.

"Hey, I'm going to go to lunch," she said.

"Don't tell me, tell your boss."

"I can't find him. I figured you'd see him eventually."

"I don't know where he is."

She set the water back into the mini-fridge and swiped her time card.

Sara passed her on the way to the deli case.

"Hey, you closin' tonight?"

"Looks like it. Emanuel was a 'no call, no show.' Unless he got arrested his ass is fired."

"Could have happened. Said last week cops stopped him on his bike, asked him if it was his. They've got a problem with thugs stealing bikes from campus."

"Emanuel ain't no thug. He's a pussy-ass college student. How you gonna hock a fuckin' ten-speed anyway?"

"True," Sara said. "But hey, cops is racist out here."

"I don't wanna close, but if he's outta here. I'm glad."

"Yeah, I heard he was all up in your shit. Some sayin' that kid was creepy. Is it true?"

"That he was in my business?"

"That he asked you out twice."

"It's true."

"Shit, how old was that kid? Nineteen?"

"Something around there."

"Fuck no."

Sara shook her head and wheeled the bread cart down the aisle.

Starla walked toward the sushi case on the opposite end of the chicken rotisseries. She searched the bright case for something without cucumber slices, eventually picking up the six-dollar tray of Philadelphia rolls. Only two of the cash registers were open. She waited in line and drummed her finger on the clear plastic, mashing the dollop of wasabi against the pink slices of pickled ginger. She felt someone pull the tray from her hands. She jerked her head to the left where Zing stood smiling at her without saying a word the way she always did. The short Burmese woman in her stark-white Irahiro sushi uniform, jet black hair wrapped in a bun and caged by a hairnet, clandestinely replaced the bar code sticker with a new one she had had stuck to her gloved pinky. She gave Starla a wink and handed her the tray. She had just turned a six-dollar tray into a two-dollar seaweed salad.

"Ka tiis twal," she attempted to say in Zing's own idiom.

The Burmese woman smiled at her like a mother and walked away.

Starla read the cover blurbs of the magazines while she waited in line for Carol to ring her up. Bugs saw her from across the cafe as he stirred honey and cinnamon into his coffee. He locked eyes with her and pointed to his register. She broke through the long line of young women yoga pants and college freshmen clutching bento boxes and backpacks to slide into first place at the furthest machine from the service desk.

"Ya'll going to lunch now?" Bugs asked her.

"I am," she said.

"Well, if I don't see you later, you have a blessed day."

"I will."

She sat alone by the juice bar and ate lunch. When she was finished, she stepped outside to smoke and drink another cup of coffee, sitting Indian-style on top of the cardboard stacks in the back alley. She tapped her ash without looking at her right hand over the side of the bail while she scrolled through her phone.

She had four minutes to go. She stared into the distance beyond the asphalt at the trees and grass and noticed a pile of dead leaves that reminded her of a prairie dog poking it's head up from a mound of dirt, its teeth forcing open its whiskery lips like a walrus.

When the manager of the store—a portly Ecuadorian woman named Lucinda—forced Starla to clock out at seven-thirty to avoid overtime, Sara asked her if she had Thursday off. A group of friends from her roller-derby club were going out for drinks. Starla hadn't committed, but said she was interested. She pulled her things from her locker and walked out the front door.

Her ears were first to go red, then her cheeks. It was much colder than the night before. She glanced, only for a moment, at the 7-Eleven across the street, then walked away without stopping in to buy cigarettes. She disappeared into the dark of the evergreens where the rusted over washing machines had been dumped and the branches were tangled in the listing strands of yellow caution tape blown over from the road. She came out on the other side where the wind picked up in the sudden absence of other trees. While working, the clay beneath her feet had frozen. It was so hard, it was as if she were walking on asphalt. The wind was funneling through the cold steel of the construction equipment and the sound of living wood creaked with every lurch of the evergreens behind her, an ominous noise that reminded her of a suspension bridge. Winter was finally settling over her town. It would come and go, interrupted by day-long periods of unwelcome heat, before staying on through February. Rain would come after that, and then, once again, the Southern heat would arrive to stay.

When she got close she noticed that she smelled no smoke. Tonight it was finally cold enough for a bonfire and LaShay hadn't lit one.

She walked down the path toward the trailers. There was light coming from the closed windows of the double-wide across from her. The same white pickup was parked in the lot beside the door. Music blared from the living room: heavy metal, old Sabbath. She could smell aluminum, sour gasoline, and the caked odor of a thousand compacted cigarettes tossed into the waste bins. Little wafts of cannabis came her way as she approached her front steps, floating south with the wind.

The front door wasn't locked.

Inside it was dark.

She stepped in, feeling her way to the couch. Her hands traced the arm to the side table where she took hold of the lamp turning the small black dial until it clicked to life.

In the incandescent light, she saw that the kitchen table was broken. A bong and a bottle of Pompeian were shattered on the floor. Murky water and olive oil soaked the carpet were the cheap pre-fab floor ended.

Lonnie was sitting in a folding chair beside the front door. He had a gash on his left temple which bled down the side of his face. A wedge of green glass was lodged in the center of the half-coagulated wound. He carried a long pump-action Browning which he held with one hand, pivoting the weight by clasping the stock in his armpit. It looked like he'd break his wrist the moment he pulled the trigger. His jacket was covered in beige grass and smears of red clay. He had a beard now and his hairline had receded even further.

He kicked the door shut, keeping the barrel pointed at her chest.

"Hey there, pretty lady," he said.

Starla froze.

"That black girl you livin' with can fight. I can see why you keep her around. She makes some good money too. Sure that helps," he said, patting his breast pocket before smoothing his hair back. "I know dark-skinned girls can fight, but I've never run into a light-skinned girl with that much gumption. She half-white, ain't she? Then that's where she gets that spunk from."

She didn't respond.

He picked at his wound and finally pulled out the glass shard, looked at it, then flicked it away.

"How's you brother?"

"He's coming to town."

"No, he's not."

"Two to one you're wrong, just like last time."

"No, I think not, I think he's still in Kentucky. And I think he's sitting tight 'cause he might be looking at probation for failing a drug test. Ya'll motherfuckers talk too much on Face-book."

She stepped toward the kitchen.

"Hold up. You park it right there and drop them bags."

She threw the backpack on the couch.

"Where is my girlfriend?" she said, her teeth clenched.

He laughed.

"You're serious ain't you? You're dead serious, no foolin'? You and her were living one those nasty alternative lifestyles. Did I ruin you for dudes or what?" He kept laughing. "Well, not anymore you ain't. That's long gone. You can't screw me like this anymore. This is my goddamned house."

"It's not yours. It never was."

"This place belongs to me and you took it," he said, reaching for a cigarette. "Now sit your ass on that couch. Wait! Second thought, you got a light?"

She nodded.

"Come, give it here."

She walked across the room and handed him a Bic.

As he took it from her, he whipped the stock of the shot-gun out from his armpit and, with better control than it initial-ly seemed, cracked her in the side of the head .

She fell to her knees.

He stood up and swung the gun like baseball bat into the

center of her back, knocking her to the floor. He pressed down on her face with his boot as he lit the menthol Basic.

All she could see were the fibers of the carpet. He tossed the Bic onto the coffee table turned the shotgun around. He dug the barrel of the shotgun into her shoulder blades as he removed his foot from her face.

"You're a funny fuckin' thing aren't cha?" he said, puffing on the cigarette. "Goddamned crazy-ass, bitch. Why me? Huh? Why do you keep doin' this shit to me."

She didn't answer.

"You're cruel," he said. "You don't care who you hurt. You make people think they're the bad guy. You can't just use people up and kick' em to the curb. You should be thankful that I care about you so much. Or else you'd get yours in a big way. You think I care if a woman shits on me? I will always defend myself. But you, you really twisted me up this time because I thought you were my friend."

"I didn't do a thing to you that you didn't deserve," she said.

"That's you trying to fuck with my head. But you can't fuck with my head anymore. You knew damn well this day was comin'. That's why you had to throw your lesbian partner under the bus in front of you."

"What the fuck did you do to LaShay?"

He puffed on the cigarette and tapped his ash into her hair.

"Well, fuck," He sniffled. "That's not on me. She came at me. I didn't do a thing you wouldn't have done. So that's that."

"You shot her you son of a bitch."

"I did not shoot her!" he yelled. "I didn't have this goddamn gun when I came by. She attacked me. She fell backwards into the sink. She was drunk as shit. Don't you go putting this shit on me!"

"So what are you gonna do now. You're gonna shoot me! Go ahead! Shoot me! I'd rather be dead that spend another second alive with you, you piece of shit! You hear me!"

She turned over in spite of the shotgun barrel and spit at him.

He took two steps back.

"You fuckin' bitch. You don't even know what you just did."

He took another step back and tossed the smoldering cigarette onto the carpet.

"You stupid, stupid woman."

He held up the shotgun, pressing the stock against his shoulder in correct form and aimed.

She spat on the carpet in front of her, rising to her knees.

He drew his left foot back to stomp her and slipped on the olive oil covered linoleum. He fell flat on his back. The shotgun fell to the side and discharged through the front door.

He had everything he wanted. He sat on the couch in his boxer shorts, socks, and white undershirt. His head bobbed up and down with the music: Snowblind from Black Sabbath. He turned up the volume up a few notches on the turntable, reached for the open hard pack of Marlboros and pulled out a crisp cigarette. He lit a match, transferred the fire to the cigarette, inhaled, blew to the side and tossed the extinguished wooden stick into the ashtray. He sucked on the filter, moving his hands with the rhythm of the music, a smirk on his face.

"Do you have any Hendrix?" the dark man called into the kitchenette.

"Not on vinyl," the woman said. "Do you take bitters with your bourbon?"

"What kind is it?"

"Maker's," she said.

"Yeah put some bitters in that stuff. It's got no bite."

"I have Wild Turkey."

"I'd rather have some that," he said, yelling over music.

"With bitters?"

"No."

"No?"

"No."

"On ice?"

"Sure," he said.

"Just a little?"

"Just get your ass back in here."

The older woman with flame-red hair in a black night-gown walked back into the living room with a garnished glass of whiskey and a gin Gibson.

"What the fuck is that on the toothpick? A lychee fruit?"

"Pickled onions," she said, taking the seat next to him.

He wrapped his hand around her shoulder and took his drink.

"Yuck."

"I made you a Gibson. They come with onions."

"I didn't know that," he said, smirking. "I tried to order one for my boss a couple days ago, a Gibson or something. I guess that's why she changed it to a Manhattan. It comes with a cherry."

"A Manhattan? Is your boss my age?"

"No," he said, sipping the drink. "She's young. Younger than me."

"She must watch Mad Men then."

"What's that?"

"A TV show," she said, resting her head on his shoulder.

"I don't watch TV."

"You don't live on this planet," she said.

"Seems like it sometimes."

She interlaced her fingers with his.

"I don't know. It's kind of refreshing to meet someone unusual who's not interested in doing anything weird."

"What constitutes weird?"

"I get some weird ones."

"I bet you do."

"I get a lot of younger guys asking me to pretend to be their moms."

He laughed.

"I'm serious," she said.

"I know you are," he said, still laughing. "After everything I've seen, nothing freaks me out."

She paused to sip her drink and pull the needle off the record as it came to an end. A moment of silence passed between them.

He smoked his cigarette and looked at her.

"Were you really in C.I.A?" she asked.

"No," he said. "I wasn't."

"Why did you lie?"

"I didn't lie. I was in the CSIS."

"What's that?"

"A big fuckin' waste of time," he said bursting to laughter.

"You're already a little drunk aren't you?"

"Nah," he said, reeling his head back. "I'm just having fun."

"Yeah?"

"Yeah."

"I bet you can't even get it up."

He set the drink on the table and wedged the cigarette in

the notch on the crystal ashtray.

"You brought this on yourself," he said, pulling down his boxers.

She leaned over grabbed his rapidly growing penis.

"You actually cleaned yourself this time."

"If you had let me use your shower like I asked."

"Nobody uses my shower," she said, pulling the condom over his cock.

"Put a record back on," he said.

She groaned.

"You like noise too much."

"Keeps me from thinking," he said.

She stood up from the couch and leaned over to the turntable.

The double bay window in front of her exploded . The momentum of what seemed like an explosion pinned her against the wall. Her chest had caved in. She was covered in blood.

The tall man dove onto the glass-covered floor. He crawled to his pants, folded on the easy chair, and pulled out the snub-nose revolver.

Lonnie hoisted himself off the slick floor.

The shotgun lay at an oblique angle beside couch. Smoke lingered in the air with the smell of tobacco and cordite. The splintered hole in the front door was the size of a volleyball. Through it, Starla could see the curled screen within the frame of the outer door.

She jumped to her feet and dove for the shotgun.

Lonnie knocked her to the couch with a left hook and grabbed it instead.

She pushed herself away with her feet, sliding on her back across the floor, letting her jacket peel away from under her.

Lonnie pulled the trigger nervously.

Nothing happened.

He looked down at the shotgun, pressed the stock against his pelvis, and racked the pump. The shell ejected onto the carpet almost without sound. He lifted it back to his shoulder and fired, blasting away a chunk of the wall.

Starla watched as he missed again.

"God damn it!" he yelled, tossing the shotgun to the side. "This isn't the way it was supposed to be!"

Starla remained behind the wall, peering over the corner. She flattened her body against the carpet, keeping as low as she possibly could.

Lonnie raised his hands in surrender.

"I'm done," he said. "I can't do this anymore. You've finally pushed me to the limit."

Neither of them spoke.

Wind bellowed through the hole in the door.

"Starla, baby—"

Lonnie stopped as the door swung open.

A shivering man emerged through the threshold: a tall man wearing only socks a white undershirt and pair of striped boxers. He held a small platinum-colored revolver with a leather grip, which he kept aimed at Lonnie.

The man glanced at the shotgun on the floor.

"What happened?" he asked.

Lonnie said nothing.

"Why?"

"The..the gun went off," he managed to stutter.

He looked at the buckshot embedded into the wall and

noticed Starla on the floor. She stared into his eyes.

"You tryin' to kill her?"

"Shoot him! Shoot him!" Starla screamed.

The tall man emptied the revolver into the Lonnie's chest.

"Anyone else in the trailer?"

"Just me," she said.

He picked up the shotgun, ejecting the spent the shell.

"Don't lie to me," he said.

"I'm not," she yelled. "Please, don't kill me."

"Stand up slow with both hands where I can see them. Walk toward me."

Starla pushed out both of her hands and separated her fingers. Slowly, she set them on the carpet and pushed herself up. Her legs quivered as she moved into the door frame. She was an open target.

"Who else was here?"

She said nothing.

"I heard you scream something about your girlfriend," he said. "Was that the woman looking at me through the window this morning?"

Starla looked up at him.

"You saw us?"

"Yup," he said. "She was your girlfriend?"

She nodded.

"And now she's dead?"

She nodded and said 'yes.'

"I'm going to assume this is the ex?"

"He killed her," she said.

"Figured as much," he said quickly ·as he lowered the shotgun. "You're gonna have a hell of a time explaining this to the cops. And I'm not gonna stick around and deal with 'em. I can't afford it." He sat down on the couch.

Starla remained in the same position, frozen. Her, her muscles grew growing weak.

He stayed seated in thought.

"If I burned down both trailers, it'd look like you did it," he said.

"But if we clean this place up a little, get any prints off the shotgun and tuck it back in his hands, put my gun in your girlfriend's hand. We could extinguish your trace from this." He turned to look at her. "Could you deal with that? Stick with the story? If we changed the scene?"

"I don't know," she managed to say.

He nodded his head.

"Yeah, it's quite a mess. You know your ex here shot my hooker."

"What?"

"Yeah, that hole in the door there. Went all the way across the road. Killed my prostitute."

"I'm...sorry," she said, confused.

He scratched at the stubble on his chin.

"There's enough in play to stump a small-town CID. But, of course, you'd have to lie to the police. Can you do that?"

She nodded.

"No, you can't. Two hours in little room with overweight detectives. All that Mountain Dew breath and hellfire. You'll crack like that," he said, snapping his fingers. "Here's what we can do. I'm about to cut you the deal of a lifetime how does that sound?"

"Good," she said.

"No, it doesn't. It sounds like garbage to you right now. Why not just come clean to the cops about the strange Indian with the dead hooker? You have nothing to lose, if they buy the story that is, because by the time you disclose this story, I'll be long gone either way. But you have to understand, other than the goodness of my heart, there's nothing keeping me from just killing you and walking away from this."

"Okay."

"You're still in shock. I've seen it before. It'll help...for now."

"No really anything sounds better than this. What kind of deal are you planning on giving me?" she said.

4.

It started with the lost dogs.

Beau woke up that morning and sat on the edge of the bed were his wife used to sleep. She never switched sides. He kept most things the way she had them out of reverence. With the furniture positioned just so, the same pictures and decorations around the mantle, the cushions fluffed, Yankee candles burning in the evening, and the front yard mulched by his nephew, he could keep up the same feeling of ease his surroundings had afforded him even when she was suffering all those years. By then, he already knew how to take care of them both.

In spite of these rituals, he still had his little acts of defiance. Smoking in the house was one of them. He massaged his back and whittled the long grains of tobacco from tip of the half-burned butt and tucked in a pinch of the cannabis his nephew had given him. He lit up, clamping the Zippo shut, squinting to the keep his eyes clear of the rising smoke. His knees creaked like floorboards as he stood.

The Krupps percolator was still frothing when the phone in his office rang. The woman on the phone seemed delusional, frantic, but strangely lucid when he mentioned his fee. She was convinced her neighbor had kidnapped her Boston terriers to train his pit bulls to kill.

He checked his datebook, agreed on a time, and hung up.

The job was a bust. He drove across town anyway. He ended up driving into an affluent subdivision: Glen Crest.

The woman was blonde, older, dressed casually. Too casual, as if she had just gotten out of bed. Her name was Lisa Anders. Her property was tacky, filled with ridiculous memorabilia, wind chimes, lawn gnomes, things purchased in beach front knick-knack shops. She said her dogs had been missing for three days. She last saw them in her backyard. He noted that her yard did not have a fence, not that it mattered. He listened to her long story about her neighbor and the shady things he did with his friends on the weekend like smoke cigarettes on the porch and leave behind a landfill's worth of beer bottles. He noticed the Margaritaville sign in her backyard. She led him into the kitchen as he scratched down rudimentary notes and offered him a cup of coffee which he declined. Mrs. Anders then reached into the back of the china curio and pulled out a bottle of sambuca from its hidden space behind a tilted mirror. She poured a few fingers into her coffee and took an immense swig from the bottle.

"Watch this," she said with a mouthful of liqueur, pulling a Bic from the cutlery drawer.

"Mrs. Anders, please."

"Just watch," she gurgled, lighting the sambuca in her mouth.

Nothing happened.

She swallowed.

"Too much saliva," she said. "Here, let me dry my mouth out."

"Really, that's okay."

He glanced at the collection of prescription bottles on the counter.

She took another swig and set the pool in her open mouth alight. A blue flame spread inside her mouth. She swallowed and smiled at him.

"What do you think of that?"

He had visited briefly with the neighbor, sitting on his couch beside the amicable pit bull. The neighbor, a young man in a Minnesota Vikings jersey, explained that Mrs. Anders was bi-polar. He spoke strangely as if he had prepared his statement in advance, or perhaps he had told it so many times that he had lost his connection to his own words. The dog did more to convince him than the neighbor. The beige pitbull never growled once, allowing Beau to pat him firmly on the side and scratch behind his ears. He was impressed the young man let the dog sit on the furniture. That would change when he got married, if he got married.

He gave up and took a walk on the nature path on the farther east side of Glen Crest. The sky was gray, the air chilled and moist. His hands grew stiff, his sciatic pain returning in his back. He found a park bench and fished the copper-plated cigarette case from his jacket. He scanned the perimeter for other people and smoked a thin joint. He lit a cigarette to mask the smell, then stubbed it out on the waste bin. His cellphone rang. He swiped the iPhone with his loosening thumb.

"Beau Cutler."

"It's been a long time, Beau."

 He winced

"What do you need, Rob?"

"How about lunch?"

"I guess I'm paying then?"

"Well, if you insist, I wouldn't turn down the offer."

"This about another police report?"

"Yup. Top dollar for this one, Beau. I've really got something here. You're gonna..." He paused. "It's gonna blow you away."

"I can tell. You sound more off-putting than normal. You blowing off class for this?"

"You gotta pay for school somehow. Can you meet me or not?"

"I'll be there."

"Awesome, see you in an hour?"

"Alright."

He ended the call and slipped the phone back into his breast pocket before standing up to stretch his back. There was a construction site at the end of the path where another subdivision had been expanding toward this one. The backhoes and unmanned bulldozers sat in the silence of the field where the red clay was still visible beneath the scattered hay and fresh blades of new grass. In his jacket pocket, he played with his Zippo, flipping it back and forth, lost in thought.

Cutler walked into the empty Mexican restaurant. He had exhaled three times before pushing open the shabby red door. The floor creaked as he stepped past the leather booths. Rob sat at the bar, slouched over his iphone as he texted frantically with both thumbs. A neglected cigarette burned in the ashtray beside his whiskey. From a distance, with the ashtray hidden behind the glass, the whiskey could have been a steaming cup of tea. Cutler noticed a pile of clothes in a plastic hamper tucked beneath the brass footrest of the bar, a computer case wedged in the side. Rob had a backpack and a gray American Traveler suitcase on the floor as well.

"What?" Are you moving in, Rob?"

He looked up from his phone and smiled.

"The man of the hour. Long time, no see."

Rob took the half-burned cigarette from the ashtray and

took one inhale before stubbing out the rest. He had a gut now and a grown man's five o'clock shadow instead of his old wispy adolescent mustache. His eyes were sunken, dark around the lids.

"You're allowed to smoke in here?" Cutler asked.

Rob looked around the room. His neck turned to jelly.

"Yeah, man. Nobody's here. I got a friend who knows the owner. They're not gonna kick me out. I just needed to get out of that fuckin' shitbag apartment. Four-hundred bucks a month for that off-campus concentration camp."

"You look like shit," Cutler said.

"Yeah," he said, nodding in agreement, sipping his whiskey as if it would remedy the blow to his vanity. "Everybody's telling me I look like Jian Ghomeshi."

"Who?"

"That syndicated motherfucker on Canadian radio. They used to play him on NPR at night. Q Radio? Radio Q? Ever heard of it? You know that guy was going to jail 'cause he choked a bunch of temps or whatever and told his producer he wanted to hate fuck her. What do want though? He's part Persian. Even the Canadians can't dilute that kind of genetically inherited violence. Towel-heads and sand niggers hate women, you know. 'Course, you never struck me as a public radio guy. What do you listen to? Alex Jones. Go fuck yourself!"

"You're rambling about nothing."

"No," Rob said, pausing to swallow his drink. "You're just old and can't keep up anymore with your informants."

"You're not an informant."

"No?"

"No, you're a thief who happens to suite my needs for now."

"Well, I'm not going to lie to you Detective Cutler. I feel

like a whole lot less these days. I'm not young. But I'm not old like you yet either."

"What's that matter with you?"

"You mean besides—"

"Besides being shit-faced at one in the afternoon."

Rob chuckled.

"Campus life is overrated," he said. "Some people have to live in tents, but if you've got a car, you're golden. You don't have to feel that wind howling on your bones. I'm blessed compared to those folks."

He laughed harder.

"I'm fuckin' blessed."

"Do you need some money?"

"For starter's, you can let me bum a cig."

He took out his cigarettes and gave one to Rob.

They both lit up.

Another young man emerged from the kitchen.

Cutler flagged him down.

The kid was dark like Rob with gelled hair and Barcelona soccer shirt, an expensive watch on his wrist.

"Whatchu need?"

"A Diet Coke , and get get this guy another shot and a pitcher of water." He turned to Rob. "And some tamales to soak up the booze."

"No sauce," Rob said.

The kid reached below the counter and cracked open a cold Diet Coke.

"You don't want anything to eat?"

"No," Culter said with the cigarette dangling from his lip. He turned to back to Rob.

"You dropped out didn't you?" he asked.

Rob nodded without looking at him.

"When?"

"A week and a half ago."

"Why?"

"Why do you think? The money ran out."

"Fail your classes?"

"As if. Dad lost his job."

"His division get moved to India too?"

"No, he lost it the old-fashioned way."

"He's drinking again?"

"He never stopped. Not really, anyway. He wasn't as dead-obvious about it like before when I'd have to carry his fat ass to bed, but he never learned how to be discreet either. Those jugs of spring water in the fridge just never froze."

"Still getting corn whiskey on the regular."

"Yeah."

"Sorry, Rob. It isn't like you can't go back later on. Get another scholarship, a Pell Grant."

Rob snorted.

"A fuckin' Pell Grant. For a Journalism Major?"

"World needs honest reporters."

"The world needs honest cops, Beau. How's that working out for everybody?"

"Nothing's that simple."

"A question I always wanted to ask you: You ever coerce a member of the African-American community with violence in your long and distinguished career with the Mecklenburg County Police Department?"

Cutler coughed, massaging his temple.

"What did you call me down here for, Rob? I am busy."

Rob scoffed.

"Sure, must be tough going door to door asking about a stolen lawnmower."

Cutler reached for his coat as he stood up from the stool. "Pay for your own goddamned tamales."

Rob tapped his ash and waved him back over.

"Come on back. Come on, don't make me beg."

Cutler said nothing.

Rob straightened himself in his bar stool and raised his voice.

"Marc Vandergreven is dead."

Cutler turned back.

"That was your last case, right? The one that went nowhere. Then you retired all shameful and quiet-like. Were you embarrassed? Worried that people were talking?"

Cutler stepped back toward the bar with his fists clenched.

Rob stood up quickly, his hands in the air when he tripped over the hamper and fell flat on his back.

Cutler offered him a hand to help him up. He didn't accept it. He kept his arms together to shield his face as if he were about to be stomped on.

"How do you know?"

"Before I dropped out I was still on the police blotter. I xeroxed the whole report."

"Yeah?"

"Hardly anyone knows about it. I never published the story."

"Why the fuck would the University rubber-gun squad know anything about that?"

"'Cause he killed himself in the parking lot of the basketball stadium. And by-the-by, the police there ain't a fuckin' rubber-gun squad. You remember Michael Pala? The frat kid that got his nose split open? They're all the fuckin' Ferguson P.D. castaways. I've seen those guys chase down track and field stars."

"So you have a copy of the report? The official report?"

He nodded.

"You copied it just to sell it to me?"

"Two weeks before finals. I had no money. My classes locked me out already. But...I still needed that last student paper check for beer and weed."

"And that's when you thought of me."

"I've given you a leg up a few times already. You gonna forget that? When I actually had something to lose in those days."

"In those days? A year and half ago? You ripped me then off too. Now, you've got more incentive."

Rob braced himself.

"Get up! I'm not gonna hit you."

Cutler gripped his wrist and pulled him from the floor.

Rob crawled back into the bar stool.

"It's not just you, if it makes you feel any better."

"What are talking about?"

"I'm auctioning all of my valuable shit off."

"All that serial killer crap."

"My Gacy original, the letters, even my Ramirez Vietnam Polaroids. Got a guy offering real money for the two. A grand a piece."

"Some people get rid of their gold clubs and guitars. You're not getting two thousand for a stolen report."

"One then."

"No."

"Seven hundred."

"You can go to hell."

"Okay, five-hundred. How's that?"

Cutler sipped the Diet Coke.

"I'll give you two-hundred dollars for it."

Rob sipped his whiskey.

"Alright."

Cutler fished out his checkbook and a pen, flattening the paper on the bar top.

"So, who the hell is dumb enough to pay you two grand for some war photos?" he asked as he pretended to write.

"They're not just war photos. You remember Richard Ramirez? The Night Stalker?"

"Serial Killer, Los Angeles, I know."

"He had an older cousin he looked up to who had gotten away atrocities while deployed in Vietnam. He raped and killed women. Tied children to tree branches with their own broken limbs. Set old men on fire during raids. He photographed the whole thing. Kept them in an old cigar tin and showed close friends. I own two of them."

"That's really sick Rob."

"I suppose it is. But it's history."

"Are they genuine?"

"They're genuine," he said. "By the way, cashing a check is a huge hassle for me."

"Too bad. Now, let me see the report."

He unzipped his computer case and handed Cutler the pages. Cutler read slowly, nodding his head.

Rob held out his hand for check.

"Give me second. None of this is abridged?"

"I photocopied every goddamn page."

"I'll bet you anything the xerox job is still logged onto the police station copy machine's history," Cutler said. .

"They don't look at that shit."

"Yes, they do."

"Can I have my money?"

Cutler handed him the check as he stuffed the folded report into his coat pocket.

"There's nothing written on this thing!"

He snatched blank check from Rob's fingers and punched him in the gut.

"Son of a bitch," Rob managed to wheeze.

He took another swing, knocking him off the stool.

Cutler caught his breath as he pulled out his wallet and let a twenty flutter to the ground.

"Enjoy your lunch," he said, as he flicked the butt of his cigarette into the hamper.

* * *

Cutler sat up in bed with a hot cup of ginger tea and a bottle of Jim Beam on the side table. With his reading glasses resting on the edge of his nose and the book light propped up on the banister above him, he read through the xeroxed report.

A university police officer was on a routine patrol of the rock gardens and the North Carolina Wetlands Restoration grounds near the Basketball Stadium. Unknown to most, the woodlands east of the of the stadium surrounding the walking path and the disc golf course by the lake was owned and maintained by the university. The modest cluster of acreage was the last bastion of the town that hadn't been paved, making it the center of the local deer population and a magnet for hunters willing to pouch on private land instead of driving forty miles north into the foothills beside the Blue Ridge Parkway. The university police took to removing clandestine deer blinds once, sometimes twice a week. Following a tip from a groundskeeper who alleged to have heard a gunshot from within the woods, the officer had headed into the forest to inspect a popular clearing. Usually, campus police found the deer blinds set up, both on the ground and in the trees, within a thirty yard radius of that particular clearing. The woodlands, even in the pitch black of the cold night, were like anything else that seemed initially complex and foreboding: once you knew where to go, where to look first, all of the bends and twists where as familiar and simple as a hometown main street. All things could, in time, be broken down into simple relationships and, despite the looming fear of the complete unknown, be learned like a map. It wasn't uncommon for the police to find trails of blood or even whole carcasses of deer left behind in the woodland as they approached. Folks would rather lose a month's worth of meat than be caught, lose their hunting license, go to jail and probably pay a fine.

This time, the officer found no deer. A few 30-30 Winchester shell casings had been left in the center of the clearing, still warm, still reeking of fresh combustion. It wasn't common to find casings in the clearing. No seasoned deer poacher stood in the open ground. The officer eventually spotted a doe with his flashlight on his way back to the patrol vehicle just before it bounded into a thicket. He kept on with the normal routine when he noticed the car parked in the handy-cap space beside the stadium entrance. It was a red Acura. He parked closer without turning his lights on. He could see fine beneath the stadium lights. The man in the front seat had a Ziploc freezer bag over his head sealed off around his neck with a collar of rubber bands and electrical tape. There was an envelope on the dashboard and half a bottle of vodka in the cup holder. The local CID would later find an empty bottle of Xanax and two opened packages of Zquil tablets on the floor, consistent with the toxicology report. There were three pages inside the envelope. All three were left blank.

Three years after Marc Vandergreven's daughter went

missing, his wife Bishop LaBlanche Vandergreven filed for divorce. The divorce was never finalized.

Culter about back to Darvin McIntire: the boy who claimed to have known of Victoria's plan to run away. The one who had made her a fake Illinois License under the fake name Lupita Lopez. Four months after the kid was let go on ID fraud, Marc Vandergreven was arrested for assaulting him three blocks from his high school. McIntire was walking along the sidewalk when Marc blocked his path with the red Acura. He confronted him and began kicking him until he was on the ground. The elderly woman who lived nearby called the police. Cutler hadn't understood McIntire. He had spoken about Victoria as if she were still alive, a possibility that Cutler had doubted. Thinking back, his teeth clenched and he shook his left leg as if his bladder were painfully full.

The kid had been deep into the drugs, dangerous prescriptions bought and sold in the hallways and under football bleachers. McIntire had a record. He was caught once with alcohol in the locker at school and suspended for a week. He had been found with less than an ounce of marijuana in his car twice and had refused drug counseling which had landed him in juvenile hall. He was caught on CCTV footage at a local apartment complex chasing residents with a fire extinguisher. Cutler had always thought about how calm he had been until the subject a Victoria was brought up, a natural clue to some kind of guilt. Unfortunately, in had turned out that McIntire was high on liquid codeine during their initial interview. Regardless Cutler had written almost all of his comments about Victoria down. He could remember some of McIntire's less inspired remarks, things like 'sharks and dolphins look alike from behind, and that's what Vicky G was.' 'there are dark corners of the internet where women crush kittens with leather

boots,' and 'when the wings come off, those are the shoes that
fit her.' He had just turned eighteen when Marc had attacked
him. His record had been clean for two months leading up to
that. Then his mother found him on the floor of his bedroom
that winter with blue lips and a needle stuck between his toes.
He had injected himself with twice the lethal dose of heroin.
While investigation, Cutler had uncovered that Darvin's last
three Google searches that he made the night he overdosed
were: "How much is too much heroin/ can you eyeball it?",
"Vandergreven name meaning" and "Vandergreven name origin." The investigators typed in the same searches and found
a suicide instructional forum amid the plethora of drug safety
and anti-drug abuse websites, and search engine registering
Dutch-American names. Despite the evidence, his death was
ruled as accidental.

Now here Marc was dead as well, an even more clear-cut
suicide.

He set the report on the side table and took a sip of the
spiked tea, then threw off the blankets and stood. He crouched
as he stepped into the bathroom and sat on the toilet. When he
came back into the bedroom, he a seat at his computer.

He thought of Victoria's case as a reverse forest: at first
simple and neat as if the leaves were sewn together from cloth
and even the creases in the tree bark were predictable, hand-
carved patterns. But as he drew closer to the artificial landscape, he could see actual weeds growing beneath that facade.
The longer he stayed the less familiar his surroundings became.

He remembered seeing the copy of The Dying Mule on
her bookshelf. It wasn't a vanity copy either, the way suburban
housewives had crisp barely opened copies of The Catcher in
the Rye, or The Painted Bird on their coffee tables while their
bedsides were piled high with Lee Child and James Patterson

novels. The book was dog-eared until bloated, the cover peeled back like the lid of a tuna can from months of reading, notes scribbled throughout. She had even copied the first lines several times in her diary. It was a first for Cutler, seeing his own novel at a crime scene: a younger self waving back to him like an awful memory, an embarrassing mistake.

He opened up the word processor and started to write a few lines before abandoning the effort. He inched over to the small table beside the bed and grabbed the Bourbon, taking it back to the liquor cabinet in the kitchen. He didn't like to see it first thing in the morning. The faucet dripped. The refrigerator hummed. He went back to bed and sipped his tea before closing his eyes.

5.

Rob Pelanski, Cutler's sometime snitch and former news editor of the Northrop University student newspaper, operated a number of blogs online. One was dedicated to his murderbilia collection, another based on urban legends. The third was a standard media blog about rare and lesser known films, rock albums, and books that he liked. He had written about Daughter of God being perverted into the slapdash nonsense that had become the Keau Reeves' vehicle Exposed. He had written short pieces about The Brown Bunny and Doctor Jesus, and the lost tapes of Death. He wrote about the hotel recordings of Bill Mann and critiqued the works of Jodorowsky. He had also at one time, written about Cutler's novel. Cutler had read the blog post, amused. Rob, of course, had no idea about Cutler's authorship of the little-known, but infamous book. When he had read the post, Cutler imagined that it was the same kind of amusement a killer had when reading a news article about their own crime.

The post read:

"No doubt about it, The Dying Mule is a challenging novel, but unlike like some infamous works in its class, it isn't a particularly challenging read. At one-hundred and thirty-five pages in the original edition, it's almost a short-story, or a novella, though I hate to use that term. The second and third prints from Anchor Books (trust me, how a book like this was released twice on a Random House imprint is another fifty-page story) is even shorter, forcing the text into a little eighty-page wafer. The narration is also straight-forward, not once in the novel is a character's thought process illuminated, nothing is explained. This aspect of, what some critics—one of them being myself but in a more formal essay format—have described as, the " noticeably restrained prose" creates an emptiness in the main character's actions. That's why there are lit-nerd forums online that go on for ever about whether or not Aiden's choice to buy a bottle of Sunkist and toss it in the storm drain is some kind of metaphor.

My answer has always been: Probably, but that's not really the point of the story now is it?

Backing up a tad, when I call The Dying Mule challenging, I mean to say that it's deceptively simple, so basic that you could read it on a beach in an afternoon and get virtually nothing out of it besides a headache and a bad evening wondering why in hell someone wrote a book like this. The story itself is a cold and somewhat obtuse examination of racial violence, insanity, and the meaningless of culture. I'm sure that sounds like a loaded, general, hipster thing to say, but the people who champion this weird little novel are generally, loaded hipsters. That's not to say that it isn't a worthwhile read. Like most books on this level—I'm thinking mostly of Beside the Sea, The Stranger and anything DFW penned—the hollow fan base of grad-student bandwagoneers helps keep these novels acceptability high, but also leaves many biased readers to think of this novel: "well, that little piece of garbage just isn't for me."

My theory is this:The Dying Mule isn't for anyone who might want to read it. It's a novel written for people who don't want to read it. That's why it's so short. That's why it's so simple, and that's why it's like being bitten by a rattlesnake toward the end of it.

The novel begins with a eight men of indistinct national origin, though foreign, digging up heaps of garbage in a post-apocalyptic landscape completely overcome with garbage. They use shovels, pickaxes, and other tools to dig through the garbage. We aren't told anything else. In the second chapter, we're introduced to Aiden, an obese, illiterate twelve-year-old who earns money by holding a cash for gold sign on the sidewalk for a nearby jewelry shop. He waves, swings and spins the sign for twelve hours a day, walking up and down the main road of an anonymous rural South Carolina town. At night, he drives out into the farmlands with his only friend, a twenty-two-year-old felon named Robbie. Robbie is a white supremacist, and has earned a certain amount of hard knocks credibility from his time in jail. The two of them commit acts of grisly violence together. They kill Mexican-owned peach farmers. They abduct black prostitutes. They set off an old WW2 grenade in the town's only gay bar. In the daytime, Aiden goes back to holding a sign on the corner. Aiden and Robbie's violence is punctuated by more scenes of the men in the near future digging in the garbage. Slowly, it is revealed that the men are either cops or volunteers searching a landfill for dumped bodies, presumably those from Robbie and Aiden. They only find the body of a dead mule. In the last scenes, Aiden sits in an interrogation room with a black police officer. Robbie walks in full police sergeant uniform to cuff and book Aiden, who, up until this point, had no idea Robbie was lying about being a felon and a member of a Nazi organization. Confronted by this truth, Aiden confesses to the crimes without implicating Robbie's participation and goes to prison, forever loyal to their joint complicity. That's it. That's the whole story. .

Kareem A. Hrabal, the author, is almost definitely a pseudonym: a simple hybrid of Kareem Abdul Jabar and Bohumil Hrabal, a Czech writer. . There are obvious references to K.A.J. in Aiden's obsession with basketball, which seem trivial at first and later manifest into an extension of his almost religious attention to race, but there are also at least three obvious references to the work of Hrabal. In the scene where Aiden sneaks into the cow pasture, the farmer's life is described as "too loud a solitude" which is the title to a Hrabal novel. There's also fictitious town mentioned south of the real life Rock Hill, South Carolina called Polna, which is also the name of the septic tank company in the second chapter. Polna is also Hrabal's favorite brewery, which he mentions often on twitter. Lastly, in the scene where Aiden is reading the church bulletin boards he glances across an advertisement for dancing lessons at the senior center, recalling Hrabal's, comic novel Dancing Lessons for the Advanced in Age.

The references don't stop there. The first sentence fragment—"A black shopping cart in green pond scum."—recalls the work of Native American, child molester Michael Dorris's novel A Yellow Raft in Blue Water.

So what do I think is the ultimate thesis of the novel? It's all about the deconstruction of a Southern novel. It's anti-Faulkner, the exact opposite of a Cormac McCarthy folktale. It doesn't spare the violence or the grit that most Southern novelists revel in, but it doesn't exploit it either. When Robbie and Aiden kill someone, the crime is committed at a distance. They do it like cowards. The book doesn't spare the boredom of everyday life, and it often touts the ubiquity of the American landscape instead of whimsically exalting the South. It's a slice of American life without embellishment. I think the authors goal was to create a time capsule, that all the fundamental faults of our time could be preserved without the cracked lens of entertainment scuffing up the details . Why do this? Perhaps it's a nod toward hope, the hope that's absent from the book. I think he's looking for a better time in our society's future by preserving the ugliness of our time, so that we won't fall into the trap of distancing ourselves from the past like we have today, distancing ourselves from the past without solving the past's problems. The Dying Mule is saying. We are still living in the past. In all our stories, or the massive omnibus of stories that all of our fucked up lives could collectively fill, wouldn't a person looking for escape find themselves whipped to shreds by the Calvinist severity of such brutal garbage. It's like a sentence of old-world penitence. There's no celebration of youth. There are no heroes. There is no unrequited love. If this shit were a movie, or a comic book, or a novel, no one, the fuck, would read it, no one, the hell, would want to see it. These are the moments made up by the negative space in between the lives of survivors . They're ugly. They're worn. They're old-testament. These are the olden days and they're never over. As long as you have an after, you'll have the olden days."

Cutler hated Rob's writing. It was puerile, hackneyed, noticeably influenced by the magazine-writer cliches. The strong points hung on a fulcrum of weak syntactical balance passed off as clever dualism. The kid read too much Buzzfeed and not enough Strunk and White.

Most of Rob's theories concerning the book were right. In that sense, Cutler thought, the kid was cut out to be a real journalist: a great snoop hellbent on truth and facts while, at the same time, still managing to be lousy writer. He was right about the Hrabal references. Cutler, at least at the age of 34, hadn't figured any American college kid would have noticed the Czech writer's titles. He recalled having a copy of Hrabal's I Served the King of England and Milan Kundera's The Joke on his desk at the old precinct. Hrabal, of course, was the best of all the eastern block writers, better than Kocbek. He was the kind of writer whose books he kept on the bedroom side table, away from the rest of the world like a fortune. Cutler had also been basketball fan during his youth but choosing the Kareem A. at the beginning of his pseudonym had been random, something to ward off any suspicion that a white cop was the author under the collar.

The cult-status surrounding his only published novel hadn't grown until ten years after the initial publication. By then, he had abandoned creative writing. It was an easy decision. In truth, he didn't enjoy it. He had written stories in high school while he still lived in New Jersey and teachers would fawn over him as if a great poet were hiding out among the rest of the jocks. But for Cutler, theirs was no connection to the work. What he wrote then felt natural enough to seem banal to him, inconsequential even. His apparent prowess over the mechanics of language and his intuition seemed to caste a smoke screen over the more artistic students and teachers, leaving them in awe of something he couldn't even see within himself. The same phenomena happened for his readers, despite the fact that after his one book his publisher was had no interest in continuing a relationship with him. Still, something powerful bled out of his sentences and he could never figure out what: a truth, perhaps, one that he could unintentionally articulated, but he still didn't know what it was or how to recognize it. There were certain tasks in life that took effort and time and care and concentration, the way a professional sniper would learn the wind patterns and the trigonometry of dealing with the distance between the muzzle and target. But some people were natural sharpshooters. As a teen, Cutler had once won a varsity State Championship basketball game at school by tossing a perfect half-court shot. He considered The Dying

Mule a similar instance. He had written a special book for a certain kind of reader, but he never knew who that reader was. He wondered what others saw in the book that he didn't, or if the entire thing was a kind of spectral psychological hoax, and his book had just hit that special place on the roulette wheel of fate.

His initial concern, once he finally set out to write the book as a beat cop, was not forging a deep connection with his readers or establishing himself as force of nature ready to shake the Southern-Gothic literary establishment, but to keep his job. He liked police work and most of all he wanted to make detective. His creative aspirations were secondary. He wondered, sometimes, if that was what made him a better writer than others; he was so close to source material that he couldn't divorce himself from it. Other times he wondered if it made him a poorer writer. Since the book's initial failure, he hadn't published anything. He had only written only on occasion and , since the age of 35, he'd barely read fiction anymore. He preferred the movies and TV. Perhaps the job had changed him. It was a strong possibility. People were always saying that his job had changed them. But at the end of the day, he thought, Gods were like photographs: tricks of the light imprinted on vessels as thin as paper, dead, frozen in time, an exaggerated victory that only took place for a second but memorized and studied as if immortal, a false immortality, fractured, warped out of context, a fluke.

6.

He woke up easier than last morning. He didn't hit a joint to loosen his back muscles. The rain the forecasters had been promising all week fell hard on the roof, washing down the icy windows to, distorting everything caught in its lens, turning the sunken parts of the unfinished neighborhood landscape jobs into black grassland ponds. Landslides and cars hydroplaned among the potholes on the bad roads. The TV news was again full of them. A slow news day for every channel. Nobody was talking about anything else. That girl Vandergreven was old news — long gone.

Cutler kept the television on in both the kitchen and the living room, listening to the anchor's voice in both ears. He made eggs on the stove and drank black drip coffee. He had a bag of sugared miniature chocolate donuts on the top of the fridge. He took out three and ate them as he flipped the eggs.

When he was finished with the eggs, he poured another cup of coffee and took it out side to his big chair on the porch to watch the rain. The screens were soaked. Water seeped inside the porch, dampening the perimeter of the carpet, but his chair was dry and his cigarette pack was full and sturdy. The paper of the cigarettes themselves were a little damp. He lit one up. It smoked just fine, the heat drying the paper as he sucked in the smoke.

His wife's vegetable garden was drowning. He stared further out at the street. Two little boys dressed in raincoats, one blue, one yellow, and black rubber galoshes navigated the overflowing sidewalk to the bus stop. They shared a rainbow umbrella. Cars drove by kicking up gallons of dirty water in giant waves over the concrete. Cutler sniffed at the air and smelled copper beneath his fog of tobacco. For some reason, or none, he thought of his early days on the beat back when the city was the city—not yet conjugated to the empty, county borderland—and the beat was the beat. A time when silence was more common in Mecklenburg County and all the suburban buildings hadn't yet cropped up like tombstones, or an evil grin full of bad teeth, were the fields were of baled hay and rusted tractors. He thought about Officer Peters, a regional transplant like himself. Instead of from the North, the tall, thin man with a stark Slavic jawline and drifted up from a vortex in Alabama. The kid had been antsy, less than charming, and childlike in his conviction and naiveté. Who in their right mind, Cutler thought, would get excited about going to church? He had said grace over greasy sandwiches in the cruiser and quoted scripture to handcuffed kids in the backseat. The funny thing was that he fit in better than Cutler whom they called him the 'Jersey Boy.' The difference was simple. Cutler wanted to live in black and white, and shades of gray, stalking the shadows in the mists gusting up from the manhole covers. The rest of them wanted to be cowboys. Peters could shoot and he was eager and he was brash. Cutler spoke the language of the street. He could work an angle and find the big fish at the end of the line. Peters always only saw the devil in every lowlife they busted, that or a lost soul. He did the talking when it came to soccer moms and pastors, devoted fathers and pious old ladies. Cutler talked to the prostitutes and drug dealers, the mindful pimps, those with an iron grip on the necessary witnesses.

Peters, he thought, that son of a bitch who always said he was too blessed to be stressed. He laughed to himself, thinking about Peters' mood while the Rae Carruth scandal was going on, the poor schmuck. He ended up getting promoted and moved to sex crimes before eating his gun a year later. The family got nothing. He should have been a highway patrolman.

Cutler laughed to himself and sipped his coffee when the phone started ringing.

Time to leave the dream world, he thought. Now, he had to tighten his voice and narrow his mind, tear it away from the clouds through which he had been drifting and turn to stone. A detective was raw, difficult, analytical to the extreme. He had to be conservative, gruff, and unfeeling. Hesitation and rudeness, strangely enough, caught him more clients than kindness. Let them do the thinking. Let them do the worrying. Blitz them with figures, dates, numbers of any kind to show them you were a man of the tangible and empirical. Intimidate them enough to believe in you. It was the only way. . His other traits were what kept them on board for the full two-thousand five hundred dollar investigation package instead of a simple seek and search recording session. A businessman with the sensibility of a good cop, what a fuckin' oxymoron.

He made his way into his office and put the receiver to his ear.

"Beau Cutler," he said, no mention of his trade, no mention of his background.

The male voice on the opposite end hesitated. That was a good sign.

"Ahh...yes..I'm calling on behalf of the Greenpoint Market Company."

The guy on the other end was trying to regain what little authority he had lost, tossing his sack back at him, but it didn't hold a candle to the kind of credibility Cutler had.

This was the social game men had to play. He hated it, but he played it well. Besides a stint in the armed services, a police background was a virtual trump card. He could not be outdone.

"What in the hell is the Greenpoint Market Company?"

"We're a grocery retailer," the man on the other side said. "Is this the office of Beaumont Cutler, Private Investigator."

"This is him speaking."

"Yes, we're looking to employ your services. Could we schedule a consultation tomorrow?"

"Yes sir, could I have an address?"

"Yes, of course, are you ready?"

"Yep," he said, with the pad and pen on the desk.

"1125 Corporate Center Drive, Asheville, North Carolina."

"Whoa, whoa! Asheville? You understand I'm based in Charlotte?"

"Yes."

"I'm not driving all the way up to Asheville," he said. "You should find another private investigator from your local area."

"You come highly recommended," the voice said.

"Yeah, by whom?" he said, putting ironic emphasis on the 'm.'

"Our CEO specifically asked for you. I'm just relaying the message."

"I'm not interested," he said and hung up.

Cutler tinkered with the replica Navy Colt on the mantle for a few minutes before the phone started ringing again. He was honest about his disinterest. How would he make a move in Asheville where he had no credibility, no connections, no snitches, no buddy cops still hanging onto their miserable jobs to help him? Then again, he considered for a moment that they wanted him because the case had something to do with his city.

He answered the phone for a second time.

"Beau Cutler."

All he heard was silence. It seemed no one was on the other end.

"Hello?" he said, annoyed. "Eh, fuck it."

Before he pull the receiver away from his ear, a nasal voice spoke.

"You do black bag jobs, Cutler?"

"Who am I speaking to?"

"Wesley Crenshaw. I'm the CEO of Greenpoint Market."

"Oh, the Wholefoods knockoff," he said as a deliberate insult.

"I understand you have a background in law enforcement."

He sounded young, and he obviously didn't know anything about private detectives.

"Yes," he said, massaging the bridge of his nose. "I am a licensed Private Investigator in the state of North Carolina if that's what you're asking."

"And you have experience in surveillance?"

"Yes, I do."

"I'd like to offer you a generous sum for a surveillance job. Do you think we could meet tomorrow and talk face to face."

"No, that's okay. I think what you're looking for is a corporate spy not a PI."

"I'd make it worth your time, Detective."

"No," he said. "And to be honest, the next PI you call is going to say the same thing because you sound fucking creepy."

"Let me just say—"

He cut him off before he could finish.

"No, let me tell you, kid. I'm not interested, so you can take whatever you consider to be a generous sum of money and shove it up your ass. Call me or contact me in any way again, and I'll make sure the Asheville Highway Patrol turns your morning commute into the country's most expensive toll road. Do you have shit in your ears, or do you understand me?"

He got no answer.

"Now, fuck off!" he said, before hanging up.

He could hear his wife's voice.

—Oh, Jesus, you fucked that one up.

"He was just a businessman thinking his money could buy him anyone. Just a punk. It was nothing, I won't hear back from him again."

—You're slipping, she said. You're making mistakes you didn't used to make back when. Now, you're making threats you can't make happen. Remember that rapist bastard when you were fresh on the beat? You know who I'm talking about.

"Oh, come on Trish, stop bustin' my balls will ya?"

—You told that son of a bitch to stop fightin', reachin' for the knife you kicked away, or else you'd break his arm. And it wasn't even a threat. You're voice trembled like you didn't want to do it to him. And it was a matter of fact that that was what you were gonna do. He could feel his arm starting to break in your hands while you told him, as a courtesy, that he was probably gonna pass out.

"Oh, Jesus Christ, Trish. Just cut it out will ya."

Their accents returned only when they argued. It was a strange thing, as if their regions were only fit for pain. Trish had moved down south from Staten Island. Cutler was the Jersey Boy.

The phone started ringing once again.

"Oh, good god fuck," he said, grabbing the receiver.

"Look, I don't want the job. I'm sorry."

It was a woman's voice this time.

"Mr. Cutler," the young woman said. "We understand your hesitation based on our previous two calls, and I would like to apologize on behalf of Greenpoint Market. We've never worked with a private investigator in the past and we are not completely confident in the best manner to be approaching a professional such as yourself."

Flattery, he thought. It was a good start. He pictured the woman blonde, strict-looking. She must have been the only competent person in the office if she had the sagacity to fix the CEO's mess. She might have been the only good one in the bunch. He imagined the weird, young CEO's befuddled expression while still sitting at his desk as she stood over him with the phone. She'd probably say something witty like 'you're welcome', or even something more subtle after the call. It could have been, of course, more sinister and calculated than he thought. Their last effort might have been the soft female voice of an intern. Either way, it kept him talking.

He cut to the chase.

"If your case requires me to stay in Asheville, I'm not interested. You should look for a younger, more eager investigator."

"It does not, sir."

"Then where is the location of this surveillance job?"

"The border town below you, in Rock Hill, South Carolina."

"That's more reasonable."

"It involves one of our franchises," she said.

"The Northrop Commons store," he said.

"Yes."

"Okay, I'm interested. I'll be able to schedule a consultation."

"Do you think I could come to your office tomorrow?"

"I don't work out of an office," he said. "And I'd rather do the consultation today. How is four thirty?"

"We can't have a rep in Charlotte today until after five."

"I'll come to you," he said.

"You will?."

"It's standard," he said. "I just don't wanna stay up there. There's free parking?"

"Of course, we're nowhere near the city."

"Good," he said, regretting his words.

* * *

It was still raining in Charlotte when he left, but Asheville was dry and cold. A city the color of smoke, he thought. He rode along the main highway through the mountain ranges. He had a good sense of direction. Once he got passed the city, he shut off his phone and the clear female voice of the GPS stopped in mid-sentence. He had been expecting some kind of industrial park, a crowded business district where the young pedestrians walked the streets with their phones clamped to their belts like a sidearm. Cutler noticed a lot of older men doing to same; their guts hanging over their leather belts with the giant smartphone holstered at their side, body tilted sideways as if the phone case were made of solid lead. They just wanted to look like John Wayne.

Instead of the business park, he found himself driving through the country past golf courses and private lakes, opulent homes built into the sides of mountains hidden by oaks and poplars. He took the last turn up a single lane road surrounded by rhododendrons and dull evergreens. The street sign looked like a Victorian gas lamp, a whimsical design framing the municipal green with faux cast-iron leaves. "1125 Corporate Center Drive."it said in raised gold letters.

There was no one driving in behind him. Once he turned onto the little road, he stopped his silver Hyundai and checked his phone. He had three messages from Mrs. Anders. He set the phone in the empty cup holder and took out his cigarettes from the side console. He kept the Marlboro between his lips without lighting it while he fidgeted with the Zippo as he drove. He kept his eyes moving, scanning the dense woodland on either side of his sedan. Twigs and bits of grit crunched beneath his tires. He eased down a hill and came to a giant black gate. A uniformed security guard sat in a tall glass-paneled booth reading a copy of The Mountain X-press.

Cutler rolled down the window.

The guard leaned in.

"License and registration."

Cutler raised an eyebrow, taking the unlit cigarette of his mouth.

"Why the fuck would you ask for that?"

The young guard instantly frowned.

"First time?" he said.

"Yeah."

"We have different rules here, sir. I need to verify who you are for safety purposes."

"I haven't even told you who I am yet."

"Who are you?"

"Detective Beau Cutler."

"I don't know that. Show me some I.D., Mr. Attitude."

He handed him his state investigator's license in the black cred case.

The guard smiled.

"A Private eye?" he said, enjoying his new-found avenue of condescension.

"I've got an appointment with your CEO?"

"He's not my CEO."

"You know what the fuck I mean."

"Hold on for a minute," the guard said, starting to turn back into the glass booth.

"Give me back my license."

"You'll get it back."

"Give it back to me, slick."

He paused, glanced once more at the license, and tossed him the cred case.

"Wait here," he said.

"Where else would I go, prick?" he mumbled as he lit the cigarette.

When the guard returned from the booth, the automatic gates were opening. He had his hands gripped tightly around the center of his belt, a classic cop stance.

"You're clear to enter, Detective," he said, staring at him.

"Much obliged, kiddo," he said, placing the Marlboro in the side of his mouth to drive with both hands. "Oh, and a word of advice, holding your pants like that doesn't make your crotch look any bigger. Not for you, at least."

Cutler tossed the half-smoked butt from the window once he reached the roundabout. From there, he passed an outdoor handball court. He chuckled.

The Greenpoint Market corporate Headquarters was set up like a campus, a kind of hipster paradise tucked into the woods. The Quantico of over-priced food.

"Come try our free-range, premium, organic donkey piss-water. The next step in hydration," he said out loud, laughing. He followed the 'vistor's parking' sign and took the space behind the bushel of elephant grass. He stretched his legs and slammed the door. He followed a cobblestone path through a mulched garden and hiked up the steps to the translucent glass doors of the office lobby. The girl at the front desk was dressed conservatively enough with a violet turtleneck and a silver medallion. The young guy behind her at the copy machine wore a handlebar mustache and white-wall haircut that might have looked good on John Dillinger and no one else.

He approached the desk and flashed her his cred case.

"I have a four-thirty appointment," he said.

"Yes sir," she said in a lower-pitched voice than he was expecting. "I just need you to sign here." She gave him a clip board with a list of names.

He signed in cursive. It was the only name on the list in cursive.

"Lost art," he said.

"What's that?"

"Nobody writes in cursive anymore."

"I guess not," she said with a smile.

The only sound in from the lobby came from the stone fountain behind the row of ottomans.

"This place is like a church," he said. "What's with the security guard?"

"What about him?"

The young guy at the copy machine turned and made eye contact with Cutler.

"Our CEO, Wesley Crenshaw, is a former member of The Church of Scientology. He has to be extra careful."

"Explains the attitude."

The phone on the girl's desk rang. She looked at the mustached kid behind her.

"Byron, can you take Detective Cutler to the VIP lounge?"

He straightened a stack of papers against the copy machine.

"Absolutely," he said.

They walked to the elevator in silence. He shook his hand once they were inside.

"Byron Stokes, marketing. You're a detective?"

"I'm a P.I."

"Shit, man. That's cool. What are you doing here?"

"I'm about to find out."

"I gotta say, you look like a detective. You've got the five o'clock shadow. You smell like cigarettes. The loose tie, beige trench coat. It's a classic look, man."

Cutler nodded.

"Thanks," he said. " I work real hard on it."

The elevator door opened.

"I'd love to pick your brain, man."

"I'd like to pick your brain too," Cutler said.

"Yeah?"

"Sure, I've always wanted to meet a Groucho Marx impersonator."

The kid, now silent, opened up the tall oaken door for Cutler and walked away.

He could hear Trish's voice again.

—Are you going to insult everybody today?

"Get off my back. I'm in that kind of mood."

He walked into a large conference room with a high ceiling and a long table. Across from the pitcher of ice water and bulb-shaped glasses was a platter of salami and water crackers. A white smart board had been mounted to the far wall.

The door opened behind him.

A woman with jet black hair in a tight bun approached him. She wore jeans and a professional-looking blouse. An I.D.

Badge hung from the lanyard around her neck, something he hadn't noticed on anyone else so far.

"Mr. Cutler?"

"He recognized the voice.

"That'd be me."

"Narvice LaQuinn," she said, shaking his hand. "Mr. Crenshaw would like to apologize again for the lack of professionalism of the earlier phone call."

"Then he can apologize himself," he said.

"And he will. Please, make yourself comfortable."

He put another cigarette between his lips and flicked open the Zippo. To his surprise, she didn't object. He poured himself a glass of water and took another glass to use as an ashtray before taking a seat.

There was a plasma screen television in the corner.

Narvice handed him the remote.

"Mr. Crenshaw is just about to finish up with an impromptu meeting. He should be here soon."

"Likes to make a grand entrance, huh?"

A young man's nasal voice reverberated through the room like an echo sounding through a metal pipe.

"It isn't always easy getting around a building like this. But hey, that's the perk of being the boss. The meeting doesn't start until you get there."

Cutler heard jingling as if someone were rattling their car keys in the dark hallway past the open doors on the opposite end of the conference table.

An animal emerged from the dark, panting: a German shepherd with a bright yellow service vest. The man holding its leash was thin and wore black dress pants and white-collar shirt rolled up at the sleeves. He was clean shaven and wore sunglasses. His hair, unlike the rest of his appearance, was unkempt and matted around the sides. He let the dog drag him through the hall and into the room with his arm fully extended and his back tilted as if he could give a damn about where he was going. The German shepherd led him to the edge of the table. Crenshaw's hand flailed for a moment, then gripped the leather head rest of the chair. He sat down and let go of the leash. The dog sat beneath the table, silent.

"Narvice?" he said.

"Yes?"

"A glass of water, please. And if you could open a window above Mr. Cutler." He cocked his head to the side as if he were staring at the ceiling. "No offense about the smoking. I just don't want it to linger in the room."

Narvice cracked open the window first, and then set a glass of water into Crenshaw's open hand.

"Thank you for driving so far on such short notice. I'm sorry I came off a little weird on the phone, but..ah..I've been weirded out lately. I'm not eating much. Sleeping even less." He laughed nervously. "If it weren't for Narvice here, I'd be up a creek. I don't think any other P.I. would work out for this case."

"Why do you say that, Mr. Crenshaw?"

"Because, according to what we've heard, you have a good reputation for discretion."

"Cut the formal talk and lay it out for me, please," Culter said, tapping his ash.

"People have told me you keep your mouth shut."

"I'll keep it shut for the right price."

"But you were a cop."

"Almost all licensed P.I.s have some kind of law enforcement background."

"But you're willing to go that extra mile."

"Stop veiling your words, Mr. Crenshaw. If I'm going to work for you, I need to know exactly what you want. Nothing leaves this room." He sucked on the filter. Smoke drifted from his lips as he spoke. "If you're asking me to do something illegal, sure I'll do something illegal. But it all depends on what it is and how much you're willing to pay."

Narvice glanced at Crenshaw as if he could see her and glance back, then stepped around him, patting his shoulder. She took out a key and unlocked the computer keyboard at the podium beside the smart board.

"Less than a month ago, we discovered that one of our IT gurus was a selling incriminating information to a German competitor. He turned out to be a corporate spy. I'm not asking you to find him, because we already found him. He managed to leave the country and walk away with more than just trade secrets."

"His name?" Cutler said.

"That's not the important part."

"I still need his name?"

"We're not asking you to find him, I'm just setting up the situation for you."

"I still want his name. You gotta check every avenue."

"He's not a problem anymore."

"He's dead then, right?" Cutler said without changing his tone. "This employee who took your shit, he's dead. You had him killed, right?"

The smart board screen lit up.

Narvice looked at Cutler.

He didn't recognize the expression, something hidden beneath a deeper emotion.

"His name was Jonathan Ruiz," Crenshaw said.

Cutler wrote the name down.

"Continue," he said.

Crenshaw bit his lower lip before he started speaking again.

"We were able to retrieve the information before any of it was used against us."

Cutler nodded.

"But—?"

"But, in the scramble to retrieve the stolen information— of course, we hired a third party for the physical retrieval—we got more than we should have. It came back to us encrypted a thousand times over, renamed, buried. It was a mess. Of course, we received it in the form of a USB stick, which used to belong to—" he gestured with his hand to signal Cutler.

"Jonathan Ruiz."

"Yes, and that's when we discovered a series of video files and photographs. And they are really goddamn disturbing."

"What's on the videos?"

Narvice cleared her throat.

"It's not pleasant," she said almost in a whisper.

"You realize I'm going to have to watch them, right? It's the only way."

"We've isolated some of the images as well for you," Narvice said, bringing Cutler a beige folder.

He took out the glossy photographs: pixelated side profiles of a white man in his mid-thirties.

"Okay," he said, staring at the images. "So what's the bottom line?"

"We want to know who he is. See, someone else is blackmailing me. Since Ruiz is no longer a problem we think this man might be the prime suspect."

"Blackmailing you over what exactly?"

"We'd like to keep that confidential. It's personal information concerning myself, not my company."

"If the content of these videos is so egregious, I think you need to go to the police not me. They have access to databases and forensic experts who can do a better job than I could," he said, handing the folder back to Narvice.

"If we went to the cops, we'd have to explain the other man in these videos. They'd want them both. And we'd have to tell him how we got the damn things in the first place. And I don't want that. That's why we want to pay you."

"I still don't get it," he said. "Why do you want me. I chase credit-card thieves and look for cheating spouses. What keeps me concerned is why you hunted me down. Can't just be the reputation. Can't just be that." He paused for moment and stubbed out the cigarette. "Why do you want me?"

Crenshaw took a moment to stretch his neck.

Narvice stared at him.

"You keep looking at him like he's gonna look back," Cutler said to her.

"I'm not completely blind, Mr. Cutler. I can't see much. I certainly can't read or make it through a dark hallway without Scott here." He pointed to the dog below the table. "But I can make out your silhouette. Everyone is an aura of light to me."

"How did you go blind?"

"For a detective, you sure haven't done your homework. You don't know anything about me do you?"

"Take it as a reassurance," Cutler said. "I'm not here to find out about you. I'm here to work for you."

Narvice cleared her throat again.

"With all due respect, Mr. Cutler, you've seemed unwilling to help from the start."

He looked into her eyes.

"Do you ever get tired of talking like that?"

"Like what?"

"Like a lawyer."

"I am a lawyer," she said.

"Well, I'm a private investigator. I don't have the luxury to seal off my words in a decorative frame. I get paid to be honest. I get people fired from their jobs. I get people killed. You think every guy who wants proof his wife is cheating files for divorce? A lot of the time, people put me in danger. Getting stabbed isn't fun. Getting a gun pulled on you isn't fun either. Now I'm old, and, to be frank, I don't need your fuckin' money. I'm more than happy just taking the Mickey-Mouse jobs from here on out. So, if you both want me to do this job, which, by the way, you're both being horrendously vague about, I need to know why you picked me. And I don't believe it was a random decision."

For the first time, Crenshaw turned his face toward Narvice and smiled.

"I like him more than I thought I would," he said.

Narvice looked exasperated. She said nothing.

He looked back into Cutler's direction.

"I want you because you worked the Vandergreven case," he said.

"The disappearance that we couldn't solve?"

"Exactly," he said. "I just started researching the case. That's when I realized you'd become a PI. You're the only person who could possibly solve this for us. I would like to pay you forty-thousand dollars for your services."

"You just wanted me because I worked some high-profile case?"

Crenshaw smiled.

"It's time you saw the video."

***

In his imaginary world, a criminology class has commenced in the top floor of some esteemed university building. The students—assuming any of them were interested in a career in law enforcement now that the days of Ferguson, Missouri and Trayvon Martin echoed the screams of Emmet Till and Los Angeles in the sixties—watched in silence as the young and playful professor sat atop his desk in his plain clothes as he clicked the slides of his projected sideshow along via remote. He plays with these hapless kids in the darkness, half-bathing in the digital projector light, enough to warp the five-by-five images, not because he was unseasoned and fresh out of grad school, but because he is am A-class motherfucker who could have used a reality check on the handle-end of a pistol a few times over on one of his nighttime stroll. But no such luck would ever befall this hipster piece of garbage since he lived in the gentrifying sector of the once crappy part of town, with new third-wave coffee shops sprouting on every other corner. He's never walked a beat in his life and here he was, teaching the next generation of shitkickers how to cop up the goddamn streets. He was a cunt and an asshole and a fraud and Cutler didn't know why he was in his mind, flipping through the pictures, asking the students which of the drawings were done by artists, and which by serial killers. The slides moved along, slowly, painfully, pointlessly. The bird soaring toward heaven: serial killer, Richard Cottingham. The tranquil Appalachian homestead: serial killer, Henry Lucas. The eerie bisected face of a mall mannequin cradling the bottom half of another disfigured dummy: artist, Eric Fournier. Anybody could get the fucking picture. He thought of a kid raising his hand among the stupidity, a single hand reaching into the swarming dust in the crescendo of manufactured light

The professor acknowledges the raised hand, poised himself for the question.

"What about that poem by that girl?"

"Poem by what girl?" he says with a smile on his face, basking part of the way into a blue-crayon demon: another Henry Lucas.

"Vandergreven's," the kid says.

The professor gently puts his head in his hands.

"There's one every semester," Cutler imagines him saying.

***

He had seen his share of fucked-up videos, black and white CCTV shots, cell phone footage of rapes, beatings, and murders. Robberies were incidental to the greater offense in Cutler's opinion. Motive was only necessary for paperwork and the district attorney. He had never been the kind of detective to wallow in the red tape, to learn the little ins-and-outs, to mind the pitfalls. He set his sights on the end result, the truth, the moral fundamentals. This lack of strategy made him a poor detective most of the time. A better person, but a poor detective. Despite his old artistic aspirations, he didn't believe in the inner-life of a person. A human being's actions, in his opinion, made them what they are. A person was a series of physical movements, transitive and intransitive, connected by the same body, rather than introverted qualia. He found it funny when a perp was more concerned with whether or not the he believed them to be a good person, rather than getting away with the crime. He didn't care why anyone did anything. Perhaps that was the message of The Dying Mule. Watching hours worth of brutality through the static of a closed circuit TV footage had had an adverse effect on a person's worldview.

Cutler watched the smart board screen in the darkness as

Narvice loaded the MPEG files.

She clicked on the first. The clip began.

He saw a white man, not the individual from the murky photos.

"That's Ruiz," Narvice said.

The man was adjusting the digital camera on the stand, staring into the lens. He had a face that Cutler would've liked to bash in with a brick.

Ruiz got the angle where he wanted it and backed up against the unfinished drywall. He stepped out of the frame for the next few seconds. Cutler watched the footage of the drywall in silence between Crenshaw and Narvice. Crenshaw had taken off his dog's service vest and was scratching it behind the ears. A screeching noise sounded from the Dolby speakers attached to the wall. On the screen, Ruiz was pulling the steel frame of a twin bed into the frame of the shot. He moved it from one corner of the room to the next, each time walking behind the camera to check the angle.

"You ain't no fuckin' Kubrick, asshole," Cutler mumbled.

The clip ended.

Narvice clicked on the next MPEG file to begin.

Ruiz had a mattress with a plastic top sheet on the bed, the kind children with weak bladders, the elderly, and severe alcoholics used.

Crenshaw stood up abruptly. He placed his hand on Cutler's shoulder.

"I have another meeting," he said. "Narvice here will fill you in on the rest. The noises upset Scott anyway."

Crenshaw left the VIP lounge.

Narvice poured herself a glass of water and turned away.

He kept watching.

The second man in question entered the frame, along

with a woman dressed only in a leather girdle and red platform shoes. They stood for awhile until Ruiz' handed her the end of a leash. She pulled a black and white spotted great Dane into the frame.

Cutler could feel the heat rising in his cheeks and his heart shudder within his chest. The woman in the leather girdle was Victoria Vandergreven. He recognized the color of her skin and hair before he even noticed the scar on the side of her face. She was a woman now, taller, thinner it seemed. Her face had matured. The other man took the dog and forced it onto its back atop the bed. She climbed on as well and spread its legs apart. Victoria set the dog's massive scrotum in her mouth until it's red, carrot-shaped phallus extended from the speckled sheath of skin.

Cutler looked away.

"That's enough," he said. "I've seen enough."

He could hear Ruiz's labored breathing from behind the camera as he watched Victoria engage the dog.

Cutler pounded his fist on the table.

"Turn the fucking thing off!"

Narvice stood up and ended the clip.

Cutler slammed the glass of water onto the table with the palm of his hand. A few streaks of his blood splattered across the table. He pulled out the shards and wiped a bloody hand print across the conference table.

"That's why you wanted me," Cutler said without looking at Narvice. "Am I supposed to be the next best thing compared to the police?"

"We realized the girl was still alive. In researching the case, we discovered you and that your services were for hire. Those facts on top of your commitment to discretion makes you the only possible candidate."

Cutler picked up the photo of the second man.

"If she's still alive, then why the fuck would I go after this guy?"

"They're connected. You find him, you'll find her."

"Or so you think," Cutler said. "Are you aware that Vandergeven's father just killed himself? So I'm protecting your CEO from going to prison as well as undermining an active police investigation."

"That's exactly what you're going to do. And what's in it for you is the money and a chance to finish what you started, and solve the case," she said. "Or you know, you could forget about everything you've just seen. You could forget about Victoria. And Ruiz, of course, our former associate."

He went silent.

"You evil bitch," he said. "You bastards set me up."

"Come out on the other end, Mr. Cutler, and you might be a hero. Go to police or try to walk away and we might have to..."

"Shut the fuck up," he said, defeated. "I've been threatened before. I'm not afraid of you."

"I'd be afraid, Mr. Cutler. If I were you, I'd be terrified," she said. "I've seen the entire thing. After they finish, she cuts the dog up while it's still alive. There's an entire subculture devoted to these kinds of films."

"I'm aware," he said.

She took out a piece of hotel paper and handed it to Cutler.

"I won't force you to watch the rest, but it's important you read this."

"What is it?"

"It's the writing spray-painted on the wall in the last seconds of the footage. We wondered if it would help identify the location or any other significance."

He read the paper: "God smokes the lamb's breath, from the ram's horn, atop the mountain of loneliness."

His hands were trembling.

Narvice leaned over and whispered to him.

"Not so tough now, are you?"

For all he knew, there was no real threat of blackmail. He had finally fallen for the long con. The perfect long con. They had him by the balls and he knew it.

He walked out of the main office with a new briefcase filled with files and phone records and email addresses. He had a new prepaid cell phone and four SD cards. The sky outside was even grayer than before. His stomach churned. He stumbled through the cobblestone path to his car where he vomited on the asphalt. He wiped his mouth, leaving a smear of blood from his torn palm on his chin and propped himself against the tire of the Hyundai.

--You have to go to the police, Trish said in his ear. You're in over your head, Beau.

"I know," he said, reaching for a cigarette.

A young man in a sweater vest, his lanyard badge dangling, approached him.

"Are you okay, man?"

"I'm fine," he whispered with the wrinkled cigarette in his lips. He started flicking the Zippo. The wick wouldn't ignite.

The kid looked at the vomit on his shoes and the blood on his hand and chin.

"You don't look fine, man. I'm gonna call you an ambulance."

"Don't," he said.

The kid pulled out his phone.

Cutler reached into his coat and pulled out the stainless .38 with the rubber grip.

"Fuck off."

The kid started to run.

"Drop the phone on the ground!"

The kid tossed the phone aside like a piece of garbage and bolted behind the elephant grass.

Cutler hoisted himself up and walked around to the driver's door of the car. He circled the roundabout twice, giving his hands time to stop shaking, then approached the giant black gate.

The eager security guard stopped him once again, motioning with his hands to roll down the passenger's side window. Cutler opted to shut off the engine completely and walk out into the crisp mountain air beside the glass booth.

"You have a good meeting, Detective," the guard said, his boyish eyelashes flared flashing outward like clam shells.

Cutler said nothing and placed his .38 on the warm hood of the Hyundai.

"This is my service weapon," he said. " I have a license granted by the attorney general to carry this under North Carolina law as a Private Investigator."

The guard squinted.

"Okay. Why are you telling me, old-timer?"

"What about you, young man? What are you issued there?"

The guard gestured toward his service weapon.

"What's it to you?"

"You ex-police?" Cutler asked.

"Military."

"So you're used to a Berretta?"

"M-4," the guard said.

"Not used to the pistol then, huh?" Cutler said, opening the cylinder of his .38, pouring the cartridges into his hand, and pocketing them in his jacket pocket. "This is all I have to work with now. It's small but it packs a punch."

The guard hesitated for a moment; then he then removed the Glock from his holster, ejecting the clip, pulling back the slide to pop the bullet from the chamber into his hand.

"Light weight," he said. "Stiff slide, but the trigger pulls like butter. I try to get it down to the range once a week if I can."

Cutler held the two empty pistols in his hand, comparing the weight.

"Damn, that is light. I prefer a gun with a little more weight to it."

"Why?"

"It's more like holding an actual weapon in your hand, rather than a game controller, a cheap piece of plastic for the sheer hell of it. See the difference?"

He handed the two guns to the security guard.

The guard weighed them in his open palms.

Cutler took a swing, flattening the guard's nose against his face. The boy tried to stand up in the entrance of the booth, but Cutler kept kicking him in the face to the ground. He wiped the kid's blood off his shoe and took back the .38 before driving away.

He drove of the highway feeling sick, the nicotine overload of a dozen cigarettes and barely any blood sugar to carry it to term. His stomach was knotted from the stress , and he felt faint as if he were too high. The sensation of the disconnect warmed his wrists while his hands sustained a mild tremor. Finally the panic overcame him as he drove into the bare parking lot of the strip mall. He was somewhere on the outskirts of Ashville: a little extension of some unseen neighborhood. He got out of the car and walked into the first restaurant he saw. It was called Miranda's Deli. The wooden booths had no cushions like the chairs did. He couldn't read the menu on the black chalkboards behind the register, not only because of his blurring vision but, in part, due to the dull neon-colored chalk and local cursive script. It was becoming a lost art for good reason.

The girl in the black apron at the register had neon pink hair to match the menu while the opposite half of her head was completely shaved to reveal a perfectly rounded scalp as well as dark tattoo of a chrysanthemum silhouette. Her name tag read Chryss.

"What can I get you?"

"Coffee and a donut."

"What kind?"

"Chocolate."

"Creamer with the coffee?"

"Yeah."

"Rice, Almond, or Soy creamer?"

"Just plastic cow," he said, getting out his wallet.

"We're a vegan restaurant," she said.

"Oh, I didn't realize. Then Almond creamer is fine."

"Sugar?"

"No sugar in the coffee. Oh, and make that a half-caf. It's kinda late."

He wiped the sweat from his forehead.

She pulled a donut from the glass case with a scrap of wax paper and set it on a colorful porcelain dish. He paid with four blood-stained bills.

She took her time with the coffee, long enough for him to stare down at the fresh cut in the center of his palm. He hadn't picked out all of the glass yet. He took the little cake fork from the paper napkin and wiggled the metal teeth beneath his skin, trying to push out the shards. He set down the fork once he had bored an opening large enough to see the glass, and then pushed it upward with his dirty thumb. The translucent speck emerged from his skin and fell onto a napkin on the table with a few more droplets of blood.

The girl set the coffee and saucer down in front of him.

"Are you alright?"

"I think I'm having a panic attack," he said.

"We have a first-aid kit in the back let me get it for you."

"Thanks," he said, lifting the white mug with his bloody hand, smudging the handle with a crimson thumbprint as he drank.

The girl returned to his table with the kit followed by a tall young man in a dress that reminded Cutler of Olive Oil from Popeye. It didn't help that the young man had red lipstick and jet black hair parted into pigtails.

"You need us to call anybody for you?" he said in a deep voice.

"I'll be alright," he said. "Part of the job. I'm a Private Detective. Just a bad day at work."

Cutler forced a smile.

"You look shook up," the half-bald girl said.

"A little," he said.

She took his hand and started cleaning it with the alcohol swab.

"Did somebody cut you?"

"Broken glass," he said, wincing from the sting.

"Is there someone after you?" the man in the dress said.

"No."

The girl coated the superficial wound in liquid bandage.

"Wait a little while for that dry."

"Thanks," he said.

"Are you going to be alright?" the man said.

"I just need to gather myself," he said.

"Okay. Do you want any water?"

"I'm fine," he said.

"Alright. Take it easy. Stay as long as you need."

The kitchen guy walked away. The girl stayed, sitting across from him. She looked at him in silence as he sipped his coffee and took a bite of the donut.

"Can I do anything else for you?"

"I think I just had that conversation with your boss."

She observed his coat.

"There's still some blood on your coat and shirt."

"Probably," he said, wiping the coffee from his chin.

"You're a detective?"

"Private Investigator."

"Is it exciting?"

"No," he said. "Not really. Not in a good way."

"You look straight-laced. Most old guys would have reacted weird to Josh."

"The guy in the dress? Not a whole lot shocks me."

"It's not that they get shocked. They just look offended."

"I'm a creepy guy who's bleeding everywhere."

She shrugged and looked at his red knuckles.

"Are you some kind of badass?"

"I'm old," he said as if that were an answer.

"Do you like the donut?"

"It's interesting."

"It's carob."

"Like for dogs?"

"Yeah."

She looked over the booth at the register, though no one else was around.

"I gotta get back to work."

He sat alone staring at the mounting gray clouds over the trees. There wasn't much infrastructure beyond the strip mall. The highway and the neighborhood were all perched at the edge of the mountain. He sipped his coffee and felt the panic attack fade. Strange how the warmth of the liquid seemed to affect him more than the caffeine within it. He looked at a vacant lot across from the parking lot. A young boy swiped at the weeds and crabgrass, at the nettles and amethyst cudweed, with a bamboo switch.

Snow fell from the clouds.

"No fuckin' way," the girl said, peering at the window from behind the register.

Cutler glanced at the field. The boy was gone. A massive wolfhound sat upright at the edge of the lot, staring at him. The dog was motionless. It didn't blink. Snow collected onto its shaggy fur. Cutler stood up and pressed his face against the glass.

"Is everything alright out there?" she asked.

"Just watching the snow," he said, locking eyes with the dog.

7.

She spent the afternoons alone in the Red Roof Inn cuffed to the steel chain he had wrapped around the base of the bathroom toilet. The handcuffs were heavy; actual police issue the way they left a semi-indelible ring around her ankle, eating into her tendon. The tall Indian had lined the outside of the tub with pillows from the queen-sized bed and gave her a large chair cushion to sit on. He brought her cheap paper-wrapped hamburgers and bottled spring water from 7-Eleven. She had just enough slack to stand and use the toilet. Cleaning herself afterward was difficult. She had a pissed a little on the couch cushion once, so she had flipped it over.

Two days in, he brought her Chinese and a six-pack of beer, then wheeled the dresser with the television into the hallway and gave her the remote. She figured she had earned it for keeping quiet.

Starla had asked him a few times if he wanted a blowjob. She bent herself over the side of tub and lowered her black yoga pants and red panties and told him he could do whatever he wanted − though even she admitted she hadn't showered in days.

Still, he always refused, but it never discouraged her from asking. He'd smile and shake his head before leaving the room.

She managed to select a pay-per-view film. A single act of disobedience. But when she was watching it, she found that she couldn't enjoy it. Boredom took the place of dread and, as the next excruciatingly long day began, dread gave way to another bout of panic. She stared at the Jack-in-the-Box and

McDonald's wrappers piling up on the counter, then down at the bathroom trash bin and the overflow of beer bottles. The alcohol was her only source of comfort, the only way she could relax and keep herself from crying. Her adrenaline pulsed as she briefly considered that her indigenous captor was fattening her up for some arcane ritual, getting ready to eat her.

On the third night, he joined her on the bathroom floor in his white undershirt and boxers. He held a chilled fifth of whiskey in his hands and two of the squat water glasses from desk beside the empty ice bucket.

"I kept this in the freezer," he said. "So, we don't need ice."

"I don't drink whiskey," she said.

"There's a mini-bar. Gin? Rum?"

"I stay away from liquor."

"Smart," he said.

"Do you have a smoke?"

"Not so smart," he said, hoisting himself up.

He walked away for moment, leaving the bottle behind on the floor.

She looked at the bottle of Red Stag. With her hands free, she had the chance to beat him with it. She could bludgeon him to death with the almost square corner of the frosty bottle. She could break the glass and slit his throat.

He returned with a pack of cigarettes.

She didn't recognize the brand.

"What are these?"

"They're French."

She took one out of the pack.

He lit a match for her.

She smoked for a while, trying not to look at him as he stared at her.

"Do you ever blink?" she said, looking at the toilet.

He sipped the whiskey.

"Tell me a story," he said.

"I was born in Kentucky."

"Doesn't have to be yours," he said. "Unless you want it to."

"I'm from North Carolina," she said. "I'm from Tennessee."

He slugged back the whiskey and set the glass on the counter above where he sat.

"I'm from Alabama. I'm from Mississippi. I'm from Florida. My name is Becky-Sue. My name is Jillian. My name is LaShay. My name is Fixico. Texaco. Mexico. Morocco. Montgomery. My bones are made of steel and my skin is bullet proof. I live in a cave somewhere other than here. I bleed gasoline and eat poison ivy and fart the purest oxygen you'll ever breathe, the kind of pure atmosphere people in the Himalayas jar and FedEx to their dying friends. I can talk to witches and listen to moss. I hear things people can only see. I taste rocks in creek water to learn which animals have stepped on them recently."

He took a cigarette out of the dwindling pack and struck a match.

"That's a pretty good story," he said.

"Thanks," she said frowning. "Are you going to kill me?"

"No," he said. "I'm not. I know right now you probably think I will and so far you have no reason to think otherwise. And I know what I'm doing with you is disgusting."

"Then why won't you let me go?"

"Because I need something from you," he said.

"What?"

"I need you to pretend to be my wife at a dinner party."

"The fuck—?"

"I need you to pretend to be someone you're not."

"Why?"

"I have to kill someone. I kill people for money. I need a false persona to get close enough to kill this person. My persona has to have a white woman as a wife."

"Why a white woman?"

"You'll see in time," he said, dragging off the cigarette. He blew smoke at the ceiling. "For now though, let's just watch TV."

"Okay," she said.

He turned his back to her and poured more whiskey, then pointed the remote at the television.

"What do you wanna watch?"

She shrugged.

"Is Seinfeld on?"

He turned the channel to TBS.

"Friends is on," he said.

"Okay," she said, tapping her ash into the toilet.

"Do you watch Friends?"

"I did when I was young."

"I mean when I was a kid," she said. "They used to leave Friends on in the rec room at juvy. The TV was in a cage, so we couldn't change the station. Once the reruns switched over to the Family Guy they turned it to the Chapel Station, or Jack Van Imp Ministries."

"Juvy, huh? I remember kiddie prison," he said. "I ate everything with a Styrofoam stick that looked like a tongue depressor. I hated the way it scraped on my teeth."

"They gave us these firm bits of celery where I went. Made everything taste like celery. Fuckin' torture."

"You been to real prison?"

"No," she said.

"It's a lot easier to kill people in prison then it is juvy. You

have to be creative, of course. The best are American prisons, the private kind. The less government presence the better.
Some of the guys had jars of weed and crack and big screen
TVs because they knew one of the guards. Canadian prisons
are tougher, unlike what the rest of the world must think. It's
difficult to move around in a Canadian prison, they keep you
locked up in one room. I did more reading then."

"Where the fuck are you from?"

"Quebec," he said. "In Canada."

"I know Quebec is a Canadian province. I'm not an idiot
hillbilly just 'cause I lived in a trailer. Where in Quebec?"

"Oka," he said. "On the Ottawa River."

She said nothing.

He pointed to the television.

"Matthew Perry's Canadian."

"Chandler Bing?"

"The neurotic one," he said.

" I always thought the Jew with the big ass was the neurotic one."

"Which one is that?"

"That one."

"Her?" he said, pointing at the TV.

"No, not Phoebe," she said. "The other guy. Dark hair.
Long face."

"Schwimmer," he said, pouring another glass of whiskey.

"Sure, Ross" she said. "The taller guy."

"Yeah, he's neurotic, and they're both Jewish – Schwimmer and Ross," he said. "Which one do you like the most?"

"None of them," she said.

"I like Pheobe," he said.

"Why?"

"She's the only one of them that isn't trying to be something other than what she is. She's the philosophical center of the show."

She nodded and blew smoke across the bathroom.

"You can't keep torturing me like this," she said. "I need to know what you want."

"For now, I just wanna watch TV."

He extended the remote and turned up the volume to drown her out.

The laugh track sounded as tears ran down her cheeks.

8.

A black shopping cart in green pond scum sits alone on its side, an open cage, unwatchable, unhinged and oozing along with the slight trickle of shallow creek bottom waters over sludge-covered rocks like chunks of masticated bone with the broken teeth of long-last sewage and car glass and chunks of gum-colored wrought redbrick now chipped like pits of cedar mulch in the mix where the filth spreads slowly over the forgotten reeds and drainage pillars with old rubber tire and sun-bleached insignia on crushed plastic soda bottle and rotten fruit and road kill carcasses wrapped in blankets of fast-food napkins, all gone under from the blackway to a stretch of odd road in the waves of kudzu on the far side of the tea-hued, rusted chain link fence. Southern humidity. Calcified streaks of silt.

Somewhere on this discarded route between 'who the fuck lives here?' and 'why would anyone come out here alone?' was the singular point Rip Van Winkle called it his, that place where he stood alone with God and said 'because here I am and this is it.' Van Winkle. Van Zant. Van Houten. Krenwinkel. Lost Dutch-American letters of anything and everything, perhaps in them somewhat of a secret that ripples like an echo across the surface of clear water. But not here. Not in this place. This place is all mine.

—Victoria Vandergreven (Diary entry June 3rd 2006)

9.

In rain, the city slept. In rain, Cutler could think. What was this place: Charlotte, North Carolina? So far from the sultry antebellum columns and front porches of a mythical Southern town, but still managing to be just as ignorant and blunt and shotgun-wielding. A bucket of steel at the edge of Appalachia. A cold Miami with surface-level decadence, always ready to roll out the red carpet of consummate sin. He knew the rough parts of the city, the outskirts of Tyvola and South Boulevard, the parts of town that looked like Pittsburgh had fucked central Atlanta .

He walked along streets beneath the wet scaffolding of the weather. He could have been any one of the Bank of America or Wells Fargo employees loafing around the barren sidewalks.

The skyscrapers ended at the foot of the municipal brick where the short-circuit light rail crawled into the sprawling pines and willows and the hills of loose red clay toward desolate urban expanses where Spanish replaced English on the billboard ads and store signs along with little syllabic blocks of Korean and the squirming, half-familiar letters of written Vietnamese.

Cutler hunched his shoulders as he crossed over into the disconnected subset of dilapidated homes and spare part garages. He had no cover from the cold rain which poured four times as heavy from the warped eaves of the clapboard huts and low-set storefronts. It was too wet and windy to hope to light a cigarette. He walked inside a convenience store to get out of the rain for a second and was struck by an immediate sense of nostalgia. It felt like New Jersey inside, cramped and unfathomably abundant. He smiled at the black girl behind the cash register and bought a copy of The Charlotte Observer.

He held the thick newsprint over his head and kept on down the road to where the path shifted from cracked, weedy concrete to gravel.

A little yellow brick house had been converted into a bar: Mallory's. A hipster joint by night, but during the day a blue-collar booze trough. Two white guys with shredded, clay-caked jeans and cigarette packs bulging from the the breast pockets of their work shirts sat on what had once been a family's front porch, a domino trail of brown-glass bottles lined up to the edge of their boots.

Cutler tossed the soaked paper into the recycling bin at the foot of the wooden steps and acknowledged them. One of the men tipped his baseball cap to him as if he were some kind of cowboy.

John fuckin' Wayne, Cutler thought.

He stepped through the threshold of the wooden door into the cavern of liquor fumes and fry oil. A touch-screen jukebox took up a third of the entrance beside the shady-looking ATM. The bartender looked out of her element. Too clean cut, too ready for business, to work for a place like Mallory's. Her black hair was clean and trim, and her shirt a solid gray. No marks or tattoos crawled up her neck. She wore a sweatband around her arm with a flat beer-bottle opener tucked in as if business were somehow out of the control.

She gave him the same look.

"What can I get you?" she asked.

He sat down at the bar.

"A Michelob Ultra," he said.

She pulled the beer from the miniature fridge beneath the bar top and twisted off the cap.

"Bishop working today?"

The bartender paused. She looked confused.

"Not sure. The schedule's kind of erratic."

He smiled.

"Evasion comes just short of lying. It's what the half-guilty do," he said, slipping her a hundred dollar bill. "I'm not a cop. I'm a good friend from a long time ago. I'm just concerned. If she wants, she can come out here and talk to me where people can see. It's important."

"Are you a reporter?"

"No," he said. "I'm an old friend."

"Bishop doesn't have any friends," she said.

"I'd say she's got friends," Cutler said. "You protecting her like one aren't you."

"I don't work for my friends."

"That explains why you took the bribe. Am I gonna get anything for my money or do I have to ask for it back."

"Money?" she said without emotion or a shred of personality in her voice. "You mean the tip you gave me for serving you? Real generous, sure. But a simple Ben Franklin won't buy you anything near the moon these days."

Cutler sipped the beer and stared up at one of the flat screens. The Cartwright boys were riding across a desolate arroyo on a grainy, old daytime rerun.

"Bonanza," he said, pointing up at the glow of the screen. "I always preferred Gunsmoke. Bonanza was too ho-hum, you know what I mean?."

"I don't," she said, grabbing the remote to the change the channel to a local news station.

He listened to the anchor doing his best to mask his

Southern accent: "A fire three nights ago in the North Polo RV park has left four dead. Officials say the blaze was so intense that the bodies had to be identified via dental record. The victims are believed to have died of smoke inhalation before the flames destroyed the mobile home. The Rock Hill fire department will not release the identities of the victims or the cause of the fire as the investigation is ongoin'." His accent slipped at the very end of the brief, cutting off the 'g' in the last word, revealing some kind of Texan drawl.

"Old western shows. Good shows," he said. "Where's your restroom?"

She pointed across from the bar.

He stood up and walked toward the opposite end of the house's creaking wood floor.. He grabbed a wooden chair from closest table and pushed open the door beside the unisex bathroom with the notice 'Employee's Only." He could hear the bartender yell at him as he shut the door and propped the jammed the chair beneath the knob. The hallway was short, darker than he expected. Mallory's electric bill must have been close to nothing. He felt his way around until he saw a dim light behind a doorway of beaded curtains. He parted the beads and walked inside some kind of living area. There was a small work desk in the corner with printed Excel spreadsheets and a locked cash box. Scribbled-on paper piled beside the nightstand near the twin bed against the wall along with a hefty collection of half-empty prescription pill bottles. He leaned over to pick one up and felt something cold press against his neck. He jolted raised his hands in the air.

"Who the fuck are you?"

He recognized Bishop's voice.

"Depressing little pad you got here," he said. "Poured everything into the business?"

She paused for a moment.

"Detective Cutler?"

"Can I turned around without being shot in the neck?"

"Sure."

He turned, grabbing her wrist.

"I don't have a gun," she said, opening her hand to let the little metallic cylinder roll into the floor.

"That's a good trick."

"Bartender texted me that you were coming."

"I'm surprised you didn't slug me with a baseball bat."

"I panicked," she said, typing a message on her phone. "Felt like a gun, didn't it?"

He got a good look at her. She had aged twenty years in just ten.

"You here about Marc?"

"Of course, I heard," he said.

"No, are you here to ask me about it?"

"Yeah, I am."

"Police business?"

"I'm not a cop anymore," he said.

She winced.

"What are doing here, then? Here to offer condolences. I hadn't seen Marc in years."

"Did he have problems with depression, remorse, guilt? Did you hear any word through the grapevine about a weird incident. Something that might have prompted him to lose hope or—"

"I'm sorry, Mr. Cutler. But if you're not a cop, I don't see you interviewing me."

He took out his cred case and gave it to her.

"I'm in a semi-retirement stage nowadays. I'm doing some private eye work, some consulting."

She closed the cred case and tossed it at him.

"So what is it? You're looking into my ex-husband's suicide?"

Cutler sighed.

"Well, not to seem completely crass Ms. LeBlanc—"

"Just call me Bishop. None of this LeBlanc shit. You act like you never grilled me for the better part of a day in that sweat box you called an interview room. You saw me cry, you saw me beg and scream. Don't act tender now, fuckin' asshole."

"Look," he said. "I was bully. But I had to be."

"You're sacrifice was very noble, and extremely fruitful as I recall, Detective."

He said nothing in response.

"I don't have to tell you shit," she said. "Get off my property, or I'll call the police. The actual police, the ones with authority around here. How dare you come here, thinkin' I would talk to you. ? Not after what you put me through. You're a failure."

"I wanna give you my card," he said. "Have you already talked to the police about Marc? Have they contacted you in any way?"

She flicked the card out of his hand and spat in his face.

He wiped off the spittle with the back of his coat sleeve.

"Why are you still standing there?"

He took out the .38 and pressed it against her throat. He pushed her against the wall and covered her mouth with his hand.

"Shut the fuck up, bitch! Shut up!"

She tried to scream through his palm.

He pressed the barrel of the gun against her kneecap.

"I will cripple you, bitch. I will fuckin' cripple you for life. Worse off than you already are. Don't fuck with me. Did you, or did you not talk to the cops about Marc?"

She shook her head.

"Don't you fuckin' lie to me!"

She kept shaking her head.

"The deputy coroner came to the bar as a courtesy. He brought a Pastor. I sent them away. I wanted nothing to do with them. I swear to God."

"Bullshit! You'd be suspect number one. Number fucking one!"

"I'm not!"

"Then who! Then who the fuck is their suspect."

"He did it himself! Nobody thinks it was murder but you!"

"Why!"

"I don't fucking know!"

"Why was there dog blood in your house?"

"What?"

"Why was there dog blood on the steps in your house, Bishop. What kind of shit was Marc involved with?"

"I think about that every goddamn day of my life. I haven't slept since Marc died. I can't fucking figure it out."

"Think Bishop!"

Something had caught his eye.

"I can't fucking think with a gun to my head."

He holstered the .38 and backed up against the her work desk where she couldn't see his hands.

"Then let's calm down," he said, changing the tone of his voice. "So, you do think about it, huh? It is haunting you isn't it. Like I've been saying, none of it makes any sense?"

"Something like that," she said, wiping the tears from her eyes.

"I need you fill me in on your deepest thoughts, your darkest suspicions. Anything that might have crossed your mind."

"God damn it, Cutler," she said.
"Come on, I'll buy you a drink."

He stared at Bishop LeBlanc beside him as she slouched over the bar and dove into a dry gin martini. She looked less like the owner in her NC State sweatshirt and unwashed cinnamon hair and more like one of the daytime patrons, trailer park drinkers who walked in alone out of the relentless green. Cutler, who had been reared by the cocktail generation, had never particularly cared for gin and even less for martinis: the suicidal poet's translucent beverage. It was the bitter tang of the pine needles and ginger and ground cloves and ethyl that he didn't like. It was the lying smooth beginning and finish. Sure it was easier on the palate than some beers and wines, but it really was as if the beverage itself were lying to the drinker about its potency, making it all the easier too for them to kill themselves.

Bishop was a shell of a woman. Her once smooth, alabaster skin had become haggard and brittle. Stress had weighed harder on her than alcoholism. He knew alcoholics. The bloated. The pickled. The red in the face. Those who weaved as if they were bound to vomit or piss themselves at any second. The kind of men, mostly ex-cops, who lulled themselves into a willing blind streak, a forced comatose. That wasn't Bishop. She dove headfirst into the booze for anesthesia. True alcoholics drank for the perceived love of the beverage, completely unaware of the monster that chased them, looming over them in bar rooms, just outside their windows like a neon sign, or behind the vortex of the television glow as they dozed off. Bishop was not undone by being a true alcoholic; she was carrying something else.

Cutler barely sucked on his now flat beer.

"The cops seriously haven't talked to you?"

"It's like I said, the coroner showed up with the pastor."

"What was the coroner's name?"

"He introduced himself as the Mecklenburg County Coroner first. I can't remember."

"Bullshit."

She looked up from her martini too exasperated to argue.

"That's the truth. Take it or leave it."

"What about the Pastor's name?"

"Bridgemont Fowley," she said.

"Had that on the tip of your tongue didn't you?"

"Hard to forget a name like that."

"Most likely a fake. A lot of these independent Baptist ministers have a warrants in nearby states," he said. "How did these guys behave?"

She took another gulp of vermouth and gin.

"The fuck does that matter?"

"Interests me."

"How did they 'behave'? About as full of shit as you did when you first got here."

"Phony," he said. "Almost like they had another agenda?"

"They didn't have an agenda. They didn't have a clue we'd been divorced as long as we were. Why they thought contacting me first was a good idea, I'll never know. But I don't really care enough to know."

"Does anybody know why he did it? Did Marc have a reason?"

"There's never a legitimate reason," she said.

"Did you ever figure him for the suicidal type?"

"Wake the fuck up! Who do you think you're kidding? It was out of blue. Everything's always out of the blue!"

"It can sure seem that way when you don't pay any attention. Storms come out of the blue. Traffic accidents. Earthquakes. Strokes. But people's decisions. There's always something to signal it. A mounting issue. An off-the-cuff comment. You're telling me you couldn't read a man you were married to for eighteen years?"

She looked him in the eye.

"When a Northerner cop causes you to suspect your husband of killing your only child, you do your best to stop reading into every little detail and comment. Or else you'll go insane. And I'm startin' to think that that's what happened to you Detective Cutler. I think the case left you in a worse state than it did me. I think that's why you here, threatening me, questioning me."

"If that's true, then Marc was probably left the most fucked up by it all. He's the one who ended up killing himself."

"You son of a bitch!"

She swung the Martini glass at Cutler's head.

It didn't shatter, but the stem broke, puncturing her hand.

Cutler had got a gash on forehead. It only bled minimally.

Blood was gushing from Bishop's palm. Without letting it distract her, she attempted to throw a few punches at his face, missing easily, splattering pellets of blood on her coat. She had cut herself in the same place he had sliced his own hand. He wondered about the coincidence even as she got to kicking him in the shin. She knew he had a gun, but it didn't seem the matter. He didn't take it out. He backed away from her and walked out of the bar.

He retraced his steps down the gravel path until he was certain she wasn't following him. In the reasonable cover from the rain beneath large oak, he took out Bishop's cell phone which he had swiped from the room and looked through her phone contacts.

His car was parked half a mile back at the twelve-story garage. The rain had started to let up. He lit a cigarette under a length of construction scaffolding when a panhandler approached him.

"Hey, man. I'm homeless, right now. Can I get a few bucks to get a coffee or something?"

Cutler wasn't about to root around the layers of his wet clothes to fish out a few dollars.

"I'm cleaned out," he said, passing him.

The young man in the military jacket and Hornets basketball cap, who smelled of cigarettes and a kind of sweet liquor concoction, walked after him.

"Hey, man. Come on, I've been in the rain all fuckin' day."

"I can't help you," he said, dragging on the cigarette.

"Hey, asshole, maybe I ain't asking."

He could feel the kid behind him, too close. He wasn't about to shanked in the middle of the day. He discarded the cigarette as he reached into his coat in one fluid motion and took out the pistol, turning on a dime to stick it in the kid's face.

"Walk away," he said.

The kid looked more disappointed than surprised.

"I just wanted some fries or something, man. God damn it," he said, heading off into the opposite direction.

He didn't see anything in the kid's hand. That was the second time today, someone came up behind him.

Cutler took the highway south of the city. Skyscrapers ended and the little abandoned shacks tucked into the kudzu and bamboo thickets cropped up on either side of the interstate. Billboards for Chick-fil-a with plastic cows scrawling misspelled words in black paint across the white background and local dentists towered over treeline; strangely placed office buildings with for- rent banners swinging in the wind, swam by. He noticed a giant rectangle of an building from the road, a hulking vault of tinted windows and offices and papers and file cabinets, a place where facts and figures stood alone, intentions where hidden, trivialities and politics amplified, and repetition flowed like streams of dark water. He looked at the beige structures that surrounded it and felt his soul mute.

The silver Hyundai sped down the exit ramp for the Rock Hill city limit. He passed the sign that read "Welcome to South Carolina." Breaking the law was common practice for a P.I.

He parked the car behind the brick church on Main Street and wandered through the garden, sitting a while in the dry shelter of the gazebo only to quell any passerby's suspicion that he had no business with the church. When the road cleared of cyclists and passing cars, he crossed the parking lot and sneaked through three gravel driveways with basketball goals mounted to shedfronts and stepped across a blackened pit for bonfires littered with aluminum beer cans before hopping the fence onto the slope carpeted in dandelions in full bloom and crabgrass that a divorced Marc Vandergreven had called his backyard for the final years of his life. The small patio was covered in wet cigarette butts. He had smoked something fancy with a red filter, a Russian brand perhaps. The portable shed out back had no window. He put on his black powderless gloves and fumbled with the knob. The door was made of the same flimsy metal as the walls, some kind of prefab setup Marc must have bought from a Home Depot or a Lowe's parking lot, but Cutler wasn't about to kick it in. He knew his limits. He'd wait till he searched the house before spraining his ankle making a racket to get inside the shed. He checked the backdoor and walked around the side of the small residence. He peered inside the kitchenette window. Had investigators even cased the place yet?, he wondered. From what he could see, it looked like someone was still living in there. He walked around front. No for rent sign. No lingering sash of police tape flapping in the wind. Suicides were funny that way. The front door had a little welcome mat. He flipped it over. No key. Too bad. He took out the shim and jammed it into the cheap Kwikset lock. Without any real finesse, the door popped open. He was glad he didn't have to walk all the way back to his car and get the portable power drill from the trunk. He walked inside. The place smelled like cigarettes and pot. The same brand of cigarettes from out back had been extinguished on the furniture. Butts and burn holes littered the shabby orange carpet. Ash and dust had collected over everything. There were three kinds of houses in Cutler's understanding: homes, the majority of which, where people carried on with their living, traphouses where business took place which was the same thing as a stash house, and sitting-around-and-thinking-about-killing-yourself, or waiting-to-be-killed, houses. Vandergreven had been treating this place the way Cutler had seen fugitives treat motel rooms. Bad business and bad memories hung around the corridors almost like an odor. The interior of the home itself had become something of a cadaver, wrapped in the bare logic of a nightmare. He walked from the living room into the kichtenette, extending a gloved finger to flip the light switch. Artificial light hadn't touched the place in a while. But at least he knew the power was still working. It was the dirty, but it wasn't cluttered. He opened up the empty cabinets and realized that Marc hadn't owned any plates or silverware. Cans of collard greens and black beans were stacked beside empty liquor bottles. Poor bastard didn't even know what to eat. All of the cans bore the leafy store-brand logo from The Greenpoint Market. He opened up the fridge. A half eaten box of sushi and several defrosted bags of chicken wings waiting to be baked were inside. Every last item on the transparent shelves had been purchased from Greenpoint. He slammed the door shut and made his way upstairs to his bedroom. The bed had no fitted sheet, just a pillow and duvet cover. The guy was Holland after all. His desk looked suspiciously void of papers. All he had was an ashtray and a laptop. Cutler took the laptop downstairs and the set it on the countertop near the backdoor. He walked back into the living room. The stillness reminded him of his own house, a house that had once been alive with movement; his nephew doing yard work, Trish's sisters sitting in the kitchen, their husbands watching the game on his couch drinking beer. A cacophony of South Jersey accents penetrating any moment of silence. He had been horrible to all of them and failed to recognize that once Trish was gone, her family would have no more reason to be around him. After the funeral, the house had become still and empty and dead. Cutler had been alone. His delinquent nephew had still come around when he wanted to buy drugs: weed mostly, a little Xanax and cocaine from time to time – anything he might pick up during his day-to-day policing.

There was half-a-bottle of 101 proof schnapps on the coffee table beside an ashtray and a mountain of beer bottles rising up from the floor. Vandergreven had been drinking and smoking himself into a short-lived coma, something to keep himself anesthetized until whatever it was he was trying to stave off had chased him down. Either that, or he had just gotten tired of being single. He had lost his daughter. He had lost his marriage. Had he forgotten what he was living for? This little shithole of a townhouse screamed depression and this was depression's closest accomplice: boredom. While despair was is a raging waterfall, depression is a stagnant puddle.

He knelt down beside the television and thumbed through the stack of DVDs. Nothing but foreign pornography, the hard-to-come-by stuff. One titled "De Boerenerf Sletten" featured a young girl fellating a horse. He felt sick and took out his camera to flash a picture of each side of the DVD, turning off his flash to avoid any light bounce.

He opened up the back door with the laptop in hand and stared at the shed. If the bastard had barnyard porn in his living room, what kind of garbage was he hiding in the shed? Marc had never struck him as a handyman and he certainly didn't have much of a lawn to keep up. What was in there? Another butchered dog?

He sighed.

10.

That morning, he had asked her to stand and took out a length of measuring tape. Her muscles had atrophied like veal and her stomach had bloated. He measured her waist, her height, her wrist size, even the circumference of her fingers with a plastic kit.

"Are you fitting me for a ring?"

He nodded.

"It has to be convincing."

"What does?"

"You'll see soon enough," he said. "Diamond solitaire, or do you want something gaudy. Honestly, I'd rather go a little cheaper and get you a sapphire."

"Are we getting married."

"We're going to pretend."

He wrote down her measurements on a legal pad and headed for the door, slipping on his shoes.

"Could I have the sheet from the bed?"

"Why?"

"I wanna wrap myself in it while I watch TV."

He raised an eyebrow and walked over to the thermostat.

"Here, I'll just turn the heat up," he said.

He left, letting the hotel door shut behind him.

She pounded her fist against the side of the bathtub until her knuckles were raw, then cried for a few minutes. The bathroom wasn't large. She lay face down on the prefab tile, extending her body as far as possible, allowing the chain to eat further into her ankle before reaching out into the hallway toward the television. If she could reach her finger into the VCR, perhaps she could get enough of a hold to rip out the unit and use the wires. She stretched until she could feel her ankle bleeding, but could only graze the wooden cabinet housing the television.

She collapsed in tears.

"Poor little sissy fuss," she could hear her brother saying. "Always fussin' like a sissy."

"Fuck!" she screamed, pounding her fist on the floor. "Fuck! Somebody help me!"

She had tried screaming for help the previous day. It seemed no one else was close enough on their floor, above or beneath them, to hear her screams, empty as most of the hotel was. She felt that her only hope was the cleaning staff, and they'd probably have been paid off by him to steer clear of this room, or even this floor, for all she knew.

She lifted her chin to look at the plastic shower curtain and ripped it off the hollow aluminum bar. The synthetic material was impossible to tear apart just by her own hands. She took the half-drunk bottle of Red Stag, methodically wrapping the cloth of the pillow case around the handle before trying to smash it across the counter. The bottle rebounded twice. She struck the counter again. Nothing happened. She drained the remainder of the spiced the liquor into the toilet and flicked the cap away into the garbage.

Another strike against the countertop was followed by nothing.

She could feel herself hesitating.

Starla covered her eyes with her free hand to keep the glass from ricocheting into her eyes. She slammed the bottle against the rim of the sink. This time, she could feel the bottom shatter. Broken glass filled the sink like ice. One jagged shard stuck out from the rest on the remainder off the bottle.

She used the thick plastic of the shower curtain as a cover for her hands as she isolated the knife-like piece of glass by tearing away the loose shards around it. She wrapped the pillow case around the handle again, as tightly as she could, before looking at the rudimentary tool she had created. She cut the shower curtain into long strips which tied together to form a primitive lasso. Using a few beer bottles as a counter weight, she flung the transparent harness at the side table. The reflection from the old television screen was clear enough for her to see her progress.

"Here I am. Gone fishing," she said out loud, thinking of her brother again, thinking of LaShay, thinking of death and the prospect of escape, about feeling the cold porcelain toilet bowl on her bare legs. She thought of how terrified the police and the hotel staff would be to see her chained to a toilet. She knew she would make the news, if not nationally then definitely locally. She might be interviewed on the morning shows like those girls from Cleveland. A subset of virtual corpses sitting inches from Barbara Walters or some faceless, nameless blonde news anchor, talking about how brave she must have been, how courageous she was. Either that, or she would end up as the slasher-film cadaver left behind for the Mexican maid, the sweet girl who had worked her hands to bone and put up with rooms covered in vomit, melted chocolate, and seminal fluid, and now finally this.

She With her lasso, she kept fishing for the telephone on the nightstand until finally knocking the receiver off the hook and pulling it towards her.

There was no dial tone.

She squinted, staring into the dark reflection of the angled screen. The chord had been ripped out of the wall. She had no way to reach it. She'd have to saw off her foot. The idea wouldn't have been out of the question if she had only been chained by the wrist. Starla felt she had the courage to cut off a few fingers, or even a wrist, but the image of a swollen, puss-rittled foot with an exposed ankle bone as she stabbed at it with the glass blade was too much to bare.

Back to square one.

She wondered if her captor would be amused by her ingenuity, or terrified by her persistence. It was strange feeling so accomplished for having failed, still knowing that she was going to die. She curled up on the couch cushion and grabbed a pillow. The heat from the air vent spread across her neck. Sleep was her only release from the chain around her ankle. She dreamed of a crowded city in a dusky twilight as gray skies overhead, full of voices and ruffled blue clouds, dropped a steady rainfall on the moss gardens spilling over the shopfronts and baroque eaves of tall buildings, where the streets were filled with the shadows of people who lived in secret corners of crossed iron and deformed brick. She walked into a grocery store and forgot who she was. Men with Scottish accent fondled cricket mallets near public restrooms. A shaggy gray schnauzer walked by her feet, near the bin of bananas. Its fur was matted against down with some congealed slime. Somehow a bottle of Caesar dressing had fallen on the dog. She took the dog into her arms and washed its fur in the store's restroom sink. Water splashed onto her shirt. The dog didn't try to run from her. It seemed to like the tepid water. It closed its eyes and raised its neck as she picked out bits of stale anchovy from its beard. She As she washed, she began to recite poetry. The word flowed from her, effortlessly, perfectly. Her doubts disappeared. Her values became unnecessary during the recitation as if the curtain of ignorance wrapped around her brain had suddenly dropped. She had been given a glimpse of knowledge that stretched beyond her own experience as the barrier between word and concept had dissolved into the unseen perimeter in the geometry of her dream. And then the dog was on fire. And water was not water. The dark scrawl of the painted words dripped down the mirror where nothing lived alone, uncoupled and fully-formed like an echo, a reflection of itself entirely stable and without nature.

When she woke up, she couldn't remember a word of the poem. The Indian was standing over her, holding several retail bags baring designer clothing logos and two shoe boxes in the crook of his shoulder. He gestured toward the plastic lasso she had made from the shower curtain.

"Don't tell me you tried to kill yourself."

"I tried to get the phone so I could call 911."

He looked at the knife she had made from the whiskey bottle.

"You're resourceful," he said. "I left the bottle there for you. You'll need that. I'm glad I found you."

11.

He couldn't shake the dread. His morning routine seemed meaningless, but he kept on doing it. He probably never left Ashville in his mind and, in the same sense, part of him was still wandering through Vandergreven's little house. He was falling apart now, leaving behind sizable chunks of himself wherever he went. That was okay, he thought. The big cases did that to good detectives. Cutler had always been a firm believer that solving any mystery was a self-destructive act. If you came out on the other end unscathed, you hadn't discovered everything. Of course, only the big cases worked like that, the really difficult ones, the mysteries that lingered over a person's head and dared them to be solved as if they required a person to stare directly into the sun.

He brewed his coffee with the loaded .38 beside the sink. He looked out the window at his now barren garden, remembering when he first bought the house, when he was still vaguely racist in his beliefs and little naïve about his place in the world, when Trish still complained about the summertime heat but continued to garden beneath the hot sun every day wearing her deluxe big brim cotton tennis visor and those floral overalls that made her look older than she actually was. She had always been a decent gardener. Cutler used to look through the window and down at the bushels of Japanese cedars intertwining with the macabre hearts of sweet potato vine leading up to the squash and cucumbers and occasional eggplant before the beefsteak tomatoes were encircled by the basil and spearmint. Those days were short lived. He figured he'd plant some pot instead as soon as it was legal.

He poured his coffee, keeping the back door in peripheral view. He grabbed the gun and walked outside with his cup. The safety was on, the barrel jammed snugly into the loop of his bathrobe. Steam rose from the cup. The sun was out. It made him uneasy. In his experience, more people were murdered on hot afternoons than any other time. The calls always came close to quitin' time. The victim's body was usually sprawled out on the asphalt or the floor of a filthy apartment with the doors and windows open to let in as much heat as possible as sweating officers wandered in and around the premises like pilgrims before a dark shrine. "There is no god here, for what belief is worth not half a second of death's time," said the PCP fiend in the back of the squad car. And the wittiest thing the officer could have thought to counter his statement was the simple, reliable cop grunt: "Shut the fuck up!"

Cutler sat in his favorite chair. It felt like a bed of nails. Marc Vandergreven's computer lay on the coffee table inside. He could almost see it through the glass door to the patio.

Restless, he got dressed, tossed the computer into the car, and drove across the state line for the second time in a week. Rock Hill was an ugly little town for the most part. It had a quaint university campus connected to a refurbished six-block downtown with a few gamely historical buildings—the diner where the Friendship Nine held their sit in—but the majority of the city had been sullied by grime and gas station lots, by billboards and the husks of failed businesses, too far from the core, and too small to be big box. It all looked even worse in the sunshine. He made a stop at the bank before moving on to the Rose Street apartments.

Rob sat by his desk. He only wore a pair of boxers and a stained white undershirt. His was pallid. He seemed to be fighting off a hangover; the tell-tale bottle of Gatorade within his reach as he sat hunched over his laptop, Metal Mulisha stickers covering the back of his screen. .

Cutler switched on the light behind him.

Rob stood up from the office chair leaning back over the desk in a stance that told Cutler he was trying to protect his last valuable possession.

"The fuck did you get in here?"

"I broke in," Cutler said.

"How'd you get passed the front the desk?"

"They let me inside. After all, I'm your uncle and I'm worried about you. I have an imagination, you know. And that makes me a dangerous person. True evil is the upshot of the stifled imagination."

Rob recognized the quote.

"Have you been reading The Dying Mule?"

"Little bit here and there," he lied.

"What are doing here?"

"I've come to bully you again," Cutler said, presenting Rob with Vandergreven's computer. "And I've brought you something."

"I don't need a Toshiba. I've got a Mac."

Cutler set the laptop on the side of the twin bed.

"This is the late Marc Vandergreven's laptop. I don't know a lot about computers, so I'm gonna take you on as an independent consultant. I need you to show me things buried his hard drive. Tell me what he's been doing on the internet. E-mails correspondences."

"I thought you were a detective. Sounds like I'm doing all the leg work."

"I've already done the legwork. I got the thing. It's the tedious computer shit I hate doing. Plus I'm bad at it. I don't know how to find what I'm looking for."

"No," he said. "Hell no. And besides,, Fuck you, old man. You ripped me off and kicked the shit out of me."

Cutler took out the money and set it on the stolen laptop.

"That's the four-hundred for the police report. You help me and keep your mouth shut about it, I'll keep more money coming."

Rob hesitated.

"You don't have any real friends do you, Beau?"

Cutler didn't respond.

Rob sat back down on the office chair and rubbed his knees.

"What am I looking for?"

"Bestiality," Cutler said. "I want to know if guy's affinity for watching girls and animals fuck went further than just a porn collection. I wanna know if he has crush videos on the laptop. I wanna know if he was talking to anyone else about it and whether or not he had a hand in producing it. I want to know what chat rooms he frequented, and who his contacts were. I wanna know if his wife knew about it."

"You're dead fucking serious aren't you?"

Cutler took out a cigarette and his lighter, nodding.

"You still know my cell number right?"

"Yeah."

"Good. Don't call me on your cell. Use a payphone."

"I can't afford a cell phone anymore."

"Sorry to hear that."

Rob leaned forward in the chair.

"Oh, shit," he muttered, standing up and stumbling to the bathroom, pushing Cutler aside.

"Feelin' bad?"

Rob started heaving violently over the toilet. He held onto the porcelain for balance. Nothing came out even as he clenched his stomach. Finally, the kid stuck his fingers down his throat to get it over with.

Cutler looked away, lighting the cigarette as Rob vomited. Half the Marlboro was gone, turned to gray ash which he had flicked onto the hallway carpet, by the time he heard the toilet flush.

Rob emerged from the bathroom wiping his chin with a towel.

"Can you stay sober enough to help me out?"

"Probably. But if I gotta look at what you say I gotta look at, I can't exactly to do so dry."

"Do what you gotta do. I expect a call in two days. You'll get more money on the 3rd."

Rob nodded in agreement, chugging back the blue Gatorade.

"Good," Cutler said. "Take some Tylenol or smoke some grass or something. You look like your old man."

"That's low, Cutler," Rob said.

"At least, your dad isn't quite as pathetic after a bender. He knew how to carry a mistake on his shoulders," he said, walking out of the bare apartment.

12.

The thin woman found herself a comfortable and anonymous spot within a brick alcove near the piazza. A porcelain cup and saucer in front of her on the patio table, a new black leather handbag at her feet, she stirred the cream into the thick coffee with ana stainless-steel teaspoon until the liquid changed from black to the color of dried blood. She sat, sipping perfunctorily, scanning the crowd at the center of the cobblestone beside the obelisk, as well as the venders with their displays of sunglasses and bootleg wallets adjacent to the cafe. A smudge of her dark violet lipstick had rubbed off on the eggshell cup. She wiped it off with her thumb as if squashing a small insect.

The midday rain started to fall. The punk-rockers and trade-school students loitered on the stone steps of the central equestrienne monument and were undeterred.

Sounds of bubbling chemistry and shuffling pastry plates carried out from the cafe's open doorway, lifted up by the acoustics of the brick dome above her, punctuated by rapid Italian conversation.

The woman lit a cigarillo and tapped her ash into the plastic L&M ashtray in the center of the wooden table. She had waited longer than she expected she would. By the time the old man in gray took a seat across from her, she was on her second cup of coffee. The cigarillo had been stubbed out, a smear of violet lipstick on the moist yellowed tip.

The old man wore sunglasses and carried what looked like a stolen umbrella. It was yellow and stitched with the image of Minnie Mouse. He tossed it aside as if he'd never use it again and took off his sunglasses to reveal a pair of beady, dark eyes.

"Buna ziua," he said.

"I don't speak Italian."

"Clearly. That was actually Romanian."

"Is that why your handle is The Count?"

"No, I just like Sesame Street, and The Count von Count is from there."

He parted his long white hair and tucked it behind his ears.

"Berlin went without a hiccup?"

"Almost. John had a shootout with some kids. Could have been Russian."

The old man leaned forward without speaking.

She explained.

"We got the guy and the USB. But afterward, John was shot at by some street hoodlums."

"Yeah?"

"Yeah."

"Any chance he was followed?"

She shrugged.

"It seems odd that a group of kids would open fire on him in Europe, even in a bad neighborhood. He said they were using a little stick of a .22 rifle. That's consistent with a group of kids. That seems about as much as they can get their hands on. But then again—"

"Ah, yes," he said. "Then again. There is always a second moment of cold doubt. A kind of doubt that freezes dreams and keeps us shivering at night in search of brandy."

She raised an eyebrow.

"A .22 is also a professional's gun. The corporate killer type. But if that were the case, I'm not sure why they'd send a group of teenage thugs after somebody like John Delisle."

The man in gray sighed audibly, theatrically.

"Not a lot of living people know this," he said, "But John Delisle's birth name is Jean Red Cloud."

"Like Jean-Claude?"

"No, like Chief Red Cloud. Delisle came later. But most people never learn his name."

"What's your point?" she said.

"Have you considered the possibility that he's lying to you?"

"Yes."

The man in gray laughed.

The thin woman sipped her coffee.

A waitress approached the table, engaging in a long and poetic Italian conversation with the man in gray. When the girl left, he smiled at the thin woman.

"So," he said. "Where's your rogue Canadian now?"

"North Carolina."

"After Crenshaw like we discussed?"

"Yes," she said.

"You sound abhorrently unconvincing," he said.

"And you sound scripted like you wrote down what you wanted to say in your hotel room with a dictionary and a thesaurus on the table. Do you want to cut me some slack; John isn't exactly the most stable person we have in the field. I still think we could have put Yossi on it, or Ortitvosnosky."

The man took a serious tone for the first time since he sat down.

"I need my money's worth from him. Crenshaw and the club aren't my top priority. And John isn't the asset I hoped he'd be. He'll tie the end of the bow and then we'll seal the envelope. Sound good?"

The thin woman didn't answer.

The man in gray laughed,

"He stripped you naked in mid-January in a feild outside of Hartney, Manitoba because he thought you had a wire. You really give a shit about this guy?"

She glanced at her new and expensive handbag.

"How do you know so much about him?" she asked, shifting focus.

"I think you'd be surprised to know the real truth," he said.

She rolled her eyes and took out another cigarillo.

"The truth about who he is?"

He gestured with his thumb and index finger for the cigarillo.

She handed it to him and he took a quick drag. He stared at the evenly burning tip then prodded the edge of the filter with his fingernail.

"Where did you first meet John?" he said, handing it back to her.

"A bar," she said, noticing the old man's silver bicuspid for the first time. She recalled images of desert sand and sagebrush and oozing black blood.

"A long time ago, back in New Mexico," she said.

"If you can believe it, I met John when he was fourteen years old."

"I thought he was Canadian Intelligence."

The old man shook his head.

"Most of his background is a lie. When I first saw him, he was just a boy."

"In Oka?"

"He's not from Oka. He was nowhere near the crisis. He might not even be from Canada." The old man chuckled. "He might not even be Native American

"Where were you then?"

"Inner city Toronto, a place called Regent Park, where . John had been a pickpocket and a street hustler. Found him in the gravel lot of a Turkish rape club, down off Church, near the old Bijou. He was dressed up in a pink tutu and woman's makeup. The cheeks of his ass were closed shut with dried blood. Probably got snatched off the Younge Street Greyhound terminal like the others. I did what anyone would have done, I turned my back and walked away. But he stopped me. He looked at me, his nose running, a black eye, and asked me for a knife. Not help or mercy or the police. He wanted a blade. So I gave him a gun. When he was finished, he hobbled out of the doorway and handed the pistol back to me. I thought he was special that little ballerina covered in kanaker blood. But he isn't loyal like he used to be."

The thin woman tapped her ash.

"Well, your ballerina's on task," she coughing.

"Or so we think. Does he have a second on his back?"

"Yes," she said. "Off the grid. Someone who can disappear."

"A professional?"

"That's what he said."

"Terminate her as well."

She nodded.

13.

Her captor had walked into the bathroom holding a Zip-loc bag with a coroner's worth of brown powder.

"Is that heroin?" she said.

"No. I don't fuck with smack."

He poured a good amount into his hand then spread it across his flattened palm, bending his fingers back.

"What the fuck is that?"

"Scopolomine," he said before kneeling down and blowing a cloud of brown dust into her face.

Her first moments of consciousness weren't blurry; a blur would have been welcome, comforting even, compared to the sudden jolt that was. Starla's eyes sprung open and came to seated in an upright position in the backseat of a moving car, her head gently pressed against the window. Cars sped past her in the parallel fast lanes. She could see every detail of the rushing asphalt, the faces of the other drivers behind their windshield glass, the sunshine subdued by an incoming tide of silver cloud cover over the highway. She was overwhelmed by the clarity of the world around her as if ice were crystallizing between the wrinkles of her gray matter.

She wore a tight, strapless little black dress she didn't remember putting on, complete with cream dress shoes, a sapphire engagement ring and a double-loop silver necklace. A matching braided ankle bracelet covered the scar from the shackle. Her hands were bound by a black plastic zip-tie.

The driver was the Indian. He looked different, clear, less threatening. His face was cleanly shaven. He wore gray dress pants and a pink button-up with the sleeves rolled up to his elbows. His hair was cut short and he wore glasses for the first time with rectangular lenses that changed the shape of his face immensely. He parked the white pickup in the lot of a long strip mall.

"What is this place?"

"This is the Yukon Bistro Bar and Grille. I figured you might be hungry."

"How did you get these clothes on me?"

"You put them on yourself," he said. "I just told you to."

"But I was passed out."

"You just don't remember. That's an effect of scopolomine."

She lowered her head onto the front seat.

"Feelin' bad?"

"Dizzy."

"Here," he said, reaching into the side console. He handed her a bottle of spring water and a packet of Dramamine.

"Thanks."

"You'll feel better once you have a meal."

"No more burgers," she said, before swallowing the tablets.

"No more burgers," he said. "How about a steak?"

"I'm not hungry."

"You should really eat something just the same."

She raised her head, looking at the zip-tie around her wrists.

"You gonna keep me tied up in public?"

"I'm setting you free," he said.

"You're lying."

"I'm not. From here on out you're not a prisoner. You can leave this parking lot, but you'll be on your own. Remember the putty I made you bit down on?"

"You got took my dental profile?"

"You're officially dead now. The guy trying to kill you set the trailer on fire before he killed himself. That's how it looks."

"He shot himself six times in the chest?"

"I pulled the lead out of him before I set him on fire. The holes all burned up."

"Who the hell had has my fake teeth in them?"

"My hooker."

"Jesus."

"The point is you don't exist anymore. You're free to leave. But you can't be you anymore. Whoever the fuck that is. If you try to, you'll be the first suspect, having faked your death, and having the most to gain."

She snorted.

"So I don't really have a choice either way?"

"Sure you do."

"What happens if I stay?"

He looked at her in the rear view mirror.

"You're no longer my prisoner. If you stay on you'll work for me. It'll be like a job, a contract."

She said nothing.

"I need someone to pose as my wife in order to get close to a couple people."

"People?"

"People I have to kill."

"So you're blackmailing me."

"Not at all," he said. "I need someone for the job. I had someone but she's dead. Then I found another, but she's got your dental records stuffed into her dead jaw right now. If you help me I'll give you her cut."

"How much?"

"Forty grand."

"Bullshit."

"It's forty grand. Think about it. You could walk out of the truck right now with no clothes but that Nordstrom sale-rack dress, no identity and no money; or you could start over with some actual resources."

She thought about making a run for it, hitchhiking her way to Kentucky. She imagined the Indian gunning her down on the side of the highway. She kept quiet about her brother.

She sat, silent.

"Take all the time you need," he said, lighting a cigarette.

She asked for a drag and he gave it to her. She reached out with her bound hands and smoked.

He lit himself another, letting her keep hers while he was at it.

They sat in silence.

He rolled up the automatic window when hers reached the filter so she could toss it out.

"Alright," she said, "Cut this shit."

He sliced off the plastic with a stainless steel folding hunting knife.

She straightened her back.

"Let's go inside," she said.

He sucked on the last bit of the filter and followed her out of the truck, leading her inside the upscale chain restaurant with his hand on her shoulder as if they had known one another for years, but the firm, domineering grip told her that he was doing more than ensuring her balance.

She turned to him as they approached the hostess.

"I can walk on my own. Don't incriminate yourself. I'm

not gonna have bruises on my shoulder because of you."

He let go and smiled.

"You'll have to learn to walk in heels eventually," he said.

"As long as they're not stilettos, I'll do fine."

The young girl in a cocktail dress with a headset and tablet greeted them.

"Just two?"

She took them to a booth in the corner of the quaint and aphotic dining room where they could barely see each others' faces. They tilted the menus to the candlelight and while the waitress listed off the specials and cocktails selection from memory.

Starla asked for a Coors Light and a glass of Diet Coke.

He ordered a Bourbon Old-Fashioned and a glass of bottled sparkling mineral water.

When the girl left, he leaned toward Starla .

"If you're gonna be convincing. You'll have to change your taste a little bit."

"What are you talking about?"

"We're bourgeois now," he said. "I'm a full-blood Cherokee web developer from Hickory, North Carolina. And you are a freelance image consultant from Tampa Bay. We don't drink soda anymore. And cheap beer, to us, might as well be soda-pop. We care about banal things, stupid things. We think we're important. We shop at Wholefoods and try to find local fish mongers and meat markets. You like to wear a summer dress to farmer's outlets. We're liberal and wish Bernie Sanders could have been the president. We care about the little guy, but we don't really know who that is. You've gotta pretend you've never worked retail. And you don't know what it's like to work a manual labor or a retail job. Do you get it?"

"Fancy, is that it? You're askin' me to be fancy?"

"But you don't know it's fancy. You've got to act fancy, but you've also got to convince people that you don't even know how fancy you are. You've got to be a fancy person who thinks they're rustic, a squatter, a poet. You've got to believe you're Kerouac. Do you know who Kerouac is?"

"Believe it or not I read, asshole. Though I ain't never bothered to read him, but I know what On the Road and Dharma Bums is."

"Perfect," he said. "You're perfect for this."

"You're gonna take the money aren't you? You'll use my help and then kill me."

He shook his head.

"Why didn't you fuck me when I told you that you could?"

"Because I didn't," he said.

"I could stab you with this here steak knife," she said, pointing to the rolled sloth napkin.

"You could have stabbed me with the whiskey bottle, if you had hidden it right," he said. "The knife's right there. Go ahead. Take a stab at me."

A waitress approached their table with their drinks. She listed off the specials from memory once again. She told Starla and the Indian that they made a cute couple.

14.

Sgt. Pullano had his little Dixie cup with him, arching his arm every few seconds to spit out a cheek full of red tobacco juice from the side of his lip, before returning it behind the napkin dispenser away from the bartender's line of view as if he were just holding a drink.

"Marc's dead. What do you think of that, Beau?"

Cutler knocked back a shot of rye and chased it with an ugly local microbrew.

"What do you know about it?"

Pullano was another overweight Italian originally from the upper reaches of Chicago, Elmwood Park. He had a crucifix burned into his right temple as if some mafioso had set a rosary on a red stove-top coil and then pressed it against his face to mark him for life; retaliation by way of a christological puta mark. It was a rumor Pullano had started that rumour himself to hide the fact that he had seared the icon into his own skin in a college fraternity ceremony with the Alpha Phi Deltans.

"Just the unimportant details," he said. "The university police like to think they're their own county sometimes. Still they can't keep a six-foot eight West African basketball scholar from jetting on a multiple rape charges. Better to let the Rock Hill P.D. deal with' em. Pretend they're real cops."

"They write real reports don't they?" Cutler said.

"The fuck would you know about it?"

Cutler reached for the leather bag and handed Pullano the xeroxed police report.

"You seen that yet?"

Pullano looked through it.

"Nope. You know how it goes. Small town P.D. doesn't want to kowtow to the big city. We don't get as much chatter from SC. At least not anymore."

Pullano kept thumbing through the pages.

Cutler took another swig of his sour ale.

"There's gotta be inconsistencies with the Rock Hill P.D. report. There has to be."

Pullano squinted to look at Cutler over the papers.

"That's a possibility. The fuck does that have to do with me. I'm with a totally different police department in a different county on the opposite end of the state line."

Cutler smiled at him.

"Come on, don't give me that shit. You're Frankie fuckin' P. Frankie P makes shit happen."

Pullano shrugged as he turned the page.

"You don't have anybody in South Carolina anymore?" Cutler said.

"I got people. Some nice guys."

"Still got your ears to ground?"

"A little less nowadays, but I do okay. You know, I keep up," he said.

"Good, that's good," Cutler said, hesitating. "Maybe, you see what you can't come up with?"

Pullano shook his head and set down the report.

"I don't think so, Beau."

"What's up?"

The aging police sergeant spit into his red Dixie cup and leaned back in the vinyl booth.

Even through the chatter of the evening rush with ta-bles and chairs full of haunted regulars and the roar of a dis-tant crowd at some European football match—displayed in blinding color on the overhead flat screens—blasting from the stereo system in tandem with the ubiquitous 21st -century jukebox which played what amounted to a lonely-hearts ballad, Cutler felt lost in his own silence.

Pullano shifted the tobacco in his lip before he spoke.

"You don't look like you've slept, Beau. How are things?"

"They're good," he said. "I've been workin'"

"I can see that."

"Not just on this."

"You're not a cop anymore," Pullano said.

"No, I'm not."

"They why are you obsessing over this shit?"

"I'm not," he said. "I'm actually working for somebody."

"Bishop hire you?"

"No," Cutler said. "It's an old associate of Marc's looking for lost capital. Food brokerage stuff. NAFTA protocol. What's it matter?"

Pullano adjusted his watch.

"Just weird is all. Considering everything that went down with his girl. I guess I wanted to make sure you weren't spinning your wheels."

Cutler managed to laugh.

"One of us ex-cops gets pulled back into an old case routines. You watch too much Netflix, Frank."

"I knew you were never the type anyway. The job didn't mean as much to you as it did for a lot of other guys."

"So how come you can't help me out?"

"You're not a cop anymore, Beau. If I get caught, I'm fucked for life. Not this late in the game. I wanna retire too, you know. Maybe I have gone soft."

"Cherish it," Cutler said.

"You want another beer?"

"No, I'm good."

"You're gonna pout now aren't you?"

"What?"

"You didn't change. You're gonna dig your heels into the ground and pout like a little girl because you didn't get what you wanted."

Cutler laughed.

"Fuck you. I'm not the one that's gone soft."

"Come on, I'm gonna get myself a scotch. I'll get you another round. What are you drinking?"

"Get me a Bud or something that doesn't taste so god-damned bitter – bullshit craft shit."

"Let me hit the head first," Pullano said, crushing the top of his cup, effectively sealing it.

Cutler felt like going outside for a cigarette but sat in the booth. He figured he had the best seats in the bar at the moment as he watched people sitting on tall bar stools and the strange 1980s art deco seats on either side of high-top tables no bigger than a car tire. There were no more bars, no more neighborhood saloons left in America. They had all become quasi-sports-themed restaurants that served alcohol from a menu. The kinds of smoky billiard halls and blue-collar lounges where his parents had met were gone, and, for all he knew, never existed this far down into the southeast where the rougher gravel-road cesspools of blood stains and bottom-dollar whiskey sat on the outskirts of town.

Cutler pulled the Northrop P.D. report back to his end of the table and re-read his underlined notes.

Pullano returned after a few months with a double of olive oil-colored whiskey and an aluminum bottle of Coor's Light.

"Colorado piss water and some Red Label."

"What's the point of good scotch if all you're gonna taste is dip?"

"Not much different than smoking," Pullano said.

He gulped his scotch holding the top of the glass as if it were a bowel, then exhaled loud enough that the women in the adjacent booth gave them both a shitty look. Pullano paid them no attention.

"I was surprised when I heard you got your P.I.'s license."

"Didn't think Carlyle'd gimme the recommendation?"

"I didn't think you'd wanna do anymore detective work. Even the chump shit."

"How come?"

"You just didn't seem like the type that needed to keep busy with a job. I thought you'd pack up and go out to the West, Florida. Do some writing."

"Do some writing? What kind of cliched bullshit is that?"

"Weren't you a writer once?" Pullano said.

"No, never. I can't string a sentence together let alone a book."

"I never said anything about a book. You always struck me as one of those creative type guys."

"Naw," Cutler said, swilling the beer.

"You're just like the rest us then," Pullano said, smiling.

Cutler paid the taxi driver and stumbled out of the backseat to wander through his lawn. He unzipped and took a piss behind the magnolia. When he got inside, he sat down on the floor in front of Trish's old bookshelf and took out the second edition of The Dying Mule from it's hidden space above the ceramic bookends. He read over the first paragraph, then flipped to the back, reading the last few sentences fragments:

"A vault closes. Chain sounds that rattle his eye sockets with the razor sharp bite of the cuffs. Rights are mumbled through fat lips. A white man knows but a white man does not speak. A white man endures but a white man keeps silent. A white man keeps silent."

He couldn't write like this now. Even when he was writing like this, it was all imitation. He ripped vocabulary from Faulkner and tone from Camus. There were a few stolen lines too, a few of which Rob and other internet writers had picked up on. He hadn't read fiction in almost twenty years. Standing up, Cutler struggled to hoist himself off the floor. He clenched the thin book in his hand and walked into the sink. Fishing the Zippo from his pocket, he plucked the brass-colored compartment out of the its base and let the butane drip onto the cover. He shut the butane injector against the counter and lit the wick as he took a cigarette from the fresh pack beside the microwave. He took a few puffs and tossed the cigarette. The flames melted the cover back into a roll of dark carbon before attacking the pages. Black smoke had reached up to the ceiling by the time he saw the copyright pages disintegrate. He let it burn as long as he could, watching the first and second chapters melt into the tide of orange flame, then, finally, turned on the faucet. The pages hissed like burnt meat. He eventually threw the soggy paperback into the garbage and went to bed.

15.

They were still young and exuded a subtle air of unmatched experience beneath their metropolitan habits, which some might have interpreted as Appalachian rusticity. It helped them to fit seamlessly into whichever venue they happened to occupy at any given time. They were the true blue bloods in a sea of upper-echelon suburbanite trash. The web-developer husband with oaken skin and a chiseled face behind a pair of cosmopolitan glasses above his impeccably ironed dress shirts drew the most attention because of his unambiguous Cherokee heritage. By his shoulder, the deep-voiced tomboy wife: an independent and self assured big-sister prototype, with understated and relatable sarcasm, which kept the designer cocktail-fueled conversations from skimming too far along their shallow surfaces. The depth and warmth they offered made them welcome enough that their standing out could be justified by their intrigue. Working their way up the ladder as they embodied their personas , the mysterious couple managed to accrue invitations wherever they went. This was the essence of a perfect hustle, the kind of scam that demanded artistry and patience and Starla found herself surprisingly good at it.

It had just been a few weeks before they could graduate from crashing gala events and other bullshit to this. John had decided to get rid of the pickup truck and swapped it for a stolen Chrysler 200 sedan. They left the truck in a gulch on the outskirts of a soybean field and set it on fire. Starla had followed him in the Chrysler, itching to pull the car into the woods along the way and drive it off to Kentucky without him.

The next morning they had brunch with a two other couples they had met at the cocktail lounge. Starla sat beside a thin woman in yoga pants. All of them smelled of sweat and sex and fruity lotion. John's hands still smelled faintly of gasoline. Eyes wild in mid-pantomime, he drew on his experience to tell his new friends a few banal stories. Stings of half-truths and prevarications, which coaxed similar accounts and amused laughter from their ignorant company, taking on a disturbing significance for Starla; that in every French subway terminal, or seaside hut on the Persian gulf, someone had been stuffed into a compartment or merely left out in the open in a pool of blood. She imagined John dragging entire men across train tracks with dark gloves, dousing them in gasoline, plucking out their teeth, and cutting off their fingers. These people that surrounded them drinking and laughing in the early afternoon had no grasp at all of how close they sat to their potential deaths.

John was a good actor. She had to give him that. He had coached her for days on how to look, how to dress, things to know, things to say. She watched the films he had laid out for her and listened to music he had chosen. She read news articles from the Utne Reader and learned her persona's political stance. Throughout her preparation, she wasn't sure he could be as convincing as he wanted her to be. He didn't appear capable of having a personality. The thought that it would be her carrying the act was more pressure than she could tolerate, but he was effortless in his transformation, charming even. She had no choice. In the end, she would have to kill him.

With him, her inner life had been robbed of time. It felt as though years had passed since LaShay had been murdered, though it had now been exactly four weeks. She had difficultly recalling certain details of her face. In Starla's dreams, LaShay had changed into an omnipresent force, running through the unconscious landscapes as something even more tenuous than wind: something more akin to gravity. There were also dogs in her dreams and a half-built locomotive engines spilling out nuggets of coal in the configuration of human skulls.

* * *

Starla looked around the transparent-glass table on the sun-splashed veranda, reached for the cucumber water, and laughed.

"Something amusing?" someone close to her asked.

"In ten years this will be a jar of pickles," she said.

A woman in sunglasses and a wide-brimmed summer hat, the kind Starla had only seen worn by elderly black women in cramped country churches, took out her phone and plugged it into the sound system downstairs from the veranda beside the pool. It was a kind of death march. The singer spoke French. She didn't recognize it. She missed her country music. Admitting that in her present company would be like death, she mused.

The young lady who sat beside her—the girl she initially encountered at the cocktail lounge who, for all she could tell, had most likely been a hyper-sexual lesbian long before money and status had come calling for her in the shape of high-rise hangover sessions and the begrudging acceptance of the power she had over a man's penis— lightly touched Starla on the thigh to strike up a conversation separate from the group.

"What are you reading right now, Lynn?"

Lynn was Starla's fake name. John kept his own.

"I'm in between books at the moment. I just finished For all the Tea in China."

"Is that a novel?"

"It's non-fiction," she said.

The girl leaned sideways, uncomfortably close to Starla's face, and told her about the book she had been reading. It was the most wonderful book, apparently, a strange novel like nothing she had ever read before; something skeletal and pure and uniquely Southern as if it were written by Camus on crystal meth and proofread by Carson McCullers. Starla didn't know who Carson McCullers was and wasn't sure about the comparison, but she knew how to feign interest. The girl kept talking about the strange novel and, to the best of limited ability, illustrated the plot. She wasn't very good at it, which forced Starla to wonder if she had ripped her previous bombastic simile from the dust jacket of the book itself. She tried to summarize the main points, ultimately losing her way in a title-wave of details. This girl had no concept of the magician's tricks. Somehow, Starla began to recognize the story and soon realized she had been droning on about The Dying Mule.

"The Dying Mule," she said. "I've read that."

"No shit?"

"Yeah, that's old school. Rock Hill, South Carolina. I've lived there."

"Oh, cool. Is it like the book?"

"It's worse," she said. "It's a whole lot worse."

"That's awesome. Have you ever read anything else by the same author?"

Starla laughed.

"What?"

"You seriously don't know?"

"Know about what?"

She had the upper hand. This way she could end their exchange whenever she needed to.

"K. Hrabal," she said "That's a pseudonym. Nobody

knows who he is. He never wrote anything again. A lot of people think it was a rough draft that Cormac McCarthy's editor published to make up for a monetary loss. I've read stuff online by people obsessed with it and thought it was written as a joke by F. Paul Wilson."

One of the men nearby who had been listening added his own theory.

"I actually read that Clyde Edgerton wrote it as an experiment and ended up publishing it himself."

The girl turned to one of the other men and asked him if he had read it. Starla found her out and excused herself from the table. She stood up and walked down to the pool. It was still too cold outside to swim, but the tarp had been taken off the water regardless. It started to rain; a weak static in the sky punching ephemeral divots in the otherwise still blue surface. Rain drops filled empty coffee cups and highball glasses that had been left out. By the time the thunder had rolled in, John had earned the coveted invite to the Crenshaw estate. He took Starla back to the timeshare and asked about the book.

"That wasn't one of the books on the list. Good improvisation."

"Thanks I guess."

"Didn't figure you for much of a reader."

"Why? Because I'm White Trash."

"Yes."

"Well, I can read."

"Good."

"So what did Crenshaw do?"

"He hired me to get something for him."

"Didn't pay?"

"He paid."

"Why does he have to die now?"

"Someone else paid more."

John shrugged.

"We'll find out."

They were confined to a slow-going mountain road, heading north. The air was crisp and thin and reminded Starla of the cold sting of catching her own breath in winter. She thought of her many athletic afternoons chasing the baseball across the slanted lawn in rural Kentucky. She heard the air whipping against the sedan as well as stray belts of moisture above the drone of the fresh tires on the grooved pavement. From her vantage point, the horizon was a nearly burst orb of hot blown glass, and the mountain ended beneath the passenger windshield. The Indian had a police special strapped to his calve and a knife in his shoe. He kept an epi pen she had not seen before in his pocket.

"You allergic to peanuts?"

"Wesley Crenshaw is."

"You're gonna kill someone with anaphylactic shock?"

"Possibly."

"Then why the epi pen?"

"Misdirection," he said without emphasis or any trace of emotion.

"Like a magic trick," she said, staring forward.

"Like a crime," he said. "Behind every good illusion is a perpetration, a trespass against others obscured by deliberate deception. An act of distraction as an act of entertainment beneath which is an act of crime. A lie is a painkiller and what you don't see coming might still get you, but at least you won't suffer. Art is a great anesthetic. It helps us forget we've been ransacked and robbed, raped and tortured."

"Is that how you see it? You're some kind of an artist?"

He smiled.

"No," he said. "I'm a garbage man with the radio on."

He reached into the side console for a CD and set it into the player: The Grateful Dead's Greatest Hits. He sang along,

A friend of the Devil is a friend of mine
If I get home before daylight
I just might get some sleep tonight

They drove past farmland. The Zimmatic irrigation rigs looked like fish skeletons hovering over the near black foliated patches, and, once on the plateau, the land gave way to yet another tree-covered road of misty dew-slick asphalt coiled around the shapelessness of the hidden foothills in the shadows of a the mountains, the straw-colored quaking aspens shooting up with white-hot torches of flaming birch.

"The man I'm going to kill tonight is blind," he said.

"Then he definitely won't see it coming."

"He might have a handler, even a bodyguard."

"What's he do?" she said, pretending not to know the name.

"He runs The Greenpoint Markets."

"He won't have a bodyguard," she said.

"Man's already hired a couple hits. He's not above any of this."

She kept quiet about her days at her Greenpoint, nothing to complicate her situation. Darkness, surrounded her, as she recalled the vague framed images of Wesley Crenshaw plastered up high in the store where she had worked: a thin frame and gaunt face behind a pair of Jonestown aviators, kneeling in a farm somewhere in the northwest, dirt falling from his hand, as if he were out plowing fields all day instead of sitting in an office.

"Why do you kill people?" she said.

He didn't answer.

"Seriously, why do this? Why any of it? Why chain people in hotel rooms and pretend to be someone else just to shoot someone? Is it only money? No bullshit. No philosophy. What is the deal?"

"I doubt you'd understand."

"You mean you don't understand."

He paused.

"Seems like you've already got a pretty good idea . Why bother convincing you otherwise?"

"You take pride in being hard to read, being an enigma with no past. It feeds your ego and makes you think you're bet-ter than everyone else. You think you're an anomaly but it's all a show. You like controlling people. You're just another version of the same kind of man I've been with my whole miserable life.

"Seems like you get it then," he said.

"You're not gonna split the money with me. You're going to kill me. There might not even be any money."

He lowered the stereo and reached into the side console.

"What are you doing?"

"Shutting you up," he said.

She lurched forward to grab the steering wheel.

He blew a handful of scopolomine in her face.

She sat back wincing, sneezing.

A moment of silence passed between them before the Indian turned the stereo up. A strange island of a knoll lay ahead of them, gutted by a bulldozer; a grass-covered hillock sitting out among the arid, upturned soil where trees had been toppled to expose their blistered arterial roots in the flashes of clarity provided by the headlights and the chopped bronchial tubes of the leafless branches dangling upward against the surface of the vitrified dark that had eaten up the terrain since the afternoon. The effects of the psychoactive blow powder weren't as sudden as they had been the first time she'd been poisoned with it. Perhaps she hadn't taken the same dose, or, for whatever reason, the stuff had lost its potency. That was, assuming it functioned according to the same pharmacological principles as cyanide, which she doubted. The dashboard expanded like a piece of rubber growing with tension. She was high now, watching everything through a filter of heat. Perhaps she had developed a semi-functional tolerance to the drug and she'd be in control of her own facilities this time around. Her hands went numb. Her heart raced.

"It was discovered prior of Benedryl," he said.

"I hate this shit," she said.

"It's an insurance policy," he said. "I know you'll try to kill me tonight. I want to keep things even."

"Even? How the fuck am I supposed to be your wife if I'm this fucked up?"

"Those effects should wear off in a moment."

"It doesn't feel like last time."

"Effects aren't always consistent. Surrender to it."

She looked at the moon as it made its first appearance behind a dormant curtain of shredded clouds that had been hiding it from her.

"I'm good at that, surrendering," she said, "I've been doing that my whole life."

...and when the rumbling of the engine was replaced

by the trickle of tepid water, her feet searing with the pain of thorn-burst calluses below the crippling ache of contracted muscles that felt as if she had been running barefoot for miles, like a fugitive through razor-wire briers and bloodied thickets, in the ominous full dark with screaming dogs on her trail. She ducked below what seemed to be a source of pure hot alien light tucked inside the folded confines of smashed and corrugated tin sheet collection of sheds, where the night gave way to an immense hallway supported by flanked wooden beams. There she encountered a man-made marshland of green nets thrust across the black polyurethane pools alive with schools of fish. Had she run from the car before reaching the estate? Had she already killed him? There was blood on her hands, on the underside of her fingernails, along with dirt and hair. Pulling herself closer, her knees buckled and she knelt before one of the black plastic-lined pools to wash her hands clean in the fragrant warm water. Inside, she could feel the fish gathering around her hands. The sharpness of their fins and tender scales stung her palms and fingers. She pulled them out and watched them tremble in the unpleasant fluorescent lights. A sound then pierced the hall like the rattling of a cage, like knives against a rusted tin shed, echoing through the evil cavern. Whatever, or whoever had been chasing her before the drugs wore off had come knocking, rattling against the edge of the safe haven of the grass carp hatchery. A pitchfork with the body of a snake close behind, scraping at the doorway. And then the sound of a loose bucket of nails from the opposite end of the damp corridor: footfalls. She turned her strained neck to see the approaching figure.

There was no one.

She looked up at the ceiling and felt as though she could read the impressions and divot marks in the corrugated steel; a secret language of hidden glyphs in the thin metal.

A crash sounded at the entrance of the hatchery and, in the sobering blink of the fluorescence overhead, the wrinkled snarl the a German shepherd emerged. Its fur was matted by blood, paws filthy with dirt and hay. The dogs had been a hallucination. The snout curled up in a permanent growl to make it appear more marsupial than canine, as if some bastard tiger, at the edge of the gene pool, had fucked its way into shepherd's fractured lineage. The bitch looked like a demon running toward her.

She reached into the pool and grabbed a fish, tossing it forward.

The slender carp disappeared in a shower of blood of scales. She flung another which too the dog ignored. It latched onto her ankle before she could dive into the water, tearing off flesh, sinking its teeth into her muscle fiber as if her foot had been caught in a thresher. Bone ground against bone.

She screamed, dragging herself into the netting over the fish ponds. Holding her breath, she felt the panicked carp swimming around her as the dog jumped in after. It paddled toward her as she fought to untangle herself, snapping at the fluttering heads. Fish had jumped out of the pool and lay in the dry soil, gills like windows inside their carcasses heaving for oxygen. Fish with exposed bones and hunks of tissue flailing off in the disturbed water scratched against her skin. She attempted to lift herself up but felt too weak. Her body, covered in soaked clothes, had been made heavy in the water. She rolled sideways, clasping a live fish like a weapon, and beating the dog on its head with it. The dog's jaw crushed the head and tore the skeletal system from the portion of the fish she had been gripping in a single, almost crocodilian reflex. The dog balanced itself on her chest and sank its teeth into her forearm. She sunk with it below the surface, holding the dog by the tuft of fur on its neck as it ripped apart her arm, hoping it would drown before she lost the appendage completely. To her surprise, the dog let go and desperately paddled to surface for air.

A human hand reached down and grabbed hold of her and pulled out among the suffocating fish. John held the police special over her and fired once. The dog yelped and sank to the bottom.

"I don't think I can walk," she said.

John stood over her and ejected the barrel of the small, heavy-looking pistol. He plucked out the spent shell and reloaded with a loose cartridge from his pocket.

"Can you at least try," he said.

She did her best to stand and stared down at the skin just above her ankle. It looked as if it had been peeled back with a fillet knife. She focused on the exposed muscles and pieces of fat as she attempted to move it. Her arm looked better with only a few impressions from the dog's teeth, but it felt broken. She tried to hoist herself to her feet.

"Stay down for now," he said as a second dog barreled through the corridor of the hatchery. He fired twice, stopping it in its tracks. Its face plummeted toward the gravel from the force of the bullet. Its back legs whipped behind as the spine folded over. The third dog bound along the edge of the hatchery, sniffed at the dead fish, and retreated.

John reloaded once more and lifted Starla to her feet. He placed his head underneath the shoulder of her good arm. She could still walk on her injured foot. Blood drained across the metacarpal indenture all the way to her toes like melted candle wax.

"What the fuck happened?"

"I got carried away," he said.

"How?"

"I got impatient and you said a little too much. You did the right thing though, bashing that guy's skull in."

"I killed someone?"

"You had no choice."

"Are we fugitives?"

"Not from the law. Not yet."

He carried her to the edge of the hatchery and sat her against the fading gas lamp in the tall reeds.

"You have sit here and not another sound. I'll be back with another car: a silver Cadillac."

"The other dog," she said.

He handed the loaded revolver.

"It's double-action. Just pull the trigger. You don't have to cock it."

She pulled the hammer back and held it toward the field.

"Or do that."

She sat alone in the fleeting light, her back against the post as her kidnapper ran into the dark. She imagined shooting him in the back, but not once did she raise the gun in his direction. She knew the dog would sniff at the blood trail and turn the corner at any moment to rip apart her jugular, her wounds beginning to throb. The lamp above her flickered out. She waited for hours in the dark, dead silence, realizing she had pissed herself during the attack.

The silver Cadillac plowed through the reeds.

John stepped out of the stolen vehicle and opened the door to the backseat. He took her by the shoulders and hoisted her inside, laying her sore body lengthwise across the black leather.

The crack of a rifle echoed from across the field.

The bullet missed the sedan by inches and sabered off

a few tops of the reeds. John ducked inside the passenger's door and, within an almost practiced finesse, slid into the driver's seat. The door was still open as he reversed through the bulrush. A few more shots rebounded off the metal walls of the hatchery, splitting clusters of gravel as the long bullets careened into the dirt.

She stared at her bleeding foot and felt her bowels distend.

"I need to shit," she said, leaning up to pull the flailing door closed.

"Try to hold it," he said.

"I can't. It's coming."

"It's better than getting shot," he said. "Try to take a shit on the floor. In one area."

"I'll need to wipe."

He tossed over a stack of memos with the Greenpoint Market letterhead in the upper corner.

The pressure had become too much. She lowered her underwear and wrapped the bottom of her dress around her stomach, then squatted over the floor, holding herself between the backseat and the front headrest. Hot excrement poured out of her propelled by a deep flatulence. She was bleeding from between her legs.

The car sped through an iron bridge and took a sharp turn onto the interstate.

She cleaned herself as best she could with the rigid computer paper, allowing the menstrual blood to continue to trickle out over the otherwise unsoiled leather seat. .

John punched open the glove box and took out a pint of cheap vodka.

"Dump it on your foot," he said.

She took the bottle and chewed off the cap, spitting it into the sloshing puddle of blood and shit below her, then pressed it against her wounds, letting the stinging fluid fill up the holes from the shepherd's teeth.

16.

After cutting past the roadblocks on the far side of what was once called the Queen City Central, he watched the faceless men ascend the porte cochere of the Ritz-Carlton high above the fog bank of tear gas. It was the perfect vantage point for thrusting bricks. The air smelled of gasoline and sweat. Screams of defiance were punctuated by distant laughter and music. The protesters, aiming to dominate the high ground with their straps and climbing gear, looked like workmen with the exception of their heads which were wrapped in T-shirts and bandanas like a squadron of Basque separatists, or Irish Republicans. A few loose windows shattered. Arches of smoke emerged from over the human wall of plastic riot shields. Kids were throwing gang signs while others read from communist tracts. Cutler sat above the confusion on a warped building front. He flicked the butt down toward the street and got back into the illegally parked Hyundai. The engine didn't sound right to him as he headed into a narrow street where the city appeared to end suddenly, opening up to a series of corner shops and laundromats. He cringed at the thought of bending over or getting on his back to see where the excess rustling was coming from underneath the chassis, to find out whether or not he had it in him to maintain his own vehicle anymore. His garbage habits had probably added another twenty years to his age.

He slammed on the break.

A group of seven kids blocked the the thoroughfare. One of them sat on a milk crate, smoking a cigarette. The shirtless boy toiled with the black-grip handle of the Louisville Slugger. A stray beam of light glanced off iits rounded end as the tight-muscled, lanky teenager pointed the bat through the windshield into Cutler's line of vision.

Cutler curled his upper lip and shook his head.

"Don't you even fuckin' dare me to, you son of a bitch," he said

Cutler hadn't slammed on the horn yet: his only civility.

Those gathering were in no hurry. The kid with the muscles slammed the end of the bat into the asphalt with a clang and leaned on the handle.

Cutler stopped the engine.

He got out of the car.

The kid didn't make eye contact with him.

"Hey, I'm just trying to get home," he said. "Just let me pass. I don't want to be a jerk about it or nothing."

"There ain't nothing stopping you. Drive on through old man," a girl said.

"If you'd kindly move. I'd like to do just that."

The shirtless kid sniffled, rubbing his nose with the side of his arm. He stepped only a few inches from Cutler's face.

"Just drive through old man."

"Okay," he said, as he turned to get back into his car, then stopped and approached the group again. He reached into his coat pocket.

They flinched.

He cracked open his cigarette case.

"You want to hold onto these for me?"

The kid took the two joints and ran them beneath his nostrils.

"Yeah, I'll take care of these. You have a good night."

He motioned for the everyone to get out of the street.

" 'Preciate ya," Cutler said, getting back into the car.

The road appeared to stop where the street lamps had been shot out. The stoplight in the distance hung in the dark like the conical red glow of an ocean buoy. He turned his brights on and maneuvered around the upturned shopping carts blocking the way. He took the last joint out of the cigarette case, lit it, and took a long inhale. He let the thick, sour smoke ripple through his fingers and skirt the roof of the car. Pieces of glass and discarded cans crushed beneath the tires. He rolled up the window and tapped his ash. There was woman calling for help from one of the pitch-black apartment building, effectively stifling his slow building high. He ignored her and turned onto the highway exit below the iron bridge shimmering in the headlights like a polished bow of scrap metal. He passed a pile of hefty coyote roadkill resting against the concrete median; just a few strips of wet fur-coated fat and a maroon coil of intestine. The city drowned in the rear view mirror and the suburbs shut up past the tangled monolith of the Carowinds' roller coasters south of town, and all of the once empty fields monopolized by the strip malls, grocery stores and their parking lots, lay untouched, unshaped. Out here, the cop cars were more likely to stop a silver Korean sedan with a fat old carpetbagging wop in the front seat, putting in construction bids up and down the interstate. After all, he thought, if he squinted real hard from the pot smoke, he could've passed for a Mexican. Even good weed couldn't keep him from feeling the loneliness of the night; protesters fighting the cops for equality and all he could see was a bunch of doped-up iPod babies sucking off the memory of civil rights. A fucking far cry from the Friendship 9 and Swan Vs. Charlotte-Mecklenburg. No plan. No sacrifice. Just loose memories of a few good ideas. Trump was probably going to become president, again . The

Indians were getting another oil pipeline hammered through sacred land. Vandergreven and her father liked to fuck animals.

He flicked the remnants of the joint out the window and swerved down the back way flanked by sidewalks toward the old neighborhood. That's when he saw the epileptic flashing: beams from two jurisdictions syncopating like festival lights along the neighbor's walls. Police vehicles had been parked up his driveway and into his lawn, kicking up slabs of fresh sod recently laid by his nephew. He inched around the cul-de-sac and drove up onto his sidewalk.

Pullano was hiding behind Tillman and the short, stout frame of Detective Brian Downing. Downing should have been I.A. in Cutler's opinion, but probably wanted to make Chief one day. They used to call him Downer Downing back in the early days when he had been a shitkicker pretty boy who looked more suited for jean-commercial modeling than Highway Patrol. But he rose up fast, mostly because he knew whose asses to kiss and whose balls to break. He had a talent for sensing self-doubt in other cops, especially sloppy ones like Cutler. He looked older now, haggard in the face, but still fit. He wore a dark pants and a pristine white button up. His badge and his gun and his cuffs all strapped thoroughly against the dress belt.

Cutler walked up the lawn and lit a Marlboro to mask the skunk on his clothes.

"Hey, Beaumont," he said.

"Hey, fuck face," he said, blowing smoke. "Thought you'd be retired in Florida selling gym memberships by now."

"We got to talk, tough guy."

"Then let's talk."

"Let's go inside."

"We can talk out here."

"You don't want to have a drink first?"

"I don't have any fucking kale smoothies in my house."

"Worried I'll see how you're living these days?"

"You can take a look at my face and see just fine how I'm living these days."

"I was a little more focused on your waistline, tubby."

"Really? Because I could have sworn you've been staring at my dick this whole time," Cutler said.

"You were working for Wesley Crenshaw. The grocery guy?"

"Still am."

"Not anymore you're not. He's dead."

He caught Cutler off guard.

"Well, fuck."

"Where were you three nights ago around eleven pm?"

"Getting drunk with Frankie P over here," he said, pointing the cigarette at Pullano.

Pullano hid his face from Cutler.

"Asking about Vandergreven's suicide."

"We talked about a lot of stuff that night."

"Why don't we go inside, Beau?"

"You got a warrant?"

Downing smiled.

"You really want all these old timers and you're nosy neighbors to hear all of this shit?"

Cutler looked around at the convoy splayed across his lawn.

"Yeah, 'cause you really showed up all discreet-like," he said, doing his best faux-Cajun accent. "What's the plan with the Asheville, P.D. boys? They here 'cause of Crenshaw?"

"They just want to know what you were doing for him."

One of the out-of-town Detective's sensed his cue and walked up to the front without speaking.

Cutler stared at the older officer who adjusted his belt just to have something to do with his hands besides reach for a pistol.

"You smell like an outdoor concert, Beau," Downing said.

"You can ask the Asheville guys about all that. I've had a bad back for years. You gonna bust me?"

"Better watch it."

"Don't you have a riot in the city to go break up?"

"You're fixin' to make this as hard as possible ain't cha?"

"I'm not the one who's harassing an old man on his front lawn."

Cutler flicked the cigarette butt.

"Why don't you give me a good reason for you to be here, Downing? At this point, seems like a whole lot of nothing."

"How about obstruction of justice?"

"Yeah, how about it? On what grounds?"

The guys from the Asheville P.D. started to look concerned.

"Misleading conduct," Downing said. "Omitting information."

"You're not a lawyer Downing, and this isn't a court. You got shit. Charge me something. Show me a warrant. Or get the fuck off my property."

Whether he meant to or not, Pullano had implicated Cutler by mentioning the case file. As close to retirement as the poor bastard had discovered himself, he could probably taste that unholy pension coming down the pike and damned if his was going to let an A-class fuckup like Cutler put it in jeopardy.

It wasn't until the Asheville cops wanted to know what he had been doing for Crenshaw that Brian Downing saw the ideal chance to use scare tactics on Culter: obstruction of justice, misleading conduct—they had nothing concrete but Pullano's word.

He shut them down fast. Not bad, he thought, for a burn-out P.I. with a college-washout handling his video analysis. But they were definitely looking at him now, and no one from the old days was going to throw him a bone. That had become clear.

He had told the Asheville department he had been scouting Greenpoint Market store managers for giving Wholefoods and Publix surveyors info on upcoming franchise locations for cash sums and promises of corporate positions. He had pulled the explanation out of his ass and they bought it with no other questions. Downing didn't even bring up Marc Vandergreven's role a food broker for the company, showing Cutler what little he actually had.

He thought about what Downing had said, asking him if he wanted a drink first. He never thought he had a reputation at the P.D. for being a drinker, not anymore than Sanders and Rourke—and the pair where even keeled compared to the lowly inhabitants of the rubber gun squad in the records wing. Those were the real burnouts and hefty boozers. And even then, Rourke and Sanders drank more than Cutler. Well passed his rookie days, he'd have a J&B and a cigarette—back when you could have a smoke in a bar in the South—and head home for dinner with Trish. Back then, Rourke and Sanders had wives and kids too, but they skipped out of late night homework and family meals to wind up on each other's porches—it depended on the night whose—to knock back more Budweiser, suck on watermelon rinds, and share a Styrofoam box of reheated Piggly-Wiggly chicken gizzards.

"The drunk bastards," he said to himself, lingering in bed, stoned, drifting.

Charlotte was on fire and all Downing wanted to do was remind Cutler that he was a better cop .

"Okay," he said to the dark, "I'll play."

17.

She caught the first heated band of red-iron light as it slid below the jagged horizon, grasping its way across the staggered crescents and rocky valleys, slapping her right cheek with a blood-like warmth before disappearing into the frozen western shade of the next peak.

Empty vehicles, scattered like insect carcasses, marked the junkyard beneath the steep incline of the freeway and the distant pines may as well have been crudely wiped pastel.

She didn't know for sure if there were residual effects to scopolomine, or if her brain was somehow marked for life the way acid had once done her in, in what now seemed like a thousand years ago; those odd little chemical incisions, she imagined, effortlessly if not accidentally, etched into the dendrites or whatever molecular mechanism it was, like razor marks on a depressive's arm—the components that separated her 21-century blue-collar mind from the virgin psyche of a pioneer hag or a dust-bowl Okie. And she lamented her new status as yet another kind of perverse outcast of a human being while at once remaining as essential and primeval as any specimen might come: a murderer.

"Who exactly did I kill?" she said, the cool morning light ahead of the vehicle, darkness still on their side.

"Some guy with a gun. Bashed his skull in with an horderve platter," John said.

"What about the CEO, the blind man?"

"I killed him."

"How?"

"A gun."

"Did I break character?"

"No," he said.

She thought he was lying.

"Who else is dead?"

"Nobody, yet," he said.

That was her cue.

They stopped at a lookout point and John scooped up the soiled matting from the backseat and tossed it over the edge. It almost took care of the smell, which, up until that point, had been unbearable. The entire car smelled like sour shit and crotch sweat. Whatever lingered behind, Starla figured was coming from her. She prodded John in the front seat, telling him she needed tampons. He stopped at a gas station and purchased them for her. Perhaps that was his final courtesy. He drove the silver Cadillac off the freeway into a secluded field. This was he'd put a bullet in the back of her head. So much for cooperation. Perhaps the tampons were an act of respect her before executing her in the field. She knew this moment was inevitable the second she found herself chained to a toilet. He hadn't raped her, but the captivity had been agonizingly sexual in nature.

"You don't just raped with a dick," LaShay had once said.

The Cadillac crossed over a bridge, which patched together two plains of dirt separated briefly by a moss-covered gully, and parked behind a mantle of pulverized wisteria branch and fat-leafed Empress of China. She couldn't tell if they were even in North Carolina anymore, the landscape seemed so foreign and intricate. Her stomach cramped at the thought of expiring somewhere unfamiliar enough to be a dream, nowhere to look for comfort, no knowledge of the land or who might be walking close by. It was like already being dead.

She watched him put on his gloves.

"Get out," he said.

"I'll suck your dick for an hour," she said. "I'll take you pre-jack and after-cum. You can give it to me for hours. I just want one more day."

"No time."

"What the fuck is wrong with you?"

He turned to her, giving her an honest and serious look as if what she had just said truly concerned him. She hated the look. It humanized him, if only for a moment. Just in the eyes, she thought. Just his eyes seemed to be looking back at her while the face and remainder of his being—a kind of void-like presence—had turned to her out of perfunctory movement. There was yearning behind his steadily dilating pupils in the absence of light. The question may as well have been any kind of objection. She could have just screamed at him. But asking what was wrong with him appeared to be a deep question for him, an inquiry that, above anything else, terrified him. And she knew that he didn't have the answer.

She said it again.

"Get out of the car," he said.

She hung her head and opened the door.

"Do you have a smoke?"

He paused and fished around his pockets.

"No," he said.

"It's just as well," she said, still speaking like Lynn. Otherwise she might have said something like 'It don't matter.'

John walked around to the back of the Cadillac and lifted the trunk.

Starla didn't bother fighting back. She felt sick, weaker than ever. She focused on whatever psychic patterns she could see in the dirt at her bare feet: spirals of glittering mica ad sprinkled along wind-blown ripples of loose ground. Then she heard voices—the expected progression of auditory hallucinations—familiar voices, at least one of them. The other voice could have been anyone. The cadence of another woman, panicked, wounded. It came from the trunk.

"I see the demon that comes to see you," the voice said.

Confused, Starla limped over to the trunk to see the woman in a torn pantsuit stuffed writhing inside the spacious trunk. She was bound in electrical tape.

"I see the demon that comes to see you," she said.

"What the hell is she talking about?"

"She's been tripping for past few hours," John said.

"You gave the memory stuff?"

"No. LSD," he said.

"How much?"

"More than eighteen hits."

"She's gonna have a heart attack. I've seen it on TV before."

He took out the police special.

"She'll doesn't have to worry about that."

"Why didn't you even take her?"

"Collateral. Help me get her out of the trunk. Get the tape off her."

"I can't even lift my own ass."

"If you want your money we gotta tie off this loose end."

She struggled with the woman's legs as they pulled her out of the truck and lay in the weeds.

"Who is she even?" Starla managed to say over her labored breath.

"Crenshaw's assistant, Ms. LaQuinn. You two got on famously last night."

"I don't remember."

"It's an easy frame," he said as he cut off the black electrical tape with the tactical knife.

Her hands began to flail gripped at his face.

He pushed her hands away and pinned them beneath his knees as if her were sheering a farm animal.

"I've seen the girl," she said. "The girl with the scar."

"Help me get her up," John said.

"What do we do about the car? I can't walk," Starla said.

"I got hiker's clothes in the trunk," he said, wrestling with the woman. "We'll act like you had a fall."

"Who do we have to be this time."

He struggled to set the woman in the front seat and buckled the seat belt.

"Just be yourself."

"I want to go to Kentucky and be with my brother," she said.

"You can do whatever the fuck you want after next week."

"One more week?"

"You want your goddamn money?"

"There's no money worth this."

"You've come this far," he said.

"I guess I have," she said. "But what else do you need me for."

"Insurance," he said, setting the pistol in the woman's hand, looping her finger in the trigger, pressing it against her temple.

BOOK B.

0.

His face was still buried in the soft goosefeathers. Waking, Forrester allowed his right eye to open from the hypnagogic borderlands onto the white-sheet silhouette beside him as the propeller engine overhead reached its grinding crescendo pitch, shaking the roof before unloading a red cloud of flame retardant onto the scorched landscape like a bird in flight bursting its abdomen to drain its offal across the treeline: the first of the dawn in the ongoing fight to curb the flames. The smoke from the arson fires had wafted down as far as the Carolina-Georgia border where the last strands of cotton listing in the smoke filled wind clung to the brittle twig fields in places like Darlington and Savannah. The apocalyptic clouds of toxic debris rolled as far north as Kentuckiana. The first of these wildfires had been set somewhere near Chattanooga, but the apex of the major ecological disaster had been East Tennessee: an earth made of kindling. The nights flickered orange and the days took on a hue grayer than normal for the region.

The soon-to-be-retired sheriff reached his hand across the mattress to pat the black woman through the sheet. His bed partner rolled over, letting her hand fall across his pillow. He reached forward and touched her face and caressed the silk wrap around her hair. She grabbed his hand by the wrist and tossed it aside. He looked up at the ceiling and listened to the second plane hover through the valley, along the river.

Nathan rose from the bed, stretched, and walked to the kitchen, wiping the crust from his eye. He took a dirty glass from the sink and poured three fingers of Pepto-Bismol, filling the remainder with water from the dripping faucet. He held the milky glass up to the frosted window and watched the mixture turn black: coal ash. He dumped the sludge and filled the percolator with spring water from the plastic gas-station jug. It started boiling. He reached back into the fridge and took out a ceramic dish half-full of kanuchi his brother had given him on his last visit to Montana. His sister-in-law had picked the hickory nuts herself. He spooned up a plate and set it in the microwave. Samantha didn't like his Cherokee foods, but he would not permit her to bring her bran cereal and milk to his house. He took out a carton of eggs and cleaned the iron skillet in the sink. Smelling the sulfur bi-product in the foul drinking water, he gave it a quick rinse with the boiling spring water from the percolator and placed it on the stove.

He had been having sex with the receptionist of the local clinic off and on for seven years. She didn't need him as much as he needed her intimacy. He had a feeling she had been with more than one man years ago, but, as sex became even less of a necessity as she grew older, she stuck around with Forrester. He didn't know why. He looked forward to her visits every other weekend or so, whenever he wasn't working, getting things ready to stop working, or about to head back into another marathon cycle of work. She disappeared for eight months once and he figured she had gotten enough of him, or logically moved on to someone steadier who suited her life, a black man perhaps, someone to grow older with. But she had returned to his doorstep in galoshes and a gray peacoat in the dead of night, a bottle of zinfandel and a box of chocolates in her purse.

He took out the sugar and crème Samantha had brought from home for her coffee. She'd make it herself, the only way she tolerated it. He fixed his coffee black and tossed in a dollop of cinnamon, which sank to the bottom: a kind of reward at the end of the cup. He wasn't sure where Samantha came from, whether or not Tennessee had always been her home. She she wasn't the kind of person to stand on rooftops the way Nathan and his brother had when they were children; his brother pointing west toward the smokestacks of the scorched-ash horizon of Louisville, saying he'd go where the real Indians were, where they still lived like Indians and not like city boys.

"Like on the TV. With the cowboys where the black and white used to be."

Samantha took care of what was right in front of her: who was under the gun at work, how much the electric ad cost the month previous, when the accounts at the clinic where due for collections. She lived in the details and, at times may have seemed gossipy to Forrester. She did have a quality he admired greatly, an almost inability to digest wistfulness as if she had no concept of where she was going or where she came from. He looked forward to their liaisons with the giddiness of a child on Christmas morning. Anytime he found himself stuck in the office till nightfall, photocopying and filing and cleaning up everyone's mess, the memory of her kept him going, kept him fulfilled the way he had been as a young man. She'd call him on occasion, and he'd step into his office to stare at the cork board, asking when he could expect her next. It gave the rest of the day a unique shimmer. He no longer purchased con-doms at the pulpería, avoiding any suspicion that county sheriff was secretly fucking a younger woman. Sam was well on the opposite end of the change and she trusted Forrester's sexual history. Forrester knew that she had been using condoms with the other men in the first few years—the younger ones that nobody could really trust—and he figured if he hadn't caught something by now, he likely wouldn't the older they got.

He sipped his coffee and opened up the door to his back porch, pushing aside the revolving panel of half-rotted plywood that served as an extra barrier from the smoky atmosphere. He stepped through the cinder-colored fog and stared up at the dull white knot of the rising sun. The ether reeked of grease and chemical fire. He listened to hum of the distant plane and thought about his brother and, in turn, about Kentucky. Louisville had always seemed like a perfect vantage point for iron-belt nomads to dream about the West. And that was exactly what his brother had been doing on the soot-blackened fire escapes and tar-pit roofings of their apartment building all those years they had played Robin Hood. His brother had gone West looking to reinvent himself as the modern Native American, and he had been exceptionally successful at it. He met an Ojibwe girl from Lansing en route and convinced her to follow him to Big Sky country where he made his fortune selling medical supplies wholesale. He had three tall sons—all of them hyper-masculine over- achievers—and a giant ranch.

As for Nathan, he had dropped out of college and joined the army, got stationed in Fairbanks, enjoyed Alaska for a couple years, then wandered into the police academy. The events of his life carried him like a river current and he found himself living in rural East Tennessee for the rest of his life. He used to like being a small town sheriff and kept getting re-elected. Now, he was finally sick of it. He used to tell his brother that choosing to be a policeman was like choosing to bite into a piece of drywall, and the only way to retire from it was to swallow.

The kitchen light flickered on behind him. He turned and looked at Sam in the opaque window, or at least what he could see of her: a thick woman with torn-lace underwear and a white undershirt which only came down to her pot-bellied navel. He walked inside, parting the plywood slab, and stepped into the kitchen.

"It's worse today," she said.

"They said it'd be the worst today. Things'll start clearing up by tonight."

"Don't you need to get to work?"

He watched her as she cracked two eggs over the skillet.

"I don't have to be in until about ten o'clock," he said. "One of the perks of being sheriff."

"Is the water hot?" she said, pointing to the percolator.

"Yeah, it's hot," he said and gripped the handle.

She poured her grounds into the filter rig atop the thermos and he let the steaming water drip inside until the brown mushroom of watery coffee sank inward like a soufflé. She added her own creamer, the one on the counter.

"What about you?" he said.

"I have to take my niece to the mall and get her a new phone. Then I got to clean my apartment."

"Want to come back tonight?" he said, slipping his hand in her underwear.

"Naw, I gotta get myself up at five thirty tomorrow."

"Doing an opening?"

"Open to close," she said. "One of the long ones."

"Eh, too bad," he said squeezing her buttock.

"Get your goddamned hand outta there."

He slid his hand out and took hold of his coffee.

"Dirty old man," she said.

"I'm old," he said, combing his fingers through his white hair.

She flipped her eggs around in the skillet. The microwave beeped again.

"Your rice stuff has been ready," she said.

He took a spoon from the drawer and reached over her

to the cupboard take out the plate

They sat across from each other in the small living room and ate in silence. His work phone rang. He waited a moment to answer, getting up from the table to walk into the next room. He listened for a moment, responded, then hung up.

"What's going on?" she said.

Forrester shook his head.

"Somebody thinks they saw a body."

"Who's somebody?"

"A kid who sees things all the time."

"Huh."

"Keep me out of the office a little longer, I guess."

"Get some fresh air," she said, looking out the smoke-blocked windows.

Years ago, Forrester had traded in a busted El Camino his brother had given him to drive back to Cosby from St. Paul—before reaching final destination of Montana, of course—for a practical Subaru hatchback. He liked driving up on a scene in his own car, unmarked and inconspicuous. He liked to shock people with his presence since the tiny precinct only had two unmarked vehicles. Anyone could make out one of the boxy police cruisers whipping around a mountain bend. He walked out the backdoor in his uniform as a gust of dry frigid morning wind tossed a flurry of dead poplar leaves across the oblique range. The brick-colored shrivels of expired foliage, some still singed and glowing like specs of floating carbon, caught in the screen door like insects to fly paper. He fired up the Subaru and carefully weaved toward the lopsided mailbox at the edge of the winding, vertical driveway. Wearing an extra layer, the heat inside the car became oppressive immediately and he turned the dial on the AC to counteract the mild sweat he had going beneath his uniform. He had his low beams on to see through the dusty mist until he got to the highway where the wind pushed the smoke away. Several miles out, he came to a clear view of the ridge lines and saw the extended boulder-encrusted gulch where Early had been waiting for him alongside Deputy Lehrmann's cruiser. Naturally, Early only wanted to see Forrester, since Forrester humored her and the kid was paranoid and involved, if only in her own mind, with the occult. She thought only Forrester could be trusted since he had special senses being in tune with the land as an Indian.

Forrester pulled up in the hatchback parallel to the icy creek below.

Deputy Lehrmann looked mortified as he watched the sheriff lift himself out of the car.

"I'm sorry," he said. "I should have waited for you."

"He shouldn't have looked," Early said, pulling at the pink fleece as if it were her own skin.

"When was the last time you used, Early?"

"That don't got nothin' to do with it."

Forrester took a quick, barely audible inhale before speaking as if to stop himself.

"Sometimes it does," he said.

He turned to the deputy.

"And how come you're apologizing? You can take a look at something without me holding your damn hand."

Early pulled off the hood of the fleece, exposing her matted locks of unwashed blonde hair.

"This ain't for his eyes, sheriff. I need another seer like me. Connected to the land."

"Cut the Native shit."

"You're deputy has tainted whatever you're gonna see. It's

a ritual is what it is," she said.

"I didn't touch a damn thing, sheriff," Lehrmann said.

"I know."

Forrester turned to the thizzhead he had put in jail twice. "Are you fixin' to tell me what you were doing here or not?"

"I'll tell you what I know," she said.

"I don't care what you know. I want to know what you where doing."

"I spent the night at Monagan's—"

"What were you up to when you found the body?"

The tunnel yonger in warmish 'round now. I'as just tryin' to get out of the wind. This hills might be burning, but it's still damn cold down here." She turned her indignant look toward the deputy. "Smoke me a cigarette."

The deputy lowered his head and spoke in Forrester's left ear.

"I figured you'd want to take a gander before we're on parking duty for the staties."

"She find Hoffa's body?"

"It's homicide, no question."

Forrester thought for a moment.

"Okay, then.

Early poised herself.

"Not you," he said. "You'll mess up my magic Indian powers."

"Should I put her in the back of squad car?"

"She done anything?"

"She seen the poor bastard first."

"Unless she's got something else to say, I don't give a whole hell of a flip what she does."

Lehrmann looked at her.

"You wanna ad anything to your statement, Ma'am?"

"Nope."

Forrester shrugged.

"Get lost then. We've got it from here."

Early tucked her lips into the fleece and pulled at the drawstrings before stomping down the highway.

"Steer clear of the north side," Forrester called out. "You'll die of smoke inhalation."

"They said on the radio there's a good rainstorm coming up from the Gulf, gonna quell some of the fire and smog."

"It ain't smog," Forrester said.

"I know that. You should have seen Gatlinburg last weekend. Damn near looked like a Los Angeles."

"You took down Early's statement, right?"

"Yeah, 'course."

He sighed deeply.

"Alright, take me to it."

"This wasn't no drunk died in a culvert," Lehrmann said, pointing to the metallic tunnel.

They stepped inside, footfalls echoing. Deputy Lehrmann already had his flashlight handy. Forrester didn't even bother with his. He just followed the expanding beam of light as the two walked further into the dark. The body came up suddenly. First nothing but rippled metal and light glancing backward—exaggerated mechanical illumination—and then, the entire gruesome situation appeared at once: a middle-aged man in a trench coat, face down, arms spread, a long stick with a rudimentary coarse twine grip wrapped around the opposite end and plunged between the shoulder blades to exit through the base of the chest.

"Barbecue skewered."

"What the fuck? How the hell did she see this shit in the dark?"

"I didn't think about that."

"I wanna know."

"Alright."

Forrester stared at the deputy who looked back at him, hesitating.

"I want to know how she saw this."

"No problem, sir."

"Run," he said.

Lehrmann paused for another moment before chasing after the meth-ravaged girl, and Forrester was once again swallowed by the grand emptiness of the pitch black tunnel. He felt around his gun belt and took out his own flashlight, shining it on the dead man before him when he was struck by an overwhelming sense of familiarity. He saw himself in the light.

By the time the CID had taped off everything within a thirty-foot radius of the tunnel and brought in newly purchased yellow construction light stands from Lowe's to better see the body, Forrester had already identified the victim as retired Detective Beau Cutler.

"And you're sure that's the guy?" one of the young crime scene jockeys had said, no trace of a Southern accent. Most of them didn't. Tennessee was peculiar in that way. UT was almost an Ivy League institution and egghead forensic students came from all over the country to study at UT places like The Body Farm – an overrated place to be sure – dead bodies and bugs, as always, had the to best step in and take the reins even in this blink-and-miss bucolic hellhole, which honestly he preferred, where either the state police and their investigators, or the Bureau where the valley authority was concerned.

His statement was long. Forrester went into detail about

the missing North Carolina girl, the Moore Cabins, the fake name, how Cutler spent the night at the station due to the ice storm, the ongoing investigation. Hard to believe ten years had gone by, and it was all so fresh in his mind. He first recognized the poor SOB from the trench coat first, and later remembered how the ex-cop looked like he could have been his brother. It was eerie, the similarity. Having to look at himself in the center of the crime scene.

The investigators discovered Cutler had been working as a private investigator for the recently murdered organic food mogul, Wesley Crenshaw. .

"He know too much?" Forrester said, sitting behind his desk.

Lehrmann flipped through his pad.

"The CEOs assistant, that Narvice LaQuinn. They already proved she'd been stealing money from the company – well into the six figures."

"Couldn't turn a blind eye," another officer said.

The room erupted in laughter.

"She killed herself out in Severe County while on a run, right?"

"Yeah, she did – shot herself."

"That whole damn county is scorched earth now. It's like a damn nuclear bomb went off."

"Did sheriff Mason ever formerly conclude any of that."

"Open and shut case," a younger officer said.

"Yeah, well, now there's a fuckin' spear in the back of the P.I. who was trying to follow the money. None of this shit is a coincidence. There's only one thing to do now."

"What's that?"

"What do y'all want for lunch?"

He was halfway through a plate of curry chicken and bottle of North Carolina Lenny Boy kombucha, when he felt his stomach start to turn. The younger guys in the precinct called it the Greenpoint shits, saying that the open buffet food was used to being left out too long. He walked off through the dimly-lit aisles of canned beans and phony potato chips. The air smelled like rotten mahogany and cinnamon dust. He clenched as he felt the gasses pushing down on his lower stomach. He cut past the little magazine rack and stormed into the bathroom, unbuckling his belt before even closing the stall. He sat for a while, waiting for his stomach to realign itself into a state of moderate comfort. The kids had gone to town on the stalls. It was worse than a gas station. People left phone numbers for blow jobs, and white supremacist messages. One kid etched a pretty detailed poem into the synthetic gray material above the toilet paper roll:

> *God smokes the lamb's breath,*
> *From the ram's horn*
> *Atop the mountain of loneliness,*

Forrester traced the words with his fingers. He smelled his hands, then his jacket. It was hard for him to gauge the stench of his own body. He noticed his deputies and office staff stopping by his desk less. Some folks cracked the window, even when the heat was on to liberate themselves from his crusty old-man stench. His brother and him used to call it "wrinkle-neck grime." Given their olfactory surroundings in a cramped apartment shared by two families about of the Quarter Top Lounge on the West End of the Louisville, the pair had invented a plethora of pseudo-terms for offensive smells. "Crust-sock toe grease," for day-old laundry. "Dark-plaque" for the rims of the toilet. "Choke-powder" for cigarette ash. "Closet smoke," for the musty odor of old coats. The "Time Travel Smell" had been the scent of fiberglass insulation in the attic. "Dead bread" was the reek inside of their uncles' old beer bottles. He thought: "Am I getting that smelly now? Do I stink like all these things that used to make us hate life?"

He wondered what he smelled like to Sam. Was he a smoky, sour smelling, dirty old man?

He always thought she smelled wonderful, youthful even like lavender and brunt sage. And when she was wet, he could have buried his entire face in that mire of their sweet bedroom acidity and lapped it up like a dog. But he couldn't tell her that. No sir. That would have made him one sick son of a bitch. You can't tell your partner things like that, he thought, how you want to grease your skin with their bodily fluids. You just had to let that enthusiasm show in other ways and keep your own fantasies to yourself, lest it become a nightmare.

He approached the buffet at the center of the store and asked the red-bearded kid in the tie-dye apron for a recycled cardboard to-go box.

"You working with the feds?" the kid said.

"Uhhh," Forrester hesitated. "No, I'm the sheriff."

"Oh," the kid said. Handing him the box. "It's just that I saw feds eating here the other day."

"Probably just the EPA, or the fires," Forrester said, walking away from the hippie.

It came over him in the evening when the sun started dying and any possibility for the day to take a different shape was gone: a deep sense of futility, boredom, and depression. He had nothing to look forward to but a murder investigation he really didn't want, and nothing to go home to but an empty bed and a bottle of Islay malt he'd promised himself not to crack open until his retirement party. He thought about going to Hooter's for dinner or a strip club in the next county and seeing if he couldn't feed off the attention of some young girl pining for a tip; pretend he was interesting; pretend he wasn't the sheriff. He knew of some good spots for hookers up in the hills, some of them were even biological girls, but the guilt he always felt after a backseat blow job would have pushed him lower then he already was. He'd risked his job before, but couldn't now. Not this close. Not the way he looked now, as fat as he was and old. He couldn't fathom the embarrassment. But the touch and intimacy of a woman, he was addicted to it. His loneliness was pathological. His sadness lifelong.

The skeletal contours of the burned terrain in the adjacent town mirrored his own psyche. Raindrops sizzled in the smoldering pits of fire-razed homes. Crocodile-hide beams of blackened wood stuck out from the ash like the ribs of a fallen giant. Dust kicked up by the impending storm wind sifted across the road which bled out from under the mountains like a strip of over-exposed film. A billboard foreshadowing something to come had its message made cryptic by losing a third of its words. An ATV dealership had lost its inventory to flames. The vehicles had been reduced to oversized chicken cages. He passed a bulldozer scooping ash in the brick plot that must have been a house. Flames had imprinted themselves on the rock walls beside the courtyard. The tires of the Suburu had turned white.   .

His cellphone rang.

He answered it.

"Yeah?"

It was Lehrmann.

"Evening sheriff."

"Evening."

"We found the hotel room Cutler was staying at."

"Been inside?"

"Nobody yet."

"Get Trudy down there. She's the best CSS for closed spaces."

"She's on vacation in Charleston, sheriff."

"That's right. It's Thanksgiving. I forgot. Hold your horses. I'm headed back to the county. Text me the address."

"Yes, sir."

He parked on the shoulder of the scorched road and turned around.

The dark hotel room reeked of cannabis, Marlboro cigarettes, and coagulated sweat. Three deputies loitered uselessly on the second floor of the open motel balcony in the tragic glint of neon: the word vacancy all in red. The "V" pointed down at the glass-encased lobby like an arrowhead. The scene had been half-assed. DNA evidence was getting dragged out into the rain on mud-caked boot tread, smeared on shoe leather, and wiped clean from the ripped carpet. Wind and water blew into the open doorway and pushed back pages of open books strewn across the tables. Photos and documents that screamed either paranoia or progress hung from thumbtacks pressed into the drab walls.

Forrester kicked the door shut.

"It's all here," Lehrmann said. "It's a cheat sheet basically. Everything the fat bastard was up to. Right here."

"If we can make sense of it," Forrester said. "Or if it makes any sense. I figure he was up to meet somebody. Somebody who had a stake in whatever he was onto, who called him out there and skewered him."

"Why not just shoot him? I'm sorry if I watch too much TV, but that shit in the tunnel looked tribal to me."

"Tribal?"

"Like Satan and shit."

"You mean 'ritual?'"

"Yeah, that's the word. And this shit looks like some kind of terrorist's hotel room. What's the word on the body?"

"Little. It'll be another month or two. The coroner's backed up. What with all the burned bodies."

"Got it."

Forrester sat on the bed.

"Have Beverly call in a couple of pizza's from Monte Carlo's."

"We gonna be here awhile?

Forrester scanned the room, ignoring the deputy.

"What's missing? The only thing you don't see that should be here?"

The deputy looked around the room and shrugged.

"A computer, I guess?"

"Exactly. Did the owner say he had a car?"

"Man in the office said he had a red Kia Sorrento. Still missing. We got the plates and a three state call out for it.

"Good. He say anybody else came and went from this room."

"Old man kept to himself, he said."

"I bet. How long he stay?"

Lehrmann checked his pad.

"Just two weeks."

"He pay by the day?"

"Full two weeks upfront."

 Forrester lowered his head.

"What? What's wrong?"

"He paid exactly two weeks?"

"Yeah."

"To the day or does he still have a few days pre-paid?"

The color drained from Lehrmann's face and he checked his dates.

"Two weeks to the day the junkie found him."

"He knew he wasn't coming back, the bastard."

1.

The eccentric steeples plastered atop the roof of the mansion like false laterals—almost fangs—sank into the rotten dog flesh of the midnight sky. Kudzu vines wrapped like desiccated, wrinkled veins around the black iron and stone pillars which separated the ominously placed estate from the remainder of the charred woodland. The smoke, which had been thicker than fog, began to recede, revealing to the naked eye a landscape of black twigs and wasted forest that appeared to be from another world.

Inside, they ripped Starla from the makeshift bed at the corner of the boiler room and pushed her along at gunpoint through what she had come to think of as the scream chamber: cages lying upon cages where the bitches and sires growled and drooled at the first sign of movement. The tile floor was wet and painfully cold on her bare feet − clearly a concrete slab beneath. She looked down at the scars where the German shepherds had attacked her at the carp hatchery. The stranger with the gun pushed her through the hall like a prison row full of barking inmates. She was impressed they had never tied her hands or bound her once, something John Delisle would have done. They were confident she wouldn't escape. They were powerful and persistent. They...

They were whoever John had been working for. She had always assumed it had been a criminal group, a cooperate conspiracy, a government branch warped and perverted. They weren't. They were something else entirely.

A door like the entrance to a furnace, a submarine hatch,

stood at the end of the chamber and the man with the gun opened it to the outside world. There, a black Lincoln Continental was waiting for them. The lanky chauffeur had SS bolts tattooed into the strained flesh of his neck and a lazy eye. The man with the gun opened the back seat for Starla and gave her time to get inside at her own pace. He holstered the Beretta and sat beside her. . The Lincoln fired up, and the neo-Nazi chauffeur drove them out of the fantasy house of locks and dead dogs. This place was the porn mansion for the princess of darkness. The long car sailed over the ash-scraped road with ease: the kind of graceful prowess of a circling vulture. She noticed the chauffeur had a hard pack of cigarettes with a skull and crossbones on the front. Nobody could pretend to be inhuman for too long. She looked at his eyes in the rear view mirror, focusing on the lazy one bobbing from side to side in its socket. It humanized him a little more, almost like the SS bolts, which, at the very least, told her that he wasn't a stranger to pledging allegiance to bad people. Maybe, that made him an idiot. Maybe, it made him dangerous. But he wasn't a block of meat like the gunmen beside her. The six-foot-four sentient crew cut in the next seat had a militaristic bend to him. He could fake it longer, let his guard down slower. He'd end up being the barrier to getting the driver to ease up, but it still wasn't him behind the wheel. That was a small victory. She had a few of the pieces in place, and now it was her last chance to work the con.

"Can I get one of those cigarettes up there?"

The chauffeur glanced once in the mirror with his straight eye.

To her surprise, the gunman didn't object to her speaking. He didn't react at all.

Neither did the chauffeur.

"One last cigarette, right?"

They took some time to think about it. A silent conversation proceeded between the two of them. She watched and held her breath. Eventually, the gunman seemed to wash his hands of the issue, staring out at the aphotic surroundings as if they were inside a diving bell, leaving the driver to decide what the right move was. He dug into the pack and pinched out a cigarette with a red filter, tossing it back. She grabbed it and ran the tobacco under her nose.

"Smells fancy," she said.

She waited for the lighter, expecting a heavy wick Zippo. He tossed a neon-green plastic Bic. She lit the cigarette and set the Bic in the cupholder between her and gunman. She blew smoke like visible breath.

"I made a knife once. Not long ago. Seems like an eon to me now. Everything feels so distant. Anyway, I made this knife out of glass. It was a broken bottle. This was back when I was chained to a toilet. Did you guys hear about that? He fuckin' tied me to the crapper. For Weeks. The bastard. I figured I needed a weapon, or something to reach the telephone with—I can't remember. But I made this thing really well. I do remember being proud of myself, if you can believe it, I was proud of the effort I put into this little thingamajig of a brittle glass bottle knife. Shit, even he was impressed. And the only thing I can think about is how I wish I had sliced my wrists with it."

Neither of them spoke.

"Hard to believe I'm saying this but, John was a better conversationalist. A lot better. I guess that's why ya'll are trying to kill him."

No response.

"Well, that's fine. You don't have to talk to me."

She sat and smoked. The cigarette tasted like some kind of rum or bourbon dipped cigar. It wasn't a real smoking cigarette, that green-bean and tar flavor that slowly usurped the taste of one's own saliva: a working-class mouth to match the ashen flavor of reality. She ashed on the black leather.

They didn't appear to care.

"Did Hillary get elected. I haven't seen the election outcome since I got to Tennessee."

The chauffeur smirked.

She was cracking the facade.

"It's Trump's America now," he said.

She said nothing in response.

The Lincoln inched up a steep incline, reaching the arc of a smaller foothill close to the valley where, in the small window of light opened up from the shifting cloud cover, the moon reflected off the lake to reveal the devastation of the wildfires. The war zone remains lay frozen below the road. She stared through the dead trunks down the slope, through the windshield and her opalescent cigarette smoke, until the clouds shifted, and the moon took it's exit, and she may as well have been looking at a dead screen, for the dull blackness that was left.

"I guess ya'll got lucky with the fires. Could have burned down the that place. All those dog skeletons. What's with the animals anyway."

"Why don't you shut up," the gunman finally said.

She sucked on the filter, letting the smoke billow out slowly. The ash was lengthening on the end. The ember became redder as she puffed.

"Why not just kill me back at the house? Where the fuck are you taking me?"

"Shut the fuck up."

"I don't have a lot to lose here. I'm just curious about the logic," she said

The gunman pulled out the Beretta and tried to smash her face with the steel butt. She slid back trapping his hand against the leather seat, and pressed the end of the cigarette against his clenched eyelid. He jerked the gun back. She was able to weave her finger into into the trigger guard and squeeze his finger. He fired once through the radio. She pushed his hand into the backseat and squeezed again. The bullet exited through the driver's shoulder. She fired again. The bullet caught him in the side of the neck. Blood flowed over the SS bolts. She gripped the hot barrel of the pistol, searing her hand, twisting back against his hand until the man's finger had snapped. With his free hand, he punched her in the throat. She fired up the into his face, nearly decapitating him. His lower jaw stuck to his body, teeth exposed above the severed portion of lip. His brain dropped out from the burst section of his skull like a mass of tube worms, oozing down the side of his lapel. Everything else had vanished into a cloud of unrecognizable arterial spray. The chauffeur kept one hand on the steering wheel, as firm as possible. The car was still cruising along the mountain at a casual speed, his right hand free to cover the wound in his neck. Blood spilled out over his fingers, sinking into the creases in his knuckles. The wound didn't appear to be mortal, no vein burst and spurted across the leather interior, just a thick chunk of flesh grazed away by the errant bullet. The car smelled of smoldering liqueur and perfume and a sour waft of cordite; sprigs of fig leaf and tangerine rind coated the air as well, something to do with the cologne of the headless gunman, his brain tissue was whorled in his stiffening lap. The driver's windshield was cracked like a spiderweb. The chauffeur kept the Lincoln steady as he slowed and eventually shut off the engine. He jerked the emergency brake with his blood-red palm and leaned over the punch open the glove box. He took out a Derringer and racked the slide. She pulled the trigger, shattering his hand. The small pistol vanished, leaving behind a stump with three exposed bones like whittled sassafras roots jutting out of the nearly black blood which burst from the partial stump she could now recognize as his right hand. A high-pitched screech like a fox caught in a snare carried through the leather plush of the vehicle. It seemed too shrill to have come from the man. She had almost mistook it for the sound of the tires, remembering only then that the Lincoln was parked. The chauffeur's face was beet red as he screamed, then, in a hallucinatory moment, a bizarre lapse in reality as she thought of it, he went pale quicker than she had ever seen anyone's face change before, and the screaming stopped. He wasn't dead. Deep breaths bellowed from the base of his stomach to the edge of his lips. The keys were in the ignition. She didn't see the use in keeping him alive. She wasn't sure if he had much time left. Whether there was time, or no time, or some time, her objective was clearly achieved.

She pressed the barrel of the gun against the driver's temple.

"Tell me what you are. What does this organization do?"

In a split second, the chauffeur pulled out the blade of a straight razor from his vest pocket and slide it across his own throat. He still wasn't dead, but he was dying slowly, heaving, convulsing, bleeding out.

It began to rain. Water dribbled in through the cracks in the glass. She checked both of their pockets. They had nothing on them. No cellphone. No wallets. She sat alone in the car for as long as she could, then stepped out into the darkness. She kept to the side of the road and let the blood wash off. Grit covered the soles of her feet. She considered returning to the car and driving it somewhere, but she'd never make it far with that much damage and blood. She disappeared on foot. There was a clear mark on her hand from the hot barrel of the gun, which she had left in the Lincoln. She held it up against the rain. It cooled it somewhat.

Down the road, where, in the potholes and cracks, the sifted ash was washed off the black asphalt into swirling pools as if it were paint puddling in from an unseen construction site, she stepped over an iron railing into the barren woods. The shrubs and bushes had been matted into a layer of soot. As the soot mingled with the rain it turned into a paste, a paste that colored her feet stark black up to ankles. She trekked on down through the slant of the woods until she reached the pinnacle of the destruction: the remains of a neighborhood burned away. Perhaps not a neighborhood in its own right but a cluster of remote mansion-like cabins void of off-season residents for their mile-high balcony spreads. Stone chimney chasms stood alone in the cinder cubes of leftover foundation. She stepped cautiously through an archway of flecked drywall and other ubiquitous building materials torn into layers of giant pages like fossilized shale. She could feel her bones freezing as she navigated the ruins. She eventually took shelter inside one of the massive stone fireplaces with a closed flue sealed well enough to keep the rain out completely.

There, she slept through the night.

2.

You cannot be an idea. You cannot live loosely on the tips of others' tongues when recalling the virtue or the prospect of cannons and beliefs. You cannot be suspended in the moment of total assurance that your own existence is somehow in accordance to your surroundings, or inconsequential to the rest of us clambering over the huddled masses and dispossessed crowds. You cannot live frozen in a photo. You cannot be the clever word written down in immortal script no matter how long ago you and your mistakes have died. You are a breathing, ridiculous, ephemeral being. Act like it.

— Diary of Victoria Vandergreven

3.

Forrester sat in his office with the window open listening to the wind bellowing through the vacant coil of the interstate ramp, dragging the loose twigs and plastic grocery bags across the lavender fields not far off. The mountain of five-times-removed-from-the-original xeroxed sheets—their quality troublesome enough to look like old carbons—sat on his desk along with a Ziploc bag of raw almonds and a dirty Tupperware bowl with the rims streaked with garlic-smelling arrabiata from Carlo's: the Italian joint that had been making him fat. The plastic fork had been tossed into the otherwise pristine waste bin. A few of the copied pages had red thumbprints like blood stains.

Lehrmann walked into the office with his legal pad. He looked jovial.

"Spit it out," Forrester said.

"Sneeds."

"What he do?"

"I got a tip from two patrons and a bartender from The Stumphouse Tavern and Billiards. Cutler was asking about getting a new license plate and a forged registration. Met up with old Sneeds the day before he stopped showing up at the motel."

"And the car went missing," Forrester said.

"Bring the garage monkey in?"

"Keep it loose. He strikes me as the running type. But put a leash on him. Soft surveillance. I'll pay him a howdy. See him about another case, run it by him. He's not too smart. The folks at the tavern turn Cutler onto him?"

"Appears so."

"So Sneeds thinks he's a regular criminal mastermind now."

"Maybe."

Jim Sneeds was an auto-mechanic from the mountain who learned his trade on a Melungeon gypsy scrapyard as a boy. Barely able to sign his own name, Forrester had seen the bespectacled little man fix a drive shaft with half a brick and a switchblade, repair the teeth on a starter solenoid gear with a butcher's stone, and whittle a functioning dipstick out of a length of deer bone. Forrester had also arrested him twice for looting the o-rings from an entire rack of oil filters at Wal-mart, and caught him with a rigged scanner changing the four-digit p-codes at the local auto store to direct more business his way. His cousin was in on the scam. There were plenty of rumors to go along with the real offenses. Some said he sold meth and purchased stolen copper wiring. Forrester wasn't sure he had enough sense to get away with anything of that magnitude if he couldn't steer clear of petty shoplifting. So the fake registration and license plate angle seemed like a fairytale, but it was the only lead they had so far into Cutler's dealings other than an avalanche of paranoid rambling about the missing Charlotte girl.

Forrester pulled into the unkempt lot of the north slope of the mountain. The weather vane above the dark garage creaked in the frigid, smoky gusts. The Melungeon mechanic sat in the tall grass on a cracked and rain-worn vinyl seat ripped from the rear of a Plymouth Voyager. He rested in his bright orange and oil-stained jumpsuit as if he were already in prison. He sipped what looked like a flat, lukewarm beer out of a brown-glass bottle of Bud Lite. Upon smelling Sneeds' breath, Forrester realized the emaciated man was drinking illicit whiskey.

"Slow day?" he said.

"It's my day off. Can't you see I'm on vacation?"

"I heard Florida's the preferred vacation stop for folks 'round here. Get out of the cold and the what not."

"Well, I ain't got no particular liking for the beach. I'm dark enough as it is. But I don't have the luxury of being no squaw like yourself, Sheriff. I might as well be a nigger with white skin for all I'm worth."

"Yeah, but you ain't, Jim. You just a white man with dark skin. Where y'all people come from anyhow?

"Ain't that the big mystery?"

"I heard it was somewhere around Portugal, Azores maybe, or Arab prisoners brought over by French trappers."

"I don't know. You seem better informed than me," he said, sipping his whiskey. "What brings you up my way? I haven't set foot in a Wal-mart in two years."

"It's got nothing to do with that, Jim. Matter of fact, it's got nothing to do with you. So, you can rest easy in your little seat there."

"I'm gonna have me a smoke," he said, pulling a soft pack of Mavericks out of the jumpsuit pocket.

"Whatever."

Sneeds set the brown bottle in the dirt beside the car seat, and struck a cardboard match to light the cigarette.

"Old boy from the city, you know, a real outsider, come up here asking 'bout some business."

"What kind of old boy?"

"Where talking old. My age. Trench coat, graying whitish

hair. Northern-sounding guy. Looked a little like me?"

"As a matter of fact, I do."

"Yeah?"

"Surely. Said his name was Cotter."

"Cutler actually. But close enough. What was he getting, an oil change?"

"No. He wanted two things. And I told him I couldn't do neither one."

"Yeah?"

"He wanted some weed. I said I don't have it. Then, he asked about speed. The real thing. And I told him it don't exist around here. You can't even find coke. It's all about meth and toilet heroin these days. I said I ain't no dealer. He wanted to know if I knew one. I said no."

"What is toilet heroin?"

"Fentanyl."

"Okay. Then what?"

"Then he wanted to know the price for the car he was driving and it's parts. I said I ain't a goddamned chop shop, and I didn't have the money to buy it from him anyhow."

"What kind of car was he driving?"

"A silver Hyundai Sonata. One of those Korean sedans."

Sneeds was getting better at lying.

"That it?" Forrester asked.

"Then he said he was a police officer. I called bullshit. He said he heard different about me and I said ' I don't give a damn what you heard. I'm a mechanic. I ain't no criminal.' Then he got sore, and pulled a gun on me. So I pulled a gun on him. Then he left. That's all."

Forrester stared at Sneeds in silence.

"You're serious?"

"Of course, I'm serious."

"He pulled a gun on you?"

"Sure did," he said, blowing smoke.

Forrester took back his original assumption about Sneeds' progress as a liar.

"You happen to catch a glimpse of what kind of gun he had on him?"

"It wasn't police issue. I can tell you that much."

"Big? Small? Automatic? Revolver?"

"It was a revolver."

"He pointed it at you?"

"He had the barrel down to the ground."

"And what did you do?"

Sneeds grinned with the beige cigarette filter clenched in his cracked blueish teeth.

"I pulled out this sucker here," he said, reaching into his jumpsuit pocket.

Forrester grasped at his service weapon. The Melungeon stopped in mid-action.

"You better think twice before you take out a gun on a damn cop, Jim."

"You wanna see it don't you?"

"Don't do anything stupid. Let me see it."

Forrester approached the car seat and took the gun from Sneeds. It was a knockoff of a Swedish pistol, probably Chinese the way most of the tactical excesses had been stripped away leaving only a nondescript little piece. On the streets they would have called it a throwaway.

"This thing loaded?"

"Yep."

"Where'd you get it?"

"You ain't gonna believe me no how."

"Humor me," Forrester said, taking his hand off his own

gun.

"Found it up by the creek near the Walker place. That weird-ass looking mansion."

"You're right. I don't believe you."

"I don't believe you either, sheriff."

Forrester ejected the clip from the pistol and struggled to push back the stubborn slide. There was no round chambered. Sneeds hadn't racked it. He sniffed at the clip and could smell the cordite. The clip was missing a cartridge.

"What don't you believe," he said.

"I don't believe you're looking for that Northern man. I think you're checking me out. Cause I'm all you got at the moment. But what it is you're looking at me for I still don't know."

"Or maybe you just won't admit it. You got a TV?"

"Do I look like I have a TV?"

Forrester gestured with the gun.

"You got a permit for this?"

"I told you I found it."

"So no, " Forrester said, stuffing the two pieces of the gun in his coat pocket.

Sneeds flicked the butt of the cigarette into the dewy grass.

"So what happened? You got the guy in custody?"

"He's dead," Forrester said. "Where were you Friday night?"

"I was changin' Marie Fletcher's oil in that beat-up Astro."

"All night long?"

"Yeah. She paid me in company. You can ask her."

"You so much as breathe outside the county line, Jim, and I'll have you in general population in a heartbeat for an unregistered firearm and soliciting a prostitute."

"Florida's beginning to sound pretty good to me now."

"I mean it, Jim. Don't go nowhere."

Forrester walked back to his Subaru and started the engine.

Upon nightfall, Forrester and Lehrmann were camped outside Sneeds' garage in a deer blind borrowed from one of the deputy's who hunted frequently before the wildfires and, when things were less bleak on the prospect, used to bring the entire department his homemade venison jerky he dried in his backyard dehumidifier, seasoned with herbs from his wife's garden. The old sheriff and the young deputy had crawled alone in the dusk shimmer up the bramble-coated woodland slope to perch themselves on the right vantage point overlooking the dead yard of the half-wit mechanic's property. Lehrmann appeared to Forrester to be absolutely giddy.

"Nice to get off diaper duty for the night. It's like a Western out here," he whispered to the sheriff. "Two lawman up the arroyo spottin' on the desperados."

"You watch too many movies," Forrester said, surprised. He genuinely didn't know that Lehrmann had a child.

Setting up the deer blind had been difficult as the light faded. The two of them watched the garage without any need for the night-vision scopes the deputy had given them as Sneeds' had the whole property lit up like a football stadium with several floodlight stands as he tinkered in the gravel stretch beneath a chassis of a Chevy hatchback. They could see his breath, floating and gray, in the stinging light.

"How do you drink that much shine and keep on under a massive car like that?"

"Stupidity," Lehrmann whispered. "You said he doesn't even know about the red Kia?"

"He told it like it was a silver Hyundai."

"That don't add up."

"None of it does."

"I don't think he was telling the truth, sheriff."

"Well," Forrester said, stretching his neck as he thought. "Hard to say with old Jim. He just ain't that bright. And as petty and low-down as a lot of what he's done, it makes no sense that he'd turn a new leaf and become this magnificent liar. You know? I don't think all of his story was truthful, but it's hard to see him as having something to do with Cutler's death, not the way it happened."

He couldn't see Lehrmann's expression in the absence of light. He could just hear the brief silence before he spoke.

"That's where you're wrong, sheriff. Killers don't just materialize out of the shadows. They start off as petty criminals, delinquents. Then they keep going. They evolve because, for the most part, society allows them to by writing them off. Peeping toms turn into burglars who turn into killers. They become addicted to that kind of morbid authorship that places them higher than the rest. His damn property looks like the perfect place to hide a bunch of bodies."

Forrester muffled his cough.

"I can't argue with you. You go to school?"

"Yeah, criminology. Four years."

"That's impressive, deputy."

"You didn't?"

"I went into the academy straight out of the army."

"Oh, yeah. I forgot about that."

Sneeds reached out from under the vehicle to grab a socket wrench.

They sat in the dark and watched him work on the car, drink a Busch Lite from the old fridge, and ultimately head to his small room adjacent the garage. After he had fallen asleep, a small coyote skulked onto the property and sniffed around, then, once an owl had made its presence known, slipped away into the grass. They had hoped to catch the mechanic tossing away evidence or making phone calls. But he looked more than content in his solitude.

"Think we're wasting our time?" Lehrmann said.

Without seeing Lehrmann's expression, in effect, isolating the cadence of his voice with the natural obscurity of the forlorn mountain, Forrester could really hear the yes-man mentality of the young deputy. Had he always been an ass-kisser?

"I think we've seen enough," he said.

4.

Neon surrounded the subterranean tunnel like hot iron bands lining a giant oven. It couldn't have been the tackiest entrance to a whorehouse she had ever seen, but it was one of the most unusual. Somewhere two miles south of Brownsville, Texas in the borderlandia where the worst of both cultures touched, the thin woman held her brown-filtered cigarillo on the ends of her fingers, leaving behind a little chimney trail of smoke, as she closed in on the entrance way: an old brick alcove adorned in succulents and dead rose petals. The underground club was called La teporocha encrucijada. She did not know what it meant. She puffed on the filter, then quickly, somewhat clandestinely, spat on the raw clay flooring which scuffed her designer shoes. She wore jeans and a blouse with several pockets, having previously chosen not to bring along her new bag. She didn't have a gun, just a switchblade and a baggie of uncut coke to barter with. Unlike the main strip where the women could work independently like the original days of Eastern block Europe, the girls down here had barcodes tattooed into their wrists and pimps that stalked the industrial catwalks over the cubicle facades of private rooms like mangy coyotes; the kinds of half-animal murder dogs thought to be chupacabras by western farmers. She noticed how their faces looked gaunt and narrow.

She stopped at the entrance and, without ever looking at the door man, thrust an ugly wad of American currency in his face. Pesos were no good.

"La Red," she said.

He spoke in rapid Spanish.

She cut him off, speaking English.

"I need to use one of your computers hooked up to the cartel's onion router. Give me a private booth. I paid for it."

The door man counted her money and called over a naked girl.

"I don't want a whore. I want the onion router. I have business."

"I got it," he said, turning to the girl, telling her what to do in Spanish.

The starved girl took her to the first black box with an open curtain and pulled back the synthetic velvet behind her. Inside was a plastic desk with a school chair, supporting a Toshiba laptop. She looked around the sticky plastic and saw the caked bottle of Vitacilina jelly beside the ashtray made from the bottom half of an apple soda can. There she stubbed out the cigarillo and took out a travel case of sanitizer wipes to wipe off down the gummy keyboard. She clicked on the TOR icon and commenced her search. She had a specific segment of footage she needed to see. She stuffed her hand into the jean pocket and felt the outline of the blank USB stick she had purchased at a local stationary shop. She intended to download the clip if she could snag a moment out of away from the eyes of the Zapotec Gestapo overhead. It was a long shot. She glanced over the last opened page on the network: child pornography. She massaged her temple and clicked out of the window. She funneled her way through several old pages that had been, without a doubt, viewed by American tourists: pages to order drugs through the mail with bitcoins, to hire assassins, prostitutes, red rooms, crush videos. Trends too extreme for the surface of the web had to sink deeper into the trenches. She erased a 'freezer bagging' page. 'Freezer bagging' was a social lifestyle from Kazakhstan and parts of mainland China as well as urban centers in the American southwest that centered around the glamorization of auto-cannibalism. They posted images of German serial killer Armen Meiwes and Slovak murderer Matej Curko. They re-blogged compilation edits, and snarky gifs of the television series Hannibal. Groups of kids would live together in squats or secret locations together and collaborate on shared recipes and, over time, videotape and mutilate one another, posting each to the fevored social responses, until there was no one left when the final member would then post a long final video of themselves eating alone in what was often called a last supper. Then the last member would join another squat, reinfecting them with the social media additction. The aesthetic of the photos was ripped off from the work of Nan Goldin and 80s heroin chic – soiled bed sheets and the light fall-off from a single underpowered flash. She erased every last page, shuddering.

The starved girl walked into the booth with a platter like a waitress. She balanced an ice-cold Corona and a shot of tequila. The thin woman shooed her and the suspect drinks away then lit another cigarillo. She sifted through a few more windows then found the search engine she needed. There was a pimp with a thick gold chain standing above her now on the catwalk as she typed in 'missing girl, dog mutilation.'

When a fight broke out on the far end of the cavern, she found the clip and downloaded it.

Once she had the USB in her pocket, she stood up and stepped out of the brothel. Walking out into the dry desert chill, she tossed the half-smoked cigarillo into a thicket of splintered cacti. She needed a drink, a real one. But every bar here was an adobe-encrusted sweat lodge full of Americans running from something and Mexicans just trying to make what living they could. The tragedy of the region had caked onto the accommodations. She walked a few paces out beyond the suspended rail line of telephone poles carrying out into the desert where lightning flashed on the edge of the horizon, inaudibly, then crossed the ATV tread marks to her rented jeep parked behind a wall of ocotillo. She drove off into the night. The jeep swayed like a canoe on the rapids until she swerved onto the sand-swept back road. Somewhere along the lonely stretch she'd find the highway. Coming back was never as ominous as going to. The underground place hadn't been as bad as she expected. She checked the rear view for company. If you knew your way around the desert well enough and the moon's shine was just so, you could manage to tail someone without the use of headlights.

This terrain reminded the thin woman of the first time she'd met John. She remembered seeing him at the edge of the bar staring at a scrap of paper he had placed over his wallet as he drank bubbly water with a fancy lime dunked in among the precious few cubes of high-priced filtered ice. The fact that he wasn't afraid to have his wallet out where everyone could see astounded her. Either he had nothing to fear, or he was a fool. It turned out to be the former. She initially took him to be a Mojave from the fort, as they called it, until he told her, curtly, that he wasn't even from the U.S. She hired him on the spot. Told him he wouldn't have to deal with the cult if it wasn't his style. They just needed muscle, somebody out in the field who needed to get paid.

She figured he was dead by now.

She felt sick now thinking about the computer images. This was her life, all of her life. She bathed in death, in blood, and hell and god, but there was no god. No more god to create for the grand absence, nor abdication of the throne. What god that looked over her, on the only plains of the far-off chaparral, as if she were already dead in this translucent wasteland, a North American Galilee, glared down from the midnight stars and must have scoffed at what she had become. She pulled the jeep over to rear her head out the window and vomit up a cup of cafe leche and a bowl of tortilla soup, down the side of the vehicle's door. After a significant amount of time as a bulimic, her autonomic nervous system began to take cues on when to vomit regularly. She leaned back in her seat and swished and spat out the window from the her bottle of mineral water, then lit a normal cigarette. It smoked faster than the cigarillos. She nursed on the filter until her stomach felt calm. Firing up the engine a second time, she took off down the lonely road.

The highway was closer than she remembered. As she pulled onto the immense belt of tarmac in the center of the desert, she could see, at least in the blurred distance, a milky film of light coating the mountain range. Now, with the city ahead of her, no longer wandering through a dark purgatory of sand and alien plant life, she felt a modicum of calm spill into her being: the kind of good feeling a thief enjoyed after getting away with something.

Her hotel stood like a monolith on the outskirts of town: a Best Western visible off the first exit. It could have been in any city in the U.S. or Europe. She pulled into the new parking lot and walked toward the automatic glass doors to the lobby. The young man behind the desk greeted her in fluid American English. She stepped past the elaborate coy fish pond to the elevator. She looked at her reflection in the stainless-steel before the doors parted to make sure she didn't have any vomit crust stuck to her chin. There was already a man in the elevator traveling up from the parking deck. He had the kind of indiscriminate look she had trained herself to watch out for.

"Which floor?"

"Eleven," she said, lying.

He pressed eleven then twelve, which had not yet been pressed. He was riding the elevator up from the parking deck without having chosen a floor.

She stepped out on the eleventh floor and waited for the doors to close. She pressed the button again and waited for the elevator to return. Inside, she pressed for the fourteenth floor. The elevator moved up one floor before stopping. She took a breath, pulled out the switchblade behind her back, and slumped into the opposite corner of the elevator. The doors opened to the same man. He walked in.

"You taking a ride again?"

"I left my makeup remover in my girlfriend's room," she said, conversationally, ready to lunge at his jugular.

"You on vacation?"

"Business."

He reached over and hit the ground floor button.

"Yeah, nobody comes out here for fun. I can't wait to go home," he said, paused, then pointed to the buttons. "I forgot my wake up call."

"You don't have an alarm?"

"I'll keep putting it on snooze," he said. "Tomorrow's do or die."

They reached the fourteenth floor.

She stepped out and said, "Good luck."

"Yup," he mumbled as the automated doors shut.

She closed the switchblade in her jacket pocket and went to her room.

She slept in that morning, having drifted off into such a deep rest that she hadn't heard the seven knocks at the door. Each was prompt and stiff, like bone against dried and stretched animal hide.

"Housekeeping," a polite voice on the other end said.

She awoke to the sound of the lock coming undone. She sat up in bed, fully clothed with the covers still spread over her lap.

The little woman carted her supplies into the room then discovered the thin woman in the bed.

"Oh, sorry," she said, carting back the fresh sheets and towels. "I'm sorry. I come back."

"It's okay. I didn't put out the 'no moleste' sign. It's my fault," she said, waiving for her to come back. "No, you can come in, I need to go eat anyway."

"Sorry, I come back."

The thin woman stood up from the bed in her pajama bottoms.

"No, really. You can come in. Clean, please. I'll leave."

"You're sure?"

"Yes, please. Come in."

"Okay. I come in."

The little woman pushed the cart back into the sizable room and shut the door behind her.

"I just need to change my pants okay?"

"Okay," the maid said, turning around.

The thin woman raised an eyebrow and smiled as she tore off her pajamas and pulled on yesterday's jeans.

The little woman turned around and pulled a 9mm from the pile of towels. She shot the thin woman through the hand and into the center of her chest. The second bullet exited through her stomach. Blood spurted over the air-conditioning unit. She fell forward onto the bed, trying to take a breath but couldn't. The maid walked up to her and rifled through her new bag and the drawers of the room. She ripped her laptop from the wall and slid it into pile of white sheets then continued searching. The thin woman coughed up a mouthful of blood and slid off the bed to the floor. The maid stood over her and checked her pockets, taking out the USB. She set it in her apron pocket.

The thin woman tried to speak. Air wouldn't even pass through as her lungs filled up with fluid. The maid didn't bother shooting her again. She left her on the floor as the thin woman weakly attempted to grab at her ankles. She left the room. The last thing the woman heard was the magnetic door lock. Then she was alone in agony.

5.

He sat alone with the open bottle of Islay malt on the coffee table beside the recliner, a gold-trimmed snifter like the glass top of a kerosene lamp smudged with the oil from his fingers in his grip. He still had his uniform on, unbuttoned to expose his undershirt. The television was off. He didn't feel like watching anything. Instead, he had an open book in his lap: What we talk about when we talk about whatever it is we're talking about, The assorted poems of Chuck Falkland. The title was a joke, as so many other writer's had made, about Raymond Carver's books. His brother's wife had given it to him a while ago through the mail. She liked to buy four or five copies of the books she enjoyed and send them to family and friends as if she were an authority on good books. He had stack of the paperbacks she had sent out over the years, which he kept on the wall stand beside the Browning with the lacquered stock to give the house more of an air of domesticity. He hadn't really read any of them: The Piano Tuner, The Time Traveler's Wife, All the Tea in China, Dimiter, Klondike, Lincoln in the Bardo, All the Light We Cannot See, The Dying Mule, The Girl that Fell from the Sky, Screwjack, By Night in Chile. He hadn't picked up one of them. He hadn't the time nor interest nor attention to commit himself to a whole book. But he did like the Falkland poems: short little observations. And he didn't have to start from page one and move all the way through the damn thing. He could skip around and find the ones he liked, and he never seemed to run out of good ones. They were sad, and weird. He liked it. Some of them rhymed. Others were just awful. Falkland wasn't the best poet in the universe and that amused him. His sister-in-law was pleased he finally found a book he liked and mentioned another poet he'd love. He couldn't remember the name. Kowalski? Something like that. He opened up the book and read over one of the poems: Ark of the Covenant.

> I screwed around
> with the plug
> > in the dark
> looking for the empty
> wall socket
> > to my little Japanese lantern
> which hangs over my bed post
> till I gave up on electrocuting myself
> > so I lit the scrappy notebook
> of raw pulp
> which I picked up in Mexicali
> with haunted cellphone light
> > like a lighter
> > like a match
> like I'm supposed to be scribbling this in army barracks
> or the county jail
> but I'm not
> I'm here, the girl's in the next room
> isn't tired yet
> > and this is all there is

He set the book down and took a sip of the whiskey, then stared at his phone. He felt like a fool, having just a few minutes ago called Sam and begged her as if he were a child, to drive out to the house and have sex with him.

"Please," he had said. "I'm so alone right now."

"I can't I'm watching my niece."

He was beginning to think the niece wasn't real.

"I understand."

"If your need someone to talk to, you should call your family."

"Yeah, okay."

Call his family? And talk about what exactly? She didn't understand the once-removed distance he had with his brother and his brother's markedly more successful life. He had to be stoic. He was the sheriff for god's sake.

He sat alone in the living room and sipped his retirement whiskey. It tasted good. He wasn't sorry he had opened it early. He opened up the gray paperback near the black and white photograph of the empty pint glass and read another poem. It wasn't as good. It was called Writing.

over time
 I learned
 not to trust
 the muse

 not to feel the words
 crashing down the mountain
 not to hurt
 with the effusive memories
 of injustice
 that we all endure

over time 1
I learned to
peel an onion
and make architecture
out of toothpicks
how to start a stalled car
and break bones if I have to

over time
  all over time
  thanks to failure and its
  curious
  necessity

"Not half bad," he said out loud, thinking to himself that he kind of understood it. He understood the metaphors at least. Perhaps this Faulkland guy wasn't full of shit after all. He flipped to back of the book and looked at the poet's photograph.

There had been a time when he smoked cigars, but those days were long gone. He had never been much of a smoker, tobacco or otherwise, nor much of a drinker. He once had an affinity for rum-dipped Swedish cigars, but, as soon as the brand was dropped from the market, he stopped smoking. He thought the only reason he smoked in the first place was to chum up to the higher command in the military, and the rum-dipped smokes were the only one that didn't make him gag. Now that he had no more ambition and those sweat black cigars were gone, what cause did he have to smoke? Boozing was similar, but far more of a conscious effort. The good stuff was good, and he stayed away from everything else. He was a cop and a Cherokee, and that was about it. He might as well have been an Irish writer with a predisposition, or something like that. He thought only briefly about taking a trip up the mountain, close to the county line, where the textile mill towered over the baby pine, then struck the idea from his immediate realm of possibility. He could see the headline already, "Sheriff disgraced one year before retirement: buys sex worker." It should have been a travesty already that he hadn't done everything in his power to close down the operations up the county, but he wasn't without his reasoning. Sex trafficking was a transient enterprise in Appalachia. No organized criminal outfit kept their slaves around as a base of operation. They used the mountains to move people the same as drugs. The prostitutes that stuck around worked for themselves and were usually hooked on meth. Meth was always involved. Back in the day, they used to smoke crack. Rock cocaine was more forgiving on the face. It was easier to talk to them, and get a promise of silence for an extra forty dollars. This new generation of shattered-glass girls, strung out on twelve-hour sessions of heightened paranoia, were all but impossible to trust. It was like visiting a leper colony. Some didn't even dress up anymore. T-shirts and pajama pants that smelled of smoke and urine. Crotches itching with crabs . It had been a long time since he paid for sex. He didn't think he'd get away with it this time. And the guilt was, of course, the worst part. Not the guilt of having aided the woes of the world but from his own blistering hypocrisy.

He corked the bottle and fell asleep, leaning all the way back.

In the morning, he got up and noticed the white stubble emerging from his olive skin and took his time to shave before showering. He put on the polo shirt from the department instead of pressing the uniform that, when he really thought about it, made him look like a ticket jockey on the highway patrol. The tucked-in polo, along with the jeans and gun belt displaying the badge at his hip, beside the defunct slot fit for a pager, made him feel like he was passing, or trying to pass. And maybe on an unconscious level he was. Although, it hadn't been his fault that he couldn't grow out his hair like his brother. He went straight from the army to the police force. But he certainly felt like he was, more often than not, seen as a white person, or at least equal or the equivalent to a white person. Being an Indian was like a being an artifact, and a strange majority of white people liked to see themselves in him. Their identity had swallowed up his race even after all they had done to it.

He walked through the kitchen. It was a mess. Outside, he got into the Subaru and drove down to the highway cross. The Huddle House was crowded with CDL drivers and the occasional lone wolf treating themselves for no apparent reason. He walked inside and could feel the tension. Nobody liked serving the sheriff. It wasn't like hallmark movies where the sheriff was a permanent fixture of the small town diner. There were no small town diners. It was all desperate chain restaurants with single mothers scraping by on minimum wage. He seated himself in a booth and ordered a patty melt and a coffee. He sipped at the brew, waiting for the temperature to drop to keep his gums from getting scalded, and listened to the monotone conversation of the other diners They had ash and grit on their work clothes that said they'd been part of the relief effort in the wake of the fires. The young men stank like a chemical fire with a bushel of tobacco thrown into the blaze. He could hear their speech peppered with the words 'spik' and 'nigger' and 'towelhead.' They discussed Trump and the wall and Boeing selling planes to Iran. The cook looked at him from behind the ticket wheel like he was spying on the room, then turned around to set the hot weighted iron on the patty melt.

He ate quickly, slathering the majority of the moist sandwich in hot sauce. His cellphone rang. It was Lehrmann, of course.

"Yeah?"

"Get to the station," Lehrmann said.

"What's going on?"

"Young man walked in driving a red Kia with matching plates. He's got what he says is Cutler's laptop. Says he wants to talk."

"Keep him."

"Alright."

"Book him if he tries to leave."

"Alright."

"I'll be right there."

He hung up his phone and set in on his belt. He had been speaking loudly and now half the restaurant was staring him down.

"What are y'all looking at," he said, tossing his money on the table before he left.

Forrester walked into the station with a burn on the inside of his nostril. Somehow, he had transferred the Texas Pete, which he ate with close to every meal, to his forefinger inevitably wiping or doing something that required him touching his consistently dripping nose. It was strange, like having a rash or a mildly aggravating mosquito bite in the summertime. He approached Lehrmann who immediately seemed to notice how Forrester was dressed down, no hat, revealing his fading white

buzz cut almost like small bits of Q-tip cotton set in the dark-
ening scalp. For the deputy, his hat was practically glued to his
head as if he were an extra on a black and white television
show.

Forrester looked at the small gathering of cops and
sucked at his tooth.

"He ask for an attorney?"

Lehermann shook his head slowly and spoke with an ag-
gressive confidence that struck almost everyone in the room as
unlike him.

"He's been given his rights and signed the papers, but he
ain't gonna stonewall us. He came here today to tell us something. He's a talker. I processed him. The kid's malleable . We
use the five steps, he'll confess."

"Who the fuck is he?"

"Rob Pelanski," a deputy named Hancock said. "Twen-
ty-two years old. College dropout. Claims he was Cutler personal assistant or something."

Forrester turned back to Lehrmann.

"Then I'll trust you and Hancock to get the confession.
And I want to know every detail of how he speared him."

Lehrmann gave him a smug look. The rest of the deputies seemed to know something Forrester didn't.

"What? What is it?"

"The kid wants to talk to you," Hancock said.

"How come?"

"You don't understand," Lehrmann said. "He knows who
you are. At least he knows of you."

"How?"

"He says he knows about you from Cutler. He claims he
worked for him like we said."

Forrester sat down in the nearest seat, squinting his eyes

in thought.

"I don't trust him," he said. "He's already trying to form a narrative. He's making requests. He walked in here on his own terms."

"And said he wanted to help us. Then we held him like he's about to be arrested."

"Do know how many good witnesses I've lost because they just got cold feet and ran back out. Or how many possible accomplices walk through the station doors of their free will?"

"I guess."

"It's a call and I made it."

He turned to the youngest deputy, a guy named Dalton.

"You take the side table. Let Lehrmann do the interoga-tion."

Hancock stepped aside without saying anything.

When Lehrmann and Dalton explained that Forrester was not attending the interrogation, Pelanski invoked his fifth amendment right. They walked back out to Forrester who stood by the water cooler.

"He just invoked his fifth."

"Alright," Forrester said. "Now he has to spend a night in general pop on suspicion of homicide."

They went back to the conference room. When they returned, they told Forrester the kid wanted to speak with a public defender, that no court would have trouble finding him indigent. He had no job and now that Cutler was dead, had no income.

"Tell him he'll get to see a court in three days. Tell him that the only lawyer we've got for him in the state will be month and half out since he's on vacation."

The deputies gave him a foul look.
He smiled and sipped his water.

The sun was setting. He was getting impatient; a day wasted on a war of attrition. Sure, there had been other things going on, short trips outside the station, but this stubborn kid was the break the whole precinct had been waiting on. When only Dalton emerged from the locked conference room, Forrester had had enough. Dalton got himself a paper cone of water from the cooler.

"This kid is fairly smart. I'm starting to think he did work with Cutler."

Forrester frowned, thinking Dalton couldn't have been a day older than Pelanski.

Lehrmann shut the door to the conference room, locked it, and came down the narrow hallway. He approached Forrester and said nothing.

"Well what the fuck now?"

"The kid basically cut me a deal."

"We don't cut deals."

"He said he wants you and a pack of cigarettes and he'll forget about a lawyer. And he'll tell us everything."

"He'll tell us everything he wants to tell us. He wants to read off a script. That's why he came on his own. We're an audience for him. The hell? Does he want a cookie too?"

"No, sir. He asked for one of the Krispy-Kremes he saw in the commons today."

Forrester crushed the paper cone and thrust it in the waste bin.

"Alright. I'll give in," he said. "He gets nothing else. No cigarettes. No doughnut. Just water."

Forrester walked into the conference room and took a quick glance at the surveillance camera in the upper corner, then sat across from Rob Pelanski. The kid looked like absolute hell. Cutler's laptop sat between them on the long synthetic table like a totem.

"Could I have a smoke, please?"

"There's no smoking in this conference room."

"What about an interrogation room?"

"This is a rural area. We're a rural police station. We have don't much room."

"Most stations would give you a coffee and some cigarettes."

"What would you know about it?"

"I'm a college washout, but I was a journalism major. Police blotter was my beat for the campus paper."

"So, you're an expert."

"I didn't say that."

"Well, I've heard all about your terms and conditions and it's not made a great impression."

"I'm sorry," the kid said.

He said it convincingly. It was a tone that Forrester had heard before from his own nephew when his brother busted him with pot in the wine cellar.

"What are you sorry for?" Forrester said, utilizing his police training.

"Cutler talked about you. He would have wanted me to speak with you first if things went south."

Forrester paused.

"I'm all ears kid."

6.

He called himself Peyton. That's the name he gave to the whores he ordered up to the rental cabin: an odd little fixture of the west-pointing slope on the mountain. It overlooked a babbling creek barely visible through the poplar brush and dead strands of kudzu, but it was the sound of the water that made it a good spot. The cabin had a brick front porch with a built-in fire pit and grill iron. The rest of the building along with the slanted roof was paneled in dark wood and, against the filament-needled pines, looked almost like an orthodox church. Behind the property, hidden from the road, was a giant terrace where the land became steep. It was the kind of boardwalk-looking veranda he might expect to see annexed to a beach-side property. The wood pillars holding it up looked splintered and worn. Beneath the boards, their crevices clotted thick with pine straw, stood a cobwebbed menagerie of yester-year's vacation equipment: croquet sets missing balls, a golf cart with a dead battery, plywood corn hole sets, a basketball goal. The cabin was typically rented out by church groups on retreat and college fraternities. He found it out of sheer luck. It wasn't easy to get whores up there. A cabin in the woods seemed like a perfect place to get killed. What he did was first create a rapport. Simple in and out blow jobs. The girls all talked to each other about who was who. Eventually a reputation set in. The guy on the hill wouldn't hurt you and he paid well. He had a big white girl in his bed lingering, snorting an eight-ball from a baggie, getting herself right with her wake up. She asked him if he wanted a hit. He was brewing coffee in the kitchen beneath the ladder to the open concept bedroom overhead.

"No, I'm okay," he said. "You drink coffee?"

"No."

She came down the ladder, then started looking for her clothes on the floor, leaning over. He stuck his index finger up her ass while pouring himself a coffee. She reeled back, still looking for her clothes, and didn't say anything. She found her clothes by the couch and put them on, then tossed the half bag of eight-ball into her small purse. She headed toward the front door and slipped on her shoes. Before she could leave, he grabbed her while still staring into the steam of his coffee and forced her to sit on his lap. He grabbed at her breast and sucked on the nape of her neck.

"Why don't you be my wife, Jan?"

"Because I'm already married."

"Forget about him. Be with me."

"I have to go."

She got up and made her way toward the door.

"See you around," he said.

She said nothing and set out on foot.

He stepped out on the terrace and took a seat at the tinted glass table. He had been drunk enough last night to forget his cigarettes and lighter outside, but miraculously the wind hadn't blown them away. He leaned back in the patio chair, listening to the babble of ashen creek water and the wood panels giving slightly under his weight. He put a cigarette between his lips then flicked open the butane wick lighter. He heard the door at the front of the cabin jostle as if Jan were trying to get back inside. She probably needed a ride somewhere. He snapped the lighter shut and headed to the front door. He opened it and saw no one. He closed the door and walked around to the kitchen and got himself a cold bottle of mineral water, then returned to the porch. He looked up at the bright but still somewhat overcast sky. He lit the cigarette. After the crackle of tobacco and paper with the first solid inhale, he heard the faint sound of a cupboard opening and froze. Without looking back into the house, he slowly reached under his seat and grabbed at a loose piece of duct tape.

It was gone.

He swallowed and set the cigarette in the ashtray. Standing up, he peered through the glass door then stepped back into the house. He sat down on the couch as casually as possible, then rifled in between the cushions. He retrieved the black .44 magnum and set it on his lap.

He waited in silence, his eyes moving, his reflexes itching. Finally, he stood up and pointed the magnum at the downstairs bathroom door. He considered blowing a hole through the wall and went as far as to pull the hammer back on the magnum, then pushed it back in place and sat back down on the couch, resting the piece on his thigh once more. Had he lost it? When they came to get him, he knew it would be sudden. But what about the Kahr cw9 strapped to the chair outside? Had he changed its location, worried somebody outside might see it on the patio chair if they were headed for the cabin from the creek, effectively scaling the side of the mountain, and take it, use it against him? No. He never got that piss-faced. And they had their own guns. That and dogs. Always the goddamned dogs. No, the missing gun was a sign. He wasn't alone.

Leaves rustled amid the kudzu beneath the window behind him. He slipped onto the floor, keeping the back of his head out of the sight and held out the magnum. He waited for what felt like ten minutes. Then he could hear the creaking of the boards outside. He could follow the distinct sound of footsteps beyond the wall of the cabin. He followed them with the magnum. If there were two of them, he knew he was dead. He could almost feel a presence behind him which caused him to whip back around as silently as he could to see there was in fact no one behind him, then return to his position on the floor, tracing the footfalls with the sight of the magnum. Once the intruder got to the glass door, he'd fire. He followed each cautious step. He reached the edge. He'd see a black shoe emerge in the glass frame and blow it off. The wood creaked. But there was nothing. He heard the leaves rustle again, then the chatter of a squirrel.

He stood up and checked each room of the timeshare, slamming doors, kicking over beds.

The refrigerator door opened, then shut. He was in the guest bedroom lined with bunk beds. He stepped to the corner of the room, just behind the light switch, holding his gun out like an extension of himself. Slowly, distributing his weight across the entire flat of his feet, he moved into the halfway without sound. When he got to the kitchen he saw the refrigerator door was closed. Had it been the ice machine? He stood in silence for a long time, without decision. Once nothing had transpired, once he felt enough empty space had passed, he let down in guard. He flipped the safety on the .44 and stuck it in his pants. When he passed the counter, he noticed the flour jar lid was lopsided. Had he done that? He opened the empty flour jar and saw the Kahr cw9 inside. It had been moved sometime in the middle of the night. He smiled and took the hulking .44 from his pants and put it inside the freezer, then returned to the porch to smoke a cigarette finally.

He couldn't blame himself for being paranoid. They'd come when they'd come. He couldn't stop it. Not in Tennessee, or any country. He could run to the edge of the globe and they'd find him. Hanging around their backyard was probably the last place they'd expect to find him.

He reached for the cigarette in the ashtray and re-lit it.

***

Lying on her back, face pointed toward the old wooden slats through which, very little of the drab, gray sunlight penetrated, she extended the shotgun erect and pressed the stock against her shoulder with the recoil pad. Racking it quickly, and fired up into the raised patio. Fire and smoke flushed out the barrel as the fist-sized glob of birdshot ripped apart the deck from below. The desiccated tufts of pine needles caught on fire. The remainder of the bird shot that didn't lodge itself in the wood tore through the chair knocking the tall man to his side. The pellets were stuck deep in the muscle and fat of his buttock. His coffee dropped from the table and spilled down through the slats like a burst pipe in a ceiling. She fired again to keep him from running to the door, then rolled out into the kudzu jumping to her feet. Starla wore clothes stolen from a church depository for wildfire victims. She looked like she had fallen into a laundry basket.

"You squaw son of a bitch," she said, firing into the patio table, letting the thick glass shatter around him in transparent chunks amid the rippling pine smoke in the margins of the cabin veranda which rose up as if it were steam.

John Delisle wasn't going anywhere. He turned himself around to get a better look at her and the shotgun she had taken. He should have thanked her for not loading it with the deer slugs. He imagined a hot D-cell battery wedged into the bloody tumor of his ass. Then again, she was probably going to kill him.

She scaled the steps and stood over him.

"You shot me in the ass."

"I researched it a long time ago. I wanted to use it on Lonnie. It's supposed to be the safest place it shoot someone."

"Why would you want to shoot someone in a safe place?"

"Because I still need you alive."

"Do you? Or are you too scared to kill somebody."

"I've already killed someone."

"You don't remember though. This will be different. You'll look in my face and know I'm going to die."

She felt her spine shudder as she pressed the shotgun's barrel against John's neck.

"It would be easier for you to just die here than let them do it."

"That's true."

"You chained me to fuckin' toilet."

"I've done worse to others. Men and women."

She moved the barrel up and pressed it against his head, pushing his skull flat against the wood.

"I really want to kill you right now."

"Sure," he said, resigned.

She took a few deep breaths. The cumbersome instrument in her hand trembled.

He moved his right hand and slowly touched the barrel to steady it.

"I already remember killing someone," she said. "I killed a man from the house. The one on the hill. The one nobody here wants to talk about."

He blinked slowly.

"Yeah?"

"I saw the girl there. She your boss?"

"Not my boss. Mine is probably dead already."

She felt sick and weak.

"Who is she?"

"If you're asking me that question, then you already know."

She jerked the shotgun out of his hand and blasted another hole in the wood. The side of John face became splintered and singed. She ejected the hot shell onto his chest, then pressed the searing barrel against his neck.

"I know who she is to me. Who is she to you?"

"You first," he said, smiling in spite of the pain.

"Do you have any food?"

"Yeah. Hungry?"

"Yes."

"Help me inside and I'll get you something."

"What about the buckshot in your ass?"

"It's birdshot and there's a first aid kit in the bathroom."

She dragged him into the living room, letting the modest streak of blood smear through the carpet fibers.

"Go pour some water on the patio," he said.

"What for?"

"I don't want the cabin to burn down."

"Fine."

She searched the kitchen and pulled one of the worn stew pots from the cupboard, filled it with water and doused the smoking patio. She went back inside and took the gun from the four jar as well as the .44 then, ejected both clips pushing the slides back and forth to check the chambers—both guns had a round drop onto the Formica counter—then set them in the sink.

"It smells like sex in here. Sex and coffee."

"I've been buying a lot whores lately."

"You have a complicated relationship with women."

"No, I have too simple a relationship with women. I wish

it were more complex."

"Well, I'm sure nobody's plucked shotgun bits out your ass before."

"Sorry, to let you down. But this isn't a first for me.

"You got liquor?"

"Check the First Aid for the rubbing alcohol."

"It's not for your ass. I need a drink."

"Trust me, you'll need a meal in you first before you can handle a bourbon."

She unbuckled his belt and pulled the zipper down, kicking him over quickly with her foot and stock of the shotgun. She peeled away his jeans, separating the bloody material from his flesh. It was like picking shattered pieces of clove from the wound. She hadn't counted on how miniscule bird shot actually was with some of the split pellets as small as a pepper grain. She'd reach in with the tweezers from the First Aid kit only to realize what had looked like a remaining shard was a singed piece of cordite-smelling hair or skin.

"What's the worst you've been shot?"

"I've not been."

"You said this wasn't a first."

"I had a butterfly knife lodged in my back. I've been mauled by a dog. A guy threw a dumbbell at my chest on the yard and cracked my rib."

"So this is a first."

"First time being shot. Not the first time getting less than stellar health care."

She picked out what she could and poured the rubbing alcohol inside the wound.

"Every toilet seat is gonna feel like an iron maiden for the next six months. Do you keep any perks or oxy around?"

"Nope," he said.

She taped up her best gauze job and helped him lie face down on the couch, giving him the half bottle of Heaven Hill. She walked into the kitchen to open the refrigerator.

"What's good?"

"I got a couple of cube steaks on the top rack. Some Canadian bacon in the crisper."

She took out a bottle of mineral water and drank it in one swallow, then started cooking the cube steaks.

"Anything to go with it?"

"Lima beans in the freezer," he said.

"These Lima beans are frozen."

"So what?"

"Cube steaks cook fast. I don't want to wait."

"It's a steamer bag. Just throw it in the microwave."

"What grocery store did you get this stuff from?"

"Piggily-Wiggily."

She cooked the food and John tried to ease his pain by getting drunk. She ate alone at the kitchen table, devouring both cube steaks with A1 and the Lima beans while drinking another two bottles of Topochico and the rest of his morning coffee. She walked back out to the patio and fished his cigarettes from the broken glass. She smoked one with last cup of coffee, then headed for the sink, popped the clip back into .44, racked the slide and sat across from John.

"You're a murderer," she said.

"Yes."

"Have you ever killed someone who you knew deserved it? Someone who deserved to die?"

"A few times, but never for money."

"Like who?"

"A guy named Kent Tiree. A CEO kind of like Crenshaw. I killed him for money actually. He was the only one who probably deserved it. But I guess they all deserve it then don't they?"he said and looked at her vacantly.

"You remember how you were sittin' there with a bottle of bourbon when you first had me tied up? And you asked me to tell you a story?"

"Yeah."

"An' I just went on with a bunch of nonsense. Because I didn't know what to say. Well, I'm gonna tell you a real story this time. And like all good stories, it has twists and turns and coincidences that don't seem like they could happen. Things you wouldn't believe could be connected get connected and for no reason."

"What is this story about?"

"I'm gonna tell you about a little girl from Kentucky. She didn't have much growing up. She didn't have a family since her half-brother got to live with his dad and she ended up having to move south with her mom. She moved to a new city in a brand new state. Where nobody know her and nobody liked her."

"Tough shit for the little girl from Kentucky."

"Yeah, it was. It was tough shit. So tough, she ended up getting jealous, jealous of people who had more, jealous of other girls. The problem was, when she finally found some friends, they were just as angry and jealous as she was. The three of them ended up being jealous of the same girl: a popular girl who had everything she wanted, or it looked like it from the outside anyway. That's when they made a plan. The three of them committed a crime. They did something awful to someone. But when they got caught, the girl from Kentucky was punished the worst because she didn't have money for legal fees or expensive diversion programs. Her mom kicked her out. She never finished school Her brother wouldn't speak to her for a long time. The only person to take her in was an asshole who constantly hung what she had done over her head."

"A couple of bullets took care of him pretty quick."

"After he murdered the only real friend I ever had."

"So what was your crime?"

"We corned a girl in the bathroom who took one of our boyfriends. Not mine, of course. The other two took turns cutting her face in. I didn't do any cutting but it was my razor. I was just 16, tried as an adult."

"You're the reason Vandergreven has that scar? You're sure it's her?"

"Nobody forgets eyes like those."

"I guess not. And the whole reason you cut her was over a boy."

"My friend said that Vicky had poisoned her dog. But to tell you the truth, I didn't believe her at the time. I didn't need a reason beyond not liking her to go ahead with the plan."

"So what do you want now? You want to kill her?"

"I recognized her when they had me inside the cage. She didn't even see me. Is she some sort of cult leader?"

"They pay. That's all I know. Hard to say what they are, but they need folks dead and they have money."

"You owe me money," she said.

"They put me in the hat. If I had gotten my fee, I would have given you your cut. But once they put the screws to you, trust me, you're not getting a cent. Consider us lucky to be alive."

"I need money to start over."

He bobbed his head back and forth in a drunken gesture.

"I never knew my dad. That's a whole half of my lineage that remains shut away. But my mom told me that nobody in this world, not even the devil, has the credit to promise you money. The people who give it to you regularly are just lucky: employers, family, the state, friends. There's no such guarantee, not in truth. You can never expect it and never really count on it and when it comes time to get yours, taking and getting are the same thing. You have to take it before someone else takes it from you."

"Your mom a prostitute?"

"Schoolteacher," he said.

"So we have to go back to the castle in the woods with all the dogs?"

He shook his head.

"It's suicide."

"What do you care? You held the gun up to your head earlier."

"Not for me. For you."

"I'm not afraid of her. I'm taking what's mine."

He scoffed, then passed out.

She sat alone in the kitchen, smoking, drinking one of the beers, listening to his snores as the day progressed. She cleaned what little of the cabin needed to be cleaned and had all the hidden guns assembled along the kitchen floor, stacking the boxes of ammunition on the table. How he had accrued so many weapons in a few weeks, she could only imagine. Perhaps it was safer to go ahead and rob him instead. The guns looked old, as though as he had ransacked a military cash from the Second World War; half-familiar weapons she may have glanced across in an old textbook before education exited her life. Images of young boys in sandy bunkers and Asian jungles, their helmets like a saucers. She picked up the loaded Gerand and aimed it at the sink set in on the counter.

7.

Cutler's death was no mystery to Pelanski. He knew who had done it. He knew how, and when. He had his story laid out for all to hear and didn't waver on a single detail despite Forrester's pressing. As for Pelanski's version of events...how could he believe the kid? It was hell of story, but how could he prove it? It was after that exact question, Pelanski may have offered his most eloquent solution: he just pointed to Cutler's laptop without another word. Lehrmann took the laptop into the next room, plugged it in and looked for the MPEG files Pelanski had named. When the deputy came back, he shook his head at Forrester.

"There's nothing there," he had said.

Pelanski went off and tried to assault Lehrmann. Forrester nearly broke the kid's arm when he cuffed him. Now, he was booked and sitting in jail. Forrester thought about how he had listened to the kid speak and now there were things in his head that no alcohol was strong enough to flush away. Hoping they would drain back out his ears from whence they had entered, these thoughts and images that he did not trust, spread along the grooves of his brain like roots and fused with the tissue.

He sat alone on the porch with the Islay malt and a can of Budweiser. A thunderstorm approached. Pink stems of electrical current like veins in the dome of the sky cracked and pulsed, lighting up the otherwise unseen tide of surging cloud cover. He tipped the can into his mouth, then licked his lips, then tipped it again, finishing the dregs, and tossed the emptied aluminum into the plastic municipal bin by the steps.

He looked up at the dark and thought about the dream: the alleged dream Cutler had become obsessed with, wherein Forrester had met him on the plains of some western snow scape. The murder palace. Had it been the Moore Campgrounds? Voices in dreams, as he had come to believe, had the propensity to dissolve into texture and would sometimes hang in the metaphysical crib just below the dissonance of the dreamer's internal dialogue. Hearing voices break through unconscious static to transcend waking life often appeared to the dreamer as dangerous and prophetic. But he didn't take stock in dreams. Forrester was not a traditional or spiritual person like his brother. He didn't go to church or attend revivals. He didn't watch mystery programs either. And he couldn't imagine Cutler as having been much different. Maybe that's why the dream had become one of his obsessions, or maybe he had been losing it long before his final days. .

The old cordless phone on the wall mount between the kitchen and porch corridor started ringing. He wandered into the dark then returned to the porch before answering.

"Forrester," he said.

"Howdy, bro. It's me calling on my new iPhone. All the way from Big Sky Country. Thought you should be the first person I call."

"An iPhone, huh. Finally with the times."

"Yeah, my eldest son bought me one. Already loaded it with an app too: the Cherokee language. Can you believe that? They got Cherokee and just about anything else you could want to learn on these things."

"I use the Spanish one for work now and then."

"Yeah....yeah," his brother said, musing to himself. "I'm surprised you're even up."

"I'm an hour behind you aren't I?"

"You're an hour ahead. Sun sets in the West, remember?"

"That's right," Forrester said. "The sun sets in the West. I'm out of my element."

"Approaching retirement throwing you off?"

"I'm not really about it. It's just close enough to be too far away," he said. "Your Kentucky accent is almost dead and buried. Every time I see you now, you sound a little bit more Canadian."

"Oh, ya," he said. "It gets in there. It's gradual, but it gets in there: the plains accent that is."

"How's the wife?"

"She started painting. I can't tell if she's any good yet, but it passes the time with both boys out of the house."

"That's right. The last one's off fightin' the man in South Dakota."

"No, that ended. He's in Great Falls doing remodeling for classic motorcycles. He's having a blast. We'll see how it pans out, though. You never know with him. He might come home next month, or we'll never see him again."

"He's a good kid. He'll be fine. He figure South Dakota was bust?"

"Well," his brother paused for a significant amount of time. "I guess he lost faith. But it's just as well, his mother was a nervous wreck the whole time he was out there. But protests don't solve shit in this fuckin' country. He wanted to go to Occupy Wall Street when he was a teenager, so I let him go to South Dakota. How are you doing? You sound down."

"I just interrogated a 20-year-old for two hours. I feel drained."

"I can understand."

"He had just about the craziest story. Sometimes I wish people would stay tight-lipped than tell me a story."

"Yeah, go all O.J. on you and keep saying they don't recall." Something rustled on the opposite end of the line. He continued, "Can I ask about the case?"

"It's homicide. I can tell you that."

"Oh, shit."

"Yeah, it's pretty strange. It's a guy I met once through work. It was a long time ago."

"With a little town like that. I'd think you know just about everybody."

"He's from out of town if you can believe it. Came all the way from North Carolina just to get himself killed in my county."

His brother paused.

"I can understand completely, man. Other day I caught a raccoon in our trash."

They both laughed.

"Listen, bro, you're welcome here anytime. Guest room is yours."

"I appreciate that.

"So how's getting older for you?"

"It is."

"No, I meant how has it been for you?"

"And that's my answer. It just is. There's not much to say about it. The mind is going. I'm not as sharp as I was. My eyes are bad, I need glasses to read. I can't take walks like I used to because of a bone spur. It never helps to complain."

"Really? I love complaining."

"Doesn't seem to do it for me."

"What does?"

"Being philosophical, the way I've always been."

"Have you found the Indian in you that you were always looking for?"

"I did. I took off his mask and found out he was a white man."

"Don't talk like that."

"It's not what you think. Financial success in life doesn't mean I'm trying to be white. Our very existence is in defiance of the white man. You being a sheriff, me doing business in plastics. We didn't become white, we beat the white man. The Indian I had been looking for, the Indian tearing up on the side of the road at litter: he was just a white man all along. The image I had been searching for was a white image sold to me. When I found out all I had to do was look in the mirror, that changed everything."

"Hmm."

"Do you get it?"

"You been drinkin' ?"

"Nope, just sitting here on my porch in the moonlight."

"I've been."

"Really? I never thought of you as much of a drinker."

"I'm not. I had a beer tonight though."

"That's hardly drinking," his brother said.

Forrester stared at the scotch bottle.

"I think about myself now as an old man and wonder what exactly I wanna do once I'm not doing this...and I can't think of a goddamned thing."

"Start painting?"

"I don't think so," he said and smirked. "So if you know who you are. Then what am I?"

"I can tell you that you're a man."

"What is a man?"

"What a man is, is a biological occurrence—it's a phenomenon like a flower or a burning match. Who a man is, is a reflection on that piece of biology. A reflection of what? The world around you? Yourself? Well...who can say? Maybe the dream of your whole life? Your experience and senses. It's a little bit of everything probably. Your whole personality, unknown to you, is an unfinished thing. It isn't written in the cosmos. But that's the beauty of it. You can mold it any way you please. And when the what dies, the who can live on, the who can carry on in your kids with a laugh or an idea, a physical trait. The reflection fades eventually, but it can stay longer than the body as long as it has something to reflect off. . That's what I believe for what it's worth."

"You don't believe in an afterlife?"

"I can't afford to."

Forrester paused.

"Well, I don't want to keep you any longer. Get some sleep," his brother said.

"Yeah, enjoy your new phone."

"I will."

He set his old phone on the wooden table then poured a little more Scotch in the snifter. Droplets of rain fell into the glass. He swigged the liquor and looked up. The rain fell faster.

His brother had always been poetic. His sons had inherited the same bug. He imagined all three of them lounging by the fireplace that really belonged in a ski lodge, talking like prophets, like something out of the theater.

Water trickled into the discard mason jars, tapping on the cans in the recycling bin. Like the ocean spilling into the mountains to make rivers, the icy water picked up while lightening tore strips in the raining-chasm overhead. He stood up in the storm, gripping the bottle and walked to the driveway. He didn't go inside the house, instead he crawled into the back of the Subaru. He wanted to be surrounded by the storm as if he were inside of a diving bell. He fell asleep. When the lightning flared, he awoke and saw the barren twigs of what remained of the treeline, desiccated and skeletal; winter brought on by fire; soggy clusters of blackened soot washed clean by yet another heavy rain. His dreams took him back to the wildfires, when waves of apocalyptic flame bled down the mountain, the stench of ash carrying through the community for months. His was mind beleaguered by the news images of tourists stuck in hotels while the flames licked the lobby windows and what he saw of his own backyard awash in a peculiar inferno. He oscillated in and out of semi-sleep as the storm only intensified. The inside of the car became cold. He thought of his brother's unique perspective on being, or perhaps it wasn't unique at all. Maybe somewhere in the world there was an entire culture that subscribed to his ideas like Japan or China. And in his bathysphere, he receded once again into sleep where he saw his brother, but not as his brother. He saw him as Cutler, and, with the over-abundance of untriggered familiarity that all dreams had afforded him, he saw Cutler as a child. Then, reincarnated before his eyes, he became an old Labrador. He followed the dog through his house chasing it, as a detective, through his kitchen, his dining room, his bedroom closet, through the walls of his bathroom; in the cramped quarters of a dust-filled attic to the steep ledge of an iron-girder above a city, and back through the window of his house where the interior had changed into a vacant office: a gray maze. There was a desk phone ringing in the corner. The dog was not there. He ignored the phone, turning the corners in vain search for the animal. The ringing got louder as if he could only hear it within himself like a tumor or a foreign object wedged in his skull. He answered the phone.

"How do you do?"

"Who is this?"

"This is Chuckaliaya Faulklandski and I'm here to cut your nads off, Sheriff."

He heard no threat in the voice.

"It's all to do with Ptolemy."

"I'm going to look for my brother now."

"You're not looking for your brother now. You're looking for a dog. You forgot what you're looking for."

"What am I looking for?"

"It's where you're looking."

He wanted it to mean something, but it was meaningless. He hung up, heard laughter behind him and shot through the cubicle wall. The dog limped out from behind, back leg raised, a bullet in his side. He sat down and listened to the rain through the phone speaker. He listened and became aware of his dream. Some part of his conscious brain had awoken while the body remained determinedly catatonic, and a strange thought came to him. What if the telephone was the connection between his dream and his sleeping body? Perhaps he could talk to his unconscious self with the phone? He pressed the call button and listened to the rain, wondering if he could speak back. But what would he say? He was asleep. He'd say nothing. He just snored back to himself. It was just a body: many pounds of old flesh, suspended in its natural state of drooling automation. He was the reflection now, torn from the reflective surface. He looked at the floor and saw the blood droplets trailing through the cubicles and followed. The little pennies of blood grew into the paw prints and half-dollar-sized splotches of intense red, into the small tunnel of indistinguishable dark. He could hear himself closing in on the wounded dog and felt a shudder down his spine. There was a rustling in the distance. He moved out of the dark where the cubicle walls had been overtaken by reeds and dead tall grass. He followed the murmurs like shadows just underneath the starlight, pushing past the reeds with the blunt end of his service weapon. There, in the night, beside the sour-looking sewage-paced trickle of creek water, he saw Cutler, gut shot, dragging himself through the sand in his trench coat. There was a tuft of bamboo growing atop of the steel culvert ahead of them. He looked down at Cutler bleeding and knew where he was headed. He tossed his pistol into the creek and walked back. He walked along the gravel mile where the women stood in the lamplight beside the ruin of the textile mill.

He woke up facing downward; the bottle of Scotch sufficiently corked, resting on the gray floor of the Subaru. Hidden birds chirped, their sound muted from behind the fogged car windows beaded with moisture. He hadn't heard birds in so long, not since the fires. He sat up with a mild stiffness in his neck and creases from the back seat on his face like scars. He opened the door. The morning air swelled the interior of the vehicle like a cold gasp. He stepped out, stretched, then noticed a cardinal. Its eyes were like black marbles. The bird pecked aimlessly at the dirt. He thought about urinating in the weeds, but decided against it. He did what he could to pop his back then grabbed the top-shelf booze, and shuffled through the gravel into the house. He smelled smoke. The distinct smell of burning tobacco carried through the hallway. He set the bottle on the kitchen counter and stepped to the living room window amid the oneiric scent. Outside he saw the black Lincoln parked in the front driveway at the end of the slope close to his mailbox. He felt ice water course through his veins.

Without making a noise he listened to the faucet drip in the kitchen behind him, then heard a rustle from his bedroom.

He reached out above the makeshift bookcase and, seeing that his untouched copy of The Dying Mule had been tossed onto the floor, took the double barrel from the wall mount. It wasn't loaded, but only he knew that.

Deputy Lehrmann, in full uniform, walked out of the bedroom into the hallway before Forrester in the living room.

Forrester lowered the empty antique.

Lehrmann had his gun drawn at his side and returned it to his retention holster.

"What are you doing?"

"You didn't answer your phone."

Forrester set the shotgun on the table .

"It's seven in the morning, how many times did you call?"

"A few times. The door was open. You scared the shit out of me."

"What's is this? A welfare visit?"

"It became one."

"You been smoking?"

"I don't smoke."

"Okay," he said, nodding in half-belief. "So what's up? The kid change his story?"

"He's in the hospital twenty miles east."

"What?"

"Slammed himself into the wall of his cell. Busted his jawbone. Tried to cut himself with a piece of glass. We got it away from him. It wasn't much bigger than a quarter," Lehrmann said, gesturing with his index and thumb.

Forrester sighed.

"He still talking?"

"His mouth is wired shut. We got him cuffed to the gurney. I mean, I guess he can still write when he isn't doped up."

"God damn it," he said, walking to the kitchen. "You

want a cup of coffee?"

"Sure."

Forrester took the jug of Greenpoint spring-water from the refrigerator and poured it into the electric percolator, then unscrewed the lid of the glass mason jar with the fresh coffee grounds.

"You take cream?"

"Yeah, cream and sugar."

"I have Sweet and Low, no sugar. Sorry, I'm old."

"Cream's fine."

"You wanna know something funny?" he said, as he scooped the blackened grounds.

"Yeah, I could use some good news, Sheriff."

"When I drove up to see Sneeds not too long ago, he mentioned the Walker place too."

"The Walker place?"

"Big house up on the western ridge. Looks like something out of London. Lucky as hell it didn't get burned down. But, I guess in a way, the fires stripped a lot of this place's secrets bare for all to see. No more trees and shadows to disappear into. That's the way I see it, at least."

"I think I know it. Old Melungeon Sneeds think that place was evil like the city boy?"

"No, he didn't say nothing that crazy. But he did have a gun on him that I confiscated. Said he found it. Just up an' found it on the ground close to the mansion."

"That's it?"

"That's all he said."

The spring-water babbled in the percolator.

"How come you're not driving a cruiser?"

"Hmm?"

"The town car out front. The Lincoln. Didn't you and

Suzy have a Honda?"

"Oh, you saw that? I just came from home. Yeah, I've had the Lincoln now for a few months. Father-in-law's old car."

"Was Suzy's daddy a chauffeur?"

The deputy laughed.

"No, he just keeps his car's up."

"Then why'd he give it to you?"

The deputy paused.

"Kindness, I guess."

"What's the license plate number?"

"What?"

"Come on, you're a cop. You gotta see things around you. You gotta know things. What's the license plate number? If it's your car, that's all I'm saying."

"You know I can't be bothered to worry about my own shit. I can't even remember my cell phone number. I save that shit for work."

Forrester took the percolator and thrust the boiling water into Lehrmann's face. The younger man stumbled backward, reaching at the retention holster. Forrester opened a drawer for a weapon and jabbed Lehrmann's shooting hand with an old steak knife. He slashed Lehrmann's palm open, kicking him into the living room. The deputy reached at his service weapon, this time with his left hand, tugging at the butt of the gun, unable to free it. Forrester jabbed him in the shoulder and forearm. The serrated edges of the blade tore his skin and uni-formed sleeve. He ducked and stabbed the deputy in the crotch, then forced the buckle open to rip off the belt. He let his muscle memory do the thinking as he pushed him on his back, binding his hands like a common assailant with his own pair of cuffs. He stood and watched him struggle on the carpet. It was as if he had never met him before now. His actions were that of another, an alien personality. He drew the deputy's weapon.

"What are you involved in?"

His deputy didn't answer.

Forrester walked around him to see his burned face.

"What the fuck, boy?"

"I gotta do what I gotta do, old man. You wouldn't know it, the way you've been alone your whole goddamned life. Well, I got a family. They brought dogs to my house. They shoved my baby in the freezer. You probably don't even know my son's name. I have to bury this stupid thing. It's just one asshole private eye. Who cares what happened to him?"

"You made it my life now. Maybe if you came clean first."

"Fuck you! Fuck you, old man! You burned my face!"

Forrester stomped his face with the callused heel of his bare foot.

"So everything the kid said at the station flies? That it?"

The deputy said nothing.

"You know , I actually like you better like this. You're more direct. To the point. And even though you haven't actually told me much. I guess the kid did your talking for you earlier. The dots aren't hard to connect. And sure, maybe they threatened your baby. You're right. I don't know what it feels like. But if you can't answer me, I'm going to take the Cracker Barrel knife off the floor and cut off your last good testicle so you can't make you another freezer baby."

"It's all fucking true. After I did you in, we were headed to the hospital to kill the kid."

"And the laptop from earlier?"

"I trashed it."

"Son of a bitch."

"Just leave, Nathan. These people don't make any sense. It's all for nothing."

"I don't think I'm gonna do that," he said, peering out the corner of the window at the bald man standing beside the Lincoln.

Lehrmann's boiled red face tensed as he struggled onto his back. Blood pulsed onto the carpet.

"I think you cut my penis off. I'm bleeding to death."

"What about the rest of the department?"

"What?"

"Who else is part of this?"

"I don't know. They make everyone feel like they're the only one to keep things in check. They have so many resources...I think I'm dying."

"You probably are, then. So who's the cue ball outside?"

"You know damn well what he is."

"Who and what," Forrester said under his breath, thinking about his brother. It meant nothing to Lehrmann whose ravaged face began to slacken.

"Do you fear a God?" Forrester said.

He nodded as best he could.

"People like me and my brother don't. We don't because we don't have a God. There's enough to be afraid of. Ain't it funny how the Godless heathens end up being the good ones." He laughed. "You sicken me you little bastard. You used to just annoy me. But now you sicken me."

Lehrmann managed to crack a smirk across his face.

"And I always hated that thing you do...when you repeat yourself like it's going to change your point or make it sound smarter. You're no Mark Twain. Never were." He lay his head back and struggled to take a nourishing breath. All he could do was pant. "In the next minute that man will expect the sound of gunshot or me coming out the front door. We both know I'm not walking out. So, if you want to get the upper-hand, we need to get him to walk up the hill, then take him down as he comes up."

"Or I could just shoot you."

"I have a kid and a wife."

"You have a story and a bare desk. Who doesn't keep photos on their desk? Hell, some cops have their kid's faces tattooed into their flesh.

Lehrmann said nothing.

Forrester looked outside again at the featureless bald man who smoked in leisure beside the black car.

"He looks mighty preoccupied to me."

He glanced at the deputy writhing on the floor.

"You look preoccupied too."

He felt as though he were still in a dream. He could sense his instinct wavering, judgment becoming moot. He had a goal other than the task at hand, and wondered if it might have been the shock or stress of the whole ordeal. He didn't want to kill the alleged bogey outside or help the man at his feet who was, in all probability, bleeding to death on his carpet. He wanted only one thing: clothes. He felt naked in only a T-shirt and underwear. He was the only one there—this is as he saw it in his startled mind—at a disadvantage.

He stepped into his bedroom while Lehrmann screamed after him.

Once he was sufficiently dressed, he returned to the living room anew. The bald man had entered the house from the open door in the back, and startled, had grabbed the shotgun from the table and aimed at him. Forrester was still holding the deputy's service weapon. The bald man stank of cigarettes. The air around him reeked like an old pool hall. Lehrmann appeared catatonic. The man said nothing. Forrester didn't bother raising the gun. He changed his expression, which gained him the necessary pause of bewilderment and curiosity from the nameless assailant.

"You know that gun isn't loaded."

"It is now," the man said

"Then pull the triggers."

"You want to be shot."

"Maybe. But whatever shells you might have loaded it with from your pocket will blow the breech clean off. The proper ammunition doesn't exist any longer, at least not made by any manufacturer. You'll only lose your thumb and index if you fire it cautious like."

The man smiled.

"Who carries shotgun shells in their pockets anyway?"

He dropped the empty gun on the floor and attempted to draw his pitch-black 9mm from his belt. Forrester buried every last bullet of Lehrmann's clip into the stranger's chest.

The man remained standing as the crater of his ribcage soaked the white shirt like a napkin submerged in a bowl of wine. He looked down at his feet, teetering, and took a deliberate step back with his polished black shoe to steady himself, then looked back at Forrester, laughing. His voice was scratchy, deeper as if a mashed bullet had punctured and simultaneously cauterized his larynx.

Blood filled the gaps in the bald man's teeth and began to run down the sides of his chin as he continued to laugh. His laughter progressed into a coughing fit. He choked up a mist of red and took out his pistol. Forrester had left his gun along with his belt on the kitchen counter, six feet away. The living man looked at his pistol and then at his wounds. He stuck a finger into his chest and removed it to see the blood on the tip in disbelief.

"I'm not dead," he said, then laughed again.

Forrester ran for the cover of the kitchen and grabbed at his pistol. The refrigerator and the several cabinets took the heavy gunfire from the other man's 9mm. Bits of woods and brittle enamel flaked off the spray of dust that drizzled down in the tainted ether above him, his home having become a war zone. He opened the cabinet to find a makeshift tool to slide his own gun belt from the counter when he saw the old dust-covered cylinder beside his cans of roach killer and the home fire extinguisher: black bear mace it said. He grabbed the canister shook it, as if that would somehow change the constitution of the liquid, and violently ripped off the safety cap. A bullet fired directly into his electric percolator, shattering the glass rims. He stood up, taking an immense chance and shot the spray at the gunman. The dead man recoiled from the stinging cloud. He fired the gun again, out of sheer reflex, toward the carpet, puncturing Lehrmann's throat. Blood frothed and bubbled over his neck as his eyes rolled back. It took Lehrmann only a moment to die. In that moment, Forrester got hold of his own pistol and shot the bald man between the eyes. The entrance wound barely bled. It looked like a Bindi the way he had shot him square in the forehead. He shot again at the man's hand to free his rigor-mortis grip on the 9mm. The bald man stumbled back, collapsing onto his back in a growing puddle of fowl-smelling blood. Forrester had never seen so much blood. It formed a pool in his living room, which he had to wade through to get anywhere near the pale phantasm. He kicked away the gun and fired another cartridge into the freshly white, bloodless scalp. He watched the smoke erupt from the man's scalp like a crushed eggshell. He stood above the man, now a butchered pile of carrion, and listened to him keep on breathing.

**

The hospital appeared from the mist like a docked barge in the center of the shallow valley. The light mist—not a true rain—moistened the landscape. It was mid-afternoon but the lights were on in the lake-sized parking lot. Forrester parked the Subaru and walked inside the automatic glass doors. There was a young black girl in pink scrubs and the front desk. He showed her his badge. A drop of semi-coagulated blood and rainwater fell from his knuckle across the laminated cred case onto the desk.

"Cocke County Sheriff's Department. Rob Pelanski, which room?"

She gave him the room number and he took off down the hall. He found the kid in the greenish fluorescence of the double-room. His wrist was handcuffed to the gurney. Forrester pulled the white curtain so he didn't have to look at the old woman with the tracheotomy. Pelanski's injuries were worse than Lehrmann had described. He His lower jaw looked crushed, held together by wires and a peculiar rig that wrapped around his face. Forrester snapped his fingers and patted his swollen cheek.

"Wake up! Come on get up."

His eyes opened and Forrester could immediately see the panic setting in.

"I'm not here to kill you. I've seen it. I've seen what's going on, but you have to tell me the truth. I just killed one of my deputy's and shot a man with enough rounds to drop an ox. He's still alive and licking at the air on the living room floor. What the fuck are they?"

Pelanski reached for the call button on the side table beside the gurney. Forrester pushed it past his reach.

"I'm the only person who can protect you. Now talk to

me."

He gave him his smartphone.

"Type," he said.

Pelanski took the phone, pressed the Notes App, and thumbed his response into the screen.

You don't stand a chance. We're both dead.

"Why didn't he die?"

Pelanski typed again then turned the screen to Forrester.

Go to the homeopathic section of the local Greenpoint Market.

"What are you fucking typing. Are you high?"

Pelanski kept thumbing the words on the screen.

Greenpoint sells a colloidal silver spray. You can coat bullets in it.

"Why do I need to coat bullets homeopathic BS for sore throats?"

It's the only way to kill them. Unless you have silver bullets?//?

"What are you saying?"

Some of them are dogs. They can be killed easy. They don't spread the condition.

"What condition?"

It's the wolves that can't be killed. There's not many of them. They're trying to cross-breed with dogs to make more.

"Jesus Christ. So why did Cutler get killed. He found them out?"

Cutler found everything. Greenpoint. Vandergreven. It was all connected. That's why the CEO was assassinated. He knew too.

"Why did Crenshaw pull him back into the fold? Why hire him?'

Keep things neat, tidy, central. Maybe he thought Cutler

couldn't resist a final shot at an old case, or he deserved to know what it was all for. .

"Who killed Cutler?"

I did.

"Why?"

He asked me to. He got bit, by a Wolf. I dipped the spear in colloidal silver. He would have been cooked in a bronze bull if I hadn't.

"What the hell are you writing?

I am screwed. What are you gonna do now?

"I guess I'm going shopping," he said, taking back his phone.

Pelanski gave him look as if he had something else to say. Forrester ignored him.

He left the hospital, the automatic glass doors parting for him as he trudged out into the rain which had begun to fall heavier now. He squinted through the fat drops as the rain fell. Close to his car, he heard a distant crash and looked back. He saw a rolling chair drop from the broken window of one of the higher floors. He stood in silence and stared at the shattered window and watched the gurney drop to the concrete sidewalk with Pelanski still handcuffed to the side. From the distance, he could see the kid's eyes closed in anticipation of the impact like a snapped-neck bird on a window sill. He traced the floors with his eyes and looked at the dark outline of a man in black standing in the open window, then got inside his car and drove away.

8.

The ever- elusive sun shone through a dense smattering of rhododendron leaves on equal sides of the bowl in the earth that might have been called a valley by some, or wherever term it was in the county that folks continued to use, arcane terms like vale, cutlark or holler. Up from that surreal, ancient terrain, parallel to the dry-run road that bisected the shadow-mountain woodland stood a respectable near-suburban home with the all too ubiquitous gravel driveway. . A boy stood on the valley slope, dandelions up to his knees, tossing a tennis ball down the way for his muscular steel-colored pitbull. The dog would fetch the neon-yellow ball and gallop back up the incline. The boy took back ball, its fibers coated in a milky, frothed saliva and repeated the ritual.

A low tremble to bubbled-up from the earth as, down the road, a beige pickup truck, its engine more akin to a motorcycle's, rattled across the silver asphalt accompanied by a curious breeze as if the presence of the truck itself were the reason for the sudden coolness in the air.

The dog caught the next ball by leaping above the weeds, and returned the slobbery glob to the kid's hand once again.

The truck came to a stop just before the porch of the two-story house. A man in all black stepped out like he was exiting a train terminal and crunched his austere jack boots across the gravel of the private property. The boy stopped his game and called to the dog to heel at his side.

"You looking for my daddy? He's out back."

The man said nothing at first. The only thing that wasn't

black on him was his confederate flag belt buckle which he framed with his hands in an angular grip as he stood like he was hiding the platinum trim.

"That's a mighty rowdy dog you got there, son," he said.

The kid didn't say anything.

"It seems to be a handful for your folks. See, I run a sanctuary up north where a dog can be a dog. Roughhouse and play with his own kind. It's a place where sick children and people from the old folks home come to visit."

"This dog ain't rowdy and he ain't a problem."

"How long you had him?"

" 'Bout a month."

"Well you see, he just a puppy. Dog's character can change mighty quick the older they get. Start eating into that nice furniture."

"He ain't going nowhere. He's mine."

The man smiled.

"I can respect that son. I sure can. But it's a good offer and it's a good life making the less fortunate smile up by this sanctuary. You're folks taught you to care for the have-nots ain't they?" he said, stepping back a few steps. "What's his name?"

"None of your goddamned business," the kid said.

"Alright, alright," the man in black said, heading back to his truck. "But let me ask you this, you ever seen a thousand dollars cash?"

The boy looked skeptical still.

"You show it to me first."

"I think I can see it from here. I ain't fuckin' blind."

"Boy you got a mouth on you," he said, reaching into the truck.

He pulled out a Glock at pointed at the boy.

"You gonna give me that dog."

The pit bull growled.

"You keep that mutt heeled at you side boy or I might as well just shoot it between its eyes."

"You trying to rob my dog!" the boy said, screaming to get someone's attention.

"You shut up. Tell that dog to get into the back of the truck."

The windshield of the man's truck shattered. The boy's father stood at the top of the driveway and fired a tactical shotgun round into the man's chest. By all accounts the man should have been dead. Instead, they told the police officer that he had driven away. He couldn't have made it far with a wound like that. His father had given the officer a description of the truck and its license number. The lone officer asked about the dog, telling the family it was standard procedure, against the boy's protests, to keep it at the humane society overnight after a traumatic event where a vet could clear it. The boy's parents begrudgingly allowed for the strange request. The boy sat on the porch and watched the dog in the back windshield of the police cruiser as it drove away.

Several miles down the road, the man in black stood waiting with the kennel ready, picking the shotgun pellets out of his chest with a buck knife.

"Don't you know these mountain people are all trained with guns?" the officer told him, laughing.

9.

The wound in his buttock was still bleeding and giving way to rampant, unhealthy-looking granulation. Starla had described the look of the shotgun blast to John after peeling back the gauze: the discoloration and the spurting gashes in the mashed tissue. Both of them could smell it. He had her find the cigar box from the beneath the sink and take out a pack of what looked like a bundle of matches. He walked her through the steps.

"Don't get it on your clothes or your skin. It's corrosive. Pull the tab and stick the bleeding parts of the wound with the Q-tip end."

The pack had little writing on it besides some Thai or Hindi letters and a warning symbol with a similar, foreign seal.

"What is it?"

"Silver nitrate. Cauterizes the wound. There's leather gloves in the drawer."

She put on the black gloves.

"These your strangling gloves?"

"Yeah."

She knelt over him holding the stick like a pen and hesitated.

"I don't know what I'm doing."

"Just stop the bleeding parts."

She poked at each gash until the bleeding appeared to quell. When she finished, she cleaned out the wound with salt water and placed another bandage over the skin.

John returned to the couch and did what he could to

fall back asleep. Starla washed her hands, took John's pack of cigarettes and his .22 caliber pistol, then climbed the ladder to the upper level bedroom. She lay in the clean bed and looked out the bubbled glass hatch where the ceiling curved downward with the roof. In the small intervals where the image of the surrounding forest wasn't warped, she could see the only light source outside: a flickering telephone-pole lamp over the dirt path. She leaned back and lit a cigarette. The smoke trail crawled up the curvature of the ceiling. She flicked the lighter and stared into the flame before tossing it on the counter nearby. She lay idly and smoked until the cigarette was gone. There was a rippled plastic ashtray—the kind she used to see at midnight diners when you could still smoke inside most places—with a couple of stubbed-out roaches in the grooves. There was an odor to them beside that obvious saccharine reek of decent weed, something sinister behind it like formaldehyde, maybe a little meth. More than likely it had been left over by the whores John had been ordering in like delivery food. She remembered that Charlotte, North Carolina was the human trafficking capital of the Southeast aside from the coyote-run south Texas. Tennessee was more like a dumping ground for faulty merchandise, fat, broken or otherwise.

She listened to John snore a while longer. Reaching for another foreign cigarette, she heard the garbage bins outside tip over and the familiar chatter of raccoons. What sounded like infighting among the group, hissing, gargled squeals, ended abruptly. She thought about Lonnie's morbid fear of raccoons. He was afraid of rats too. He used to say he hated all rodents, to which she was too obedient or scared to correct him that raccoons weren't rodents. She held the cigarette between her lips for a moment without lighting it, listening to the sounds outside.

Six loud knocks slammed against the front door. The stranger might as well have been knocking with a baseball bat. She felt her body freeze, cold fluid running down her veins to numb her hands and feet. When the adrenaline subsided she looked through the bubble glass at the flickering light.

Three more knocks hit the door. The knocks were heavy enough to house some kind of authority behind them, but no one was yelling. Usually the police announced themselves. She put the cigarette on the side table and sat up with the .22. She looked down at the living room. John stood in the center of the living room sliding into a pair of sweatpants.

"Is that a prostitute you ordered?"

"Probably that auto-mechanic pimp here to collect from the last one."

"You sure about that?"

"Nope."

She crawled down the wooden ladder and pointed the gun at John.

"Answer it," she said.

"Don't be stupid. We're not answering anyone. If it's them, they'll find their way in no matter what. If it isn't...they'll leave."

Someone continued to knock against the door. The knocks were softer, more frantic. Still no one asked if anyone was there.

John went to the cabinet.

Starla still had the gun aimed at him.

"What are you doing? Do you want me to shoot you."

"Go ahead," he said. "You'd be shooting yourself in the foot. You don't stand a chance without some help."

"I took care of two of them by myself."

"Just two?"

He held a brown apothecary while in his hand with the Greenpoint grocery seal on it. . He took out the dropper.

"Here coat the barrel in this."

He dripped the clear liquid on the end of the .22, then took out a cartridge for the M-1 Gerand rifle and soaked the bullets in the same liquid. Then took out one of the silver nitrate sticks and rubbed the silver wick around the rim of the barrel.

"What are you doing?"

"Taking precautions."

"By poisoning the bullets."

"Yup."

"I think the bullets themselves will do the trick."

He said nothing and jammed the cluster of sharp brass rounds into the top of the rifle, popping in the top with his vein-rippled, brown fist. The metal guard snapped back over the top of the gun like a deployed guillotine.

***

He stopped for gas close to the county line and passed the motel where Cutler had been staying, almost taking the turn up the mountain where Sneeds's auto-shop lingered in semi-dereliction. He bought a foil-wrapped cheeseburger at a teardrop trailer stand manned by an old woman. Having not eaten all day, he took the Subaru to the black creek by the swampy reeds in the waning dusk shine. He parked in a little cul-de-sac facing the boulder where the creek split and ate the burger as night capitalized on his surroundings. He kept the police scanner shut off, choosing not to listen to the pleas to come into the station. He wouldn't turn himself in now. He squashed the foil with one hand and tossed it over his shoulder.

The headlights glanced off the moss on the boulder in time with the roar of the engine. Backing out of the isolated lot, he headed north. He cut onto the highway for a few minutes then took the turn off parallel to the bramble-covered nature trail. The epileptic flash of state-sanctioned blue and red lit up the void behind him. A cruiser tailed the Subaru like a barracuda's shadow in the wake of a mackerel; its warning blips the sonic cadence of a deep-sea behemoth.

In all that dark steeped somewhere close to his worldview, pacing along the wooden bridge of his psyche with the memory of the day like the face of the undead man smiling at him, Nathan Forrester could see what was left of his life ahead. He parked the car onto the shoulder, then pulled his hand out of the sleeve of his windbreaker. Taking his gun to his chest, he zipped the windbreaker with his free hand and set the loose sleeve beside his left on the steering wheel.

He watched the deputy in the rear view mirror step out of the cruiser and walk on down the dirt path toward him until the rookie turned on his flashlight, blinding him, and approached his car like the Zodiac killer. Forrester didn't bother with the window and waited for the officer to lean closer to his car. He got a good shot on the kid around the time he heard him say something benign.

"Sheriff?"

Forrester went ahead and pulled the trigger. The synthetic fabric on his chest burst as the window cracked apart. The kid's face was pelted with shards of glass as he fell back from the force of the bullet distributing across his Kevlar vest. He lay on the ground as the flashlight lit up his own face. Whoever else was hiding out in the car pelted the Subaru with bullets. They shot out the tires, blasting off the young officer's foot in the process.

Unable to swerve around or aim the pistol with it caught in the windbreaker, he unbuckled and ducked down trying to avoid the barrage of sloppy fire as the back windshield shattered. He attempted to scoot his way out the passenger's door, but his back shifted the stick into neutral. The sedan rolled into the grass and sailed through the bushes before hitting a tree. It still put more distance between him and the shooters. Instead of running, he slipped out of the open door and took cover in the staggered branches of a recently fallen juniper. The evergreen foliage was like a series of enormous fans within which he could fold himself: a basic trick from ranger training in Alaska. He carefully unzipped the windbreaker and gripped the pistol, watching the two men in black somehow let themselves out of the back of the cruiser. They shot the deputy dead in the street and moved into the woodland closer to Forrester. He considered checking his clip but figured it would make too much noise. He wondered if he could even kill these men.

They came close to the juniper, guns drawn, and then passed him, heading into the dark of the woods. He hesitated to move and instead listened to their footfalls. The soft crunch of pine needles was getting louder. They were doubling back. He kept the sight of his pistol on one of their heads, but, once again, they passed him. The two men headed right back up the ridge to the police cruiser. He squinted to see what they were doing. One of them opened the door and out from the backseat leaped a giant, black dog. The black mass came charging down the ridge. It drew closer, sniffing its way toward him. Once it was tearing away at the juniper, he could see it close enough to realize it was no dog. He thought about what Pelanski had said. He felt inside the torn pockets of the windbreaker and fumbled around for the tincture he had purchased from the hippie smoke shop. He instantly felt the puncture of broken glass. Somewhere in the confusion and adrenaline, his weight had crushed the bottle. He pulled the shard out of his finger and tore off the windbreaker.

The sound was undeniable.

He could see the wolf's snout writhing through the juniper when he finally pressed the gun against its nostril and fired. He saw the top of the wolf's head peel back as if it had second mouth, and scamper away into the trees. He dove across an open patch of darkness to take cover behind an elm trunk. Chips of wood started flying as they shot after him. Fortunate for his sake, these faceless men in black had no aim. In the next second, their clips were spent and he could hear them struggle to eject the spent clips and reinsert their backups. He ran faster than he thought possible. He tripped over a root and continued to roll forward out of instinct, almost discharging the gun. Covered in leaves, he slid down an embankment, halting his free fall on a rhododendron branch. The wolf, more ghastly than before with its facial wound, dove toward him. He shot it in mid-air, changing its direction as it slammed into an outcropping of jagged rocks. Its ribs cracked.

He let go of the branch and landed hard on the edge of a gravel road. Picking himself up, he limped away as the wolf came down the slope after him.

***

They stood by the door and listened to the man on the other end finally speak.

"This is the Sheriff of Cocke County. There's a wolf after me. And two men with guns."

Starla looked at John.

"Let him in."

"No."

"Let him in," she said.

He held the carbine and thought for a moment.

"Did the wolf bite you?"

"Not yet, it hasn't."

Starla pressed the .22 to John's temple.

"Let him in."

John walked to door with the Gerand and opened the front door. An older man in a dirty police uniform staggered past the threshold. John closed the door behind him and locked it. The sheriff sat on the floor and caught his breath, looking around at them.

"What's with the guns?"

John and Starla said nothing at first.

Forrester looked at their kitchen table and saw the ammunition and other antique weapons.

"What, are you doomsday preparers?"

"Who's chasing you besides the wolf?"

Forrester sat in silence looking at both of them before drawing his pistol.

"Y'all know what's going on don't you? Are you a friend?"

John didn't speak.

"That depends. What do you think you know?" Starla said.

"Too much," he said. "If I shoot you. Will either of you die?"

"We'll both die," Starla said. "Of course, we'll die."

Forrester lowered his gun.

"Then you don't know what I know."

"I do," John said, still aiming the carbine at the sheriff's chest. "Keep your mouth shut old man."

He could see the sheriff staring at him, taking notice of

his appearance.

"These men after you," Starla said. "Are they dressed in black?"

He nodded.

"Then we're on the same side."

"He's police, Starla. He'll just fuck everything up. You want your money or not."

"You think these people are going to pay you a red cent?" Forrester said. "They're not human. They've taken over an entire precinct."

"We were going to rob them," Starla said. "They screwed us over."

"Cut your losses and get out of town," Forrester said. "What the fuck is wrong with y'all."

"There's no other way but to go for broke. They got eyes and ears everywhere. Plus, it's personal."

"Stop trading information and step away from the old man, Starla. We don't need him."

She moved in between John's line of site and the sheriff.

"You're not going to kill him. We need all the help we can get. You said yourself it's suicide anyway."

"He's not going to help us," John said.

"He needs our help."

He begrudgingly lowered the rifle.

"How many are coming?"

"Two men and a wolf," the sheriff said.

"Alright," he said, heading to the door.

The sheriff tried to stop him.

"Are you out of your fuckin' mind. Bullets won't do a thing."

"I got silver, old man."

"Jesus," he said.

The window above the kitchenette sink shattered. A thin sliver of glass broke off from the main puncture and fell into the metal square with the disposal drain like a sheet of thin ice. The next gunshot sailed through the opening, invisible through its own speed until it splintered the cheap particle board cabinets. Starla began to aimlessly fire back with the .22 until John forced her hands down.

"Stop wasting shots."

The sheriff, who had taken cover on the floor of the kitchen, had taken the clip from out of his own firearm. Just two cartridges left. He pointed to the table.

"That Winchester loaded?"

John pushed the slender, lever-action rifle across the table.

Forrester caught it in mid-air and cranked a round into the chamber.

"I need silver."

John rolled a dropper of colloidal silver across the floor. It stopped halfway.

Forrester leaned in to grab it.

The wolf leaped from the darkness into the cabin, cutting its back on the broken window, landing on the table. Its immense paws scattered the stacks of ammunition and handguns.

Forrester shot it in the neck, pivoting the stock of the Winchester on the shabby linoleum floor.

The Gerand went off like a pipe-bomb as its bullets slammed into the thick body of the wolf. John shot it once more and the beast collapsed onto Forrester, writhing, yelping in agony. The trace amounts of silver seemed to be dissolving the animal's hair around the wounds.

"What the fuck is that?"

"What the fuck does it look like," Forrester said, pulling

himself out from under the massive dog-like creature. He took the bottle of silver and wedged it in the wolf's mouth, pushing its jaws together with all his might to crack the bottle in its teeth. The liquid eroded the animal's gums like sulfuric acid. He finally pulled himself free, and the wolf was dead.

John stood up and kicked open the door.

"Where are you going?" Starla said.

He didn't respond.

"Let him do what he's gonna do," Forrester said.

She turned to the sheriff and attempted to speak, but felt she could say nothing. There was too much to say as if the thousands of words she had inside her had no order, no succession, and had become stuck in the spare threshold, keeping what little room she had for them to fill vacant, silent.

They listened to John's footfalls in the gravel and the thunderous sound of the carbine. Then screaming, screaming and pleading before a breathless interval of the silence.

John returned with the rifle over his shoulder, dragging the wounded man by the collar of his shirt. The man dressed in black had taken fire to his shin which appeared to have been split on impact.

"There was another one," Forrester said.

"He's dead."

"Well, let's kill this guy."

Starla stood up and began to rummage through the cabinets.

"I need to know a few things before, eh," John said before bashing in the man's face with the stock of the rifle. He looked into his eyes. "So how about it? My handlers, they're gone? The thin woman? The Romanian?"

The man spit blood back in his face.

Starla handed John a few sticks of silver nitrate.

"Stick these between his eyes," she said.

The man started pleading.

"The thin woman. She was shot dead in Mexico. The Romanian. He was torn apart on a pig farm outside Budapest. Vicky's got his tooth on her mantle in a little ring case. They had to dig through a field of pig shit to get it. That's all I know."

Forrester stood up, using the rifle like a cane.

"You're talking about Victoria Vandergreven. The missing girl?"

The man started laughing.

"She was never missing. Not if you what she was ."

"A skinwalker." Starla said. "She wasn't human."

The man stared at Starla.

"That scar on her face. You know the one I'm talking about. Do you know why it took? Because it was my razor. It was silver. The three us were leaning over her in the bathroom, holding the bitch down, watching that old grimy blade of mine eat into her skin like it as blow torch. Her skin burned. All we had to do was hold it down on her. We couldn't believe what we were seeing. I thought I was going insane. I never thought in a million years that's that what she was. Are you? Are you one of them?"

"No," the man said.

She shrugged.

"This should still hurt," she said, jumping on top of his chest to holding his arms down with her knees before forcing a swab of silver nitrate into the soft tissue surrounding his eye.

His screams carried through the cabin.

"Don't blind him in the other eye," Forrester said.

"Why not?"

"Might need him to show us where she is."

"I know where she is," John said. "We don't need anyone

else."

He pulled Starla off of the man and shot him in the head with the .22. The bullet went in clean through his left eye sockets and the arterial blow-back spread across the floor like the entrails of a squashed insect. .

"If you knew one thing or another about your county," John said to Forrester. "you'd know where to go too."

Forrester sighed, hanging his head.

"The Walker Estate."

John nodded.

"But we don't need you. If I were you, I'd get the fuck out of town and never come back. Go somewhere else. Go somewhere and die ."

Forrester smirked and managed to laugh.

"I'd be a fugitive. . Leaving this kind of carnage behind. I'd be in a federal prison in a month."

"Yeah, well, seems like the fires came at the wrong time, didn't they?"

Forrester took a seat on the kitchen table.

"On the other hand, just flat-out disappearing worked out for Vandergreven."

"Not after the next few days," Starla said.

Forrester stood up.

"I thank you both for the help, but I think I agree," he hesitated, "this is where we go our separate ways."

Starla chose not to protest.

The sheriff held the Winchester and looked at John.

"Do you mind—"

"Keep it," John said, handing him a box of ammunition.

Forrester headed for the door.

"Good luck," he said, just before walking out into the night.

10.

And after hours of suspension, where, at last, some modicum of truth shined through the opaque nonsense of her dream like the gray skylight glare emanating from the strip of silk curtain flanked by the heavier blackout material, she opened her eyes and decided for herself—and from no other cue—that it was morning. Yawning, stretching her limbs in the warm duvet she had had imported from Sweden, the young woman rose pleasantly and cracked her neck with a near athletic precision. She stepped out of the bed, taking the remote from the dark mahogany side table, and turned on the television across from the canopy bed: CNN—Donald Trump and Russia probe. She parted the blackout curtains to allow the light to fill the room, then opened the window to let the mountain air circulate. The white silk of the under-curtains drifted in the wind like semi-transparent ectoplasm, a slightly haunted, out-of-season chill in the atmosphere. She looked out at the overgrown courtyard just a few feet from the woods the way, she imagined, a dictator of a small conquered nation must stare out at their finite dominion.

She walked to the mirror of her private bathroom and flossed and brushed her teeth, then applied lotion to her face. Barely noticing the scars, she had become used to her own appearance. Both the long scar running down her face from the razor blade, and the cracked almost marbled look of the burn on her neck, no longer bothered her. She took out the hair tie and the bobby pin, letting her auburn hair hang naturally.

Stepping out of the comfortable sanctuary of her room

while wearing her black nightgown, she nodded to the guards on either side of her door. Neither of them stood at attention. One of them was playing a game on their phone.

"At ease, gentlemen," she said.

"Oh, come on, it's Sunday Vicky."

She stepped down the baroque steps of the antebellum mansion and, looking like she had spawned from the frame of an oil painting, as though she belonged here more than the furniture itself, she walked into the dining hall: a long, thin dining hall that any pre-secesion slave-owner, turn of the century Vanderbilt, or morphine-addled Lugosi might have been comfortable in. She ate a warm, just-prepared, soft-boiled egg and soft-buttered toast in silence and drank from a dark bottled spring water and the perfectly-sweetened lukewarm coffee.

She thought about all the violence, then took out an old book she had read more than once, flipped to a page in the very center and read. When she was finished she lay the book on the table beside her soiled china and walked away. Someone else would take away the plates and cups and set The Dying Mule back on the shelf where it belonged for her.

11.

Sneeds had his back propped up by a thin sheet cover to an old infirmary mattress which he had stretched over a patch of thistles as he toiled beneath the old Dodge Challenger the rusty color of a dried scab. In his hands he held the two cork-grips to the punch and hook of his patch kit. He took the piece of rubber that looked like a desiccated inchworm in the hook and dipped it in the open can of glue, jammed the punch into the hard rubber of the underside of the tire then stuck in the plug. He clipped off the excess with a cigar cutter and poured the soap and water over the fresh plug..

More bubbles.

"Shit," he said out loud, grabbing the can of glue before taking a long huff. He jammed another plug into the tire and poured more of the soap liquid.

Nothing this time. It was good and patched.

He felt cold steel press up against his temple, and knew that he had been too stoned t be aware of his surroundings. He adjusted his thick glasses and looked up at Forrester who held a long Winchester to his head.

"Morning, Jim," he said.

"Morning, sheriff."

"Why don't you come out from under the car and let's have you and me another conversation?"

Sneeds bent over and capped his glue can, then stood up from under the Challenger.

"You don't look particularly well, sheriff."

"You can call me Nathan now, Jimmy. This shit don't

mean anything to me anymore," he said, ripping off his badge. He tossed it to Sneeds who caught it with both hands.

"You can smelt it down and patch something with it," Forrester said.

"If you ain't gonna arrest me, how come you got the gun up on me?"

"Because I going to borrow things from you that I know you have, and I don't have the money to pay for them."

"What kinds of things."

"Guns and a working car."

"So you're robbing me? The county sheriff is robbing me?"

"We'll call it civil forfeiture, how about that?"

"Ain't nothing civil about a gun of that caliber."

Forrester smiled.

"Let's go to the shack, Jim."

He let the melungeon lead him into the garage space of the property. He saw several American Traveler suitcases lined up against the chain of the rolling door.

"You trying to take off?"

"That was the plan," Sneeds said, pulling out of cobwebbed toolbox with a Masterlock. He rolled the combination on the dial and opened it before lighting a cigarette.

"A couple of .357 magnums. A Sig Sauer. It's about all I got left."

"I'll take the whole box. Just close it back up and I'll get out the stuff later. You got bullets?"

Sneeds smirked wryly and took a drag on the Maverick.

"Yeah, I got bullets. But you're looking for a something else ain't you. My private stash, right?" he said, before letting the smoke drift from his nostrils.

Forrester looked at him.

"'Cause I know now. And you've known for a while."

"I ain't got nothing to do with them, I just knew like some other folks did. Kept my head down. Took care of my business and all that. A little pimping. A little selling. Chopping. You do it all long enough, you'll learn some things about these mountains you wished you didn't know. Then you gotta live with'em. But the shit going on now. Dogs going missing. Cops beating down doors. I figured I'd leave. Get to the West. Forget about here. Who's gonna believe us anyway?"

"I knew you were part-time pimp. I fucking knew it. What happened, your bottom bitch get ripped apart?"

"No. Nothing like that. They get high and then they go missing. Last one I had went to a client out in one of them timeshares. 'Fore she left, swiped a bag of H from one of the Stumphouse guys. She just didn't come back. But that's neither here nor there. You ain't the law no more, and you said you ain't tryin' to arrest me. What else do you want to take from me?"

"You have silver bullets?"

"I got silver-coated bullets."

"For these guns here?" he said, lifting up the toolbox.

Sneeds nodded.

"Come on 'round back. You can put the Winchester down. I ain't gonna try nothin'"

"I'd feel more comfortable keeping a bead on you," Forrester said, following Sneeds through the doorway.

They walked through a narrow path hidden by the bristled stalks of elephant grass. The broom-tipped ends shuddered in the strong winds as if coastal sand dunes lay ahead of them. Instead, the path opened into a circling of ironwood and beech trees, between which, nestled in the scruff, was Sneeds' trailer. He opened the door and hoisted himself inside. Forrester followed. Expecting disarray, he was surprised to see how clean and empty the trailer was.

"You live here?"

"I don't spend much time here. I sleep in the shack back yonder."

He rummaged through his closet and took out several grated stacks of ammunition.

"There you go. .38 special, silver coated, blade-tipped, and a few clip's worth of the CCI mini mags for the Sig. Make it count. That's all I got."

Forrester set the toolbox on the miniature counter.

"Pop'em in."

Sneeds loaded up the toolbox, then crushed his cigarette in the sink.

"Where are you planning to go west?'

"I don't know. The Dakotas."

"I got a brother in Montana."

"Guess I ain't going there," Sneeds said, heading to the fridge. He popped the top on a generic beer with a resigned expression and poured half the bottle down his nearly elastic gullet. "You gonna take the Challenger?"

Forrester shrugged.

"You got anything else I can drive?"

"How far you looking to go?" he said before finishing off the beer, tossing it through the open doorway.

"You know where I'm going."

"The keys to the Pinto round the edge there are in the Folgers can back in the garage."

"That'll work," Forrester said. "Can I ask you something else?"

"You're the man with the gun."

"What did Cutler really want from you?"

"What you've got held in your hands right there. That

and some weed."

"And you told him to get lost."

"Yep."

"Shoes on the other foot now."

Sneeds nodded as he took out a jar of moonshine from the fridge, unscrewed the cap.

Nothing but silence passed between them for the next few moment. Sneeds drank the liquor and sat down on the bunk bed.

"Get out of here. Go kill'em, sheriff. Go kill those lobos."

Forrester grabbed the toolbox and walked away.

12.

John held the wheel of the stolen Dodge Dynasty with one hand, sitting awkwardly to keep the pressure off his wounds.

"Where are we going?" Starla said.

"A bad place. Where it all began."

The weather-worn sign pointing left at the fork in the road between the charred trees read, "Moore Campgrounds."

John pulled into the dirt lot where the cabin office stood on old stilts halfway in the drained creek resembling a boat on a marsh. The dimestore sign read, "Closed."

John checked the perimeter without getting out of the car and drove straight, bisecting the dandelion and sawgrass-splotched field. The mist parted at the grill of the Dodge, leaving a wake of fresh tire prints, tilling the soil. He cut back onto the path and parked where the fog seemed to accumulate near a cabin beside a tall willow.

"We staying here?"

"I'm not staying in this shithole," he said.

"Then what are we doing here?"

"Just come inside."

John wasn't armed as fare as she knew, and she had a snub-nosed revolver on her belt. She followed him into the cabin after he kicked in the door.

"This place used to be a hub for trafficking," he said.

"Drugs?"

"Humans."

"Doesn't look like much," she said.

John limped through the bare room and opened the bathroom door, then ripped the medicine cabinet and mirror from the wall. Behind it there was a small hole in the wall where someone had stuffed a canvas bag.

"What's in there?"

"I shot a guy a long time ago not far from here. Johnson City. It was two o'clock in the morning, I was angry and hungover and nowhere near the top of my game. It was at a truck depot right after a complicated job went as wrong as it could. I knew I was gonna have to leave the country for at least 6 months. This freight kingpin who ran restaurant supplies throughout the Southeast thought he was gonna play teamster for while, ended up screwing the whole deal. We had a dead girl in an ice chest and several pounds of product floating at the bottom of the fuckin' river. I had to bleach down a truck bed pooled with a fat guy's worth of HIV positive blood. The long jobs never suited me. I didn't have to but I did . So I went back to Tennessee and caught the guy on one of the night shifts, took him to one of the lots, pressed a gun against his head. Then he told about the money he stashed all over, trying to buy his life back. This is just some of it. I honestly don't remember where the rest is."

He handed her the bag and she rifled through the stacks of sour-smelling money.

"I think that'll amount to the cut you were promised."

"Why didn't you give me this when we first got here?"

"I didn't think I'd have to. I figured they'd take you, which was always the plan. Then I'd be killed eventually too. But you got away. Then you came back and shot me. You've earned it in my book."

She said nothing.

"I'm giving you a chance to run away," he said. "Take it."

"Why?"

"What do you mean why? You're the luckiest person in the world right now. Get the fuck out of here. I'm not going to siege Vandergreven's compound with you just to get paid. You got paid. Now fuck off."

"You're right. She never really was my enemy."

"No, she wasn't," John said, lighting a cigarette.

"You were."

"Yeah," he said. "But you still gave me everything when I needed it. And you still—"

She took out the revolver and shot him through the chest. The blood didn't burst from his body rather than trickle down his clothes. She shot him again in the head and his body dropped pulling down the shower curtain. She looked at him once more, slumped over the toilet. The cigarette lay smoldering on the tile floor. She knelt down and took his keys then wrapped the bag around her shoulder, closing the door to the cabin behind her. Before driving away, she set the beg in the trunk of the car and looked around to see what else John had stashed. She got back inside the driver's side and started the engine, turning on the radio as she pulled out of the campground. She hummed along with the bluegrass on the radio.

13.

Starla approached the gothic manor where she had been held captive like a dog, driving parallel to the hedges and iron fence, parking at an oblique angle just a few feet from the main gate. She got out of the car and sniffed the cordite on her fingers, then took out the snub-nosed revolver to thumb out the spent cartridges. She snapped the gun back together after hearing a engine in the distance and watched the sputtering Pinto crawl up the hill: a familiar face behind the wheel. It was the sheriff, the old man.

He parked his car in the middle of the road and stepped out with the rifle and a metal box.

"Where's the big guy?"

"He had to go," she said.

"What happened to all your fire power?"

"I forgot it."

Forrester nodded silently.

"I didn't really think this out," she said. "I just had nowhere else to go."

Forrester set the box on the hood of the car and took out the guns, showing her the silver bullets. He kept the Sig Sauer and gave her the .357.

"Every shot counts. But each one will put them down." He stuffed extra bullets in the pockets of the beat-up jacket he had taken from the mechanic.

"I brought something special too."

"Bump stocks? Garlic?"

"You'll see."

The front gate was open. They stepped through the courtyard.

"Is this a trap?"

"I don't know," she said.

"Where do we go in."

"Where else?" she said, ringing the front door.

"Are you suicidal?" he said, backing away into hedges.

Starla took out the plastic bag of scopolomine and poured into her palm. A man in a dark suit with a Bushmaster rifle jerked open the door. She blew it all in his face before he had time to react. He stood, confused.

She waved her hand in front of him. He squinted.

Forrester kept the man in his sights from behind the hedge.

"What did you do to him?"

"It's drug I've had used on me before," she said, then turned at the man. "Take that gun and kill everyone in the house. Kill everybody accept Vicky. Bring her out here on the lawn."

"I can try," the man said.

"You'll do it. When I close this door..."

She shut the front door and came down the steps. She stuffed the gun into her belt loop and took out a pack of cigarettes.

The first gunshot sounded. They both flinched. She lit the cigarette and looked up at the manor.

"She must have known what she was all along. Figured she'd come out here to start her own empire. Live like a fucking Dracula. She did good. She did good up until now."

"Yeah, I guess she did," Forrester said.

They listened to the cacophony of screams and gunfire. Everything stopped immediately.

"Do you think he did it?"

"He at least made our job easier."

She thought about heading to Kentucky and showing up with a sack of money on the doorstep of her brother's apartment. He thought about going to Montana, the way his ears would pop as the plane landed and whether it would land at night or by day, perhaps at dawn when the plane would tilt in the direction of the horizon as though he could see the curvature of the earth. But they were both still there, standing in the lawn, waiting for a dead woman. They waited for ten minutes. Starla stubbed out the cigarette in the grass.

"I think it's safe to say—"

The window above them shattered and Victoria Vandergreven fell onto the lawn surrounded by glass. They took turns shooting her, watching the silver bullets rip into her flesh, letting her body dance in the frenetic jolt of their unpolished massacre.

Victoria Vandergreven went missing in the fall of 2007, and by 2017 she had finally died.

—Kareem A. Hrabal
October 2018
Salerno, Italy

About the Author

Connor de Bruler has been published in *The Rambler, Pulp Metal Magazine, FRESH, The Horror Library Vol. 6, Yellow Mama,* and *The New Flesh.* He has two other novels published by Montag Press, and two self-published short story collections. He lives in Columbia, South Carolina.